City of Dreams

a novel

Other Books by Stephen Lawhead

Patrick

The Celtic Crusades
The Iron Lance
The Black Rood
The Mystic Rose

Byzantium

The Pendragon Cycle
Taliesin
Merlin
Arthur
Pendragon
Grail

Avalon

The Song of Albion
The Paradise War
The Silver Hand
The Endless Knot

Empyrion

Dream Thief

The Dragon King
In the Hall of the Dragon King
The Warlords of Nin
The Sword and the Flame

Stephen R. Lawhead
Ross A. Lawhead

City of Dreams

a novel

NAVPRESS ®

Bringing Truth to Life

NavPress
P.O. Box 35001
Colorado Springs, Colorado 80935

The Navigators is an international Christian organization. Our mission is to reach, disciple, and equip people to know Christ and to make Him known through successive generations. We envision multitudes of diverse people in the United States and every other nation who have a passionate love for Christ, live a lifestyle of sharing Christ's love, and multiply spiritual laborers among those without Christ.

NavPress is the publishing ministry of The Navigators. NavPress publications help believers learn biblical truth and apply what they learn to their lives and ministries. Our mission is to stimulate spiritual formation among our readers.

ISBN 1-57683-499-9

Cover design by The Office of Bill Chiaravalle, Benjamin Kinzer, www.officeofbc.com
Cover illustration by Benjamin Kinzer
Creative Team: Jay Howver, Karen Lee-Thorp, Nat Akin, Darla Hightower, Pat Miller

City of Dreams is adapted from the original story by Eddie DeGarmo and Bob Farrell.

Some of the anecdotal illustrations in this book are true to life and are included with the permission of the persons involved. All other illustrations are composites of real situations, and any resemblance to people living or dead is coincidental.

Lawhead, Steve.
  City of dreams / Stephen R. Lawhead and Ross Lawhead.
    p. cm.
  ISBN 1-57683-499-9
  1. Government investigators--Fiction. 2.
Terrorism--Prevention--Fiction. 3. Second advent--Fiction. 4.
Conspiracies--Fiction. I. Lawhead, Ross. II. Title.
  PS3562.A865C58 2003
  813'.54--dc21

                                    2003013868

Printed in Canada

1 2 3 4 5 6 7 8 9 10 / 08 07 06 05 04 03

This story

is set in the present day
but not the present time.

History as we know it revolves around a
peasant born in Palestine more than two
thousand years ago who changed the
world forever.

But what if that didn't happen?

What if

he was born only thirty years ago
in Bethlehem . . . Pennsylvania?

What if . . .

prologue

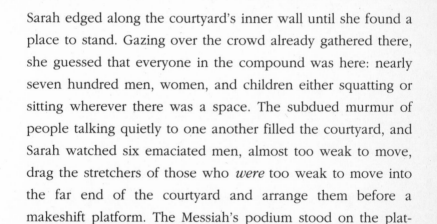

Sarah edged along the courtyard's inner wall until she found a place to stand. Gazing over the crowd already gathered there, she guessed that everyone in the compound was here: nearly seven hundred men, women, and children either squatting or sitting wherever there was a space. The subdued murmur of people talking quietly to one another filled the courtyard, and Sarah watched six emaciated men, almost too weak to move, drag the stretchers of those who *were* too weak to move into the far end of the courtyard and arrange them before a makeshift platform. The Messiah's podium stood on the platform, and Sarah wondered if the rumor was true that The Messiah would appear today.

No one had seen The Messiah for almost a week—not his closest aides, not even his concubines. He had barricaded himself in the ICON staff supervisor's office, a large room on an upper floor of the central building of the Regional Administration Center. Six days ago, around three o'clock in the morning, a loud hammering was heard coming from that office—the sound of nails being driven through the solid oak door and frame. Those who wished to speak to The Messiah—once they had negotiated their way through his ranks of official bodyguards—were forced to shout through the door, often receiving no response. If they did get an answer, it was in the form of an unintelligible grunt accompanied by a chair hurled in the general direction of the doorway.

Sarah gave a weary sigh and leaned against the cool stone of the wall. She closed her eyes and began humming to the music that blared continually from beyond the high compound walls. A week after the storming of the center, when it had become obvious that any attempt at serious negotiation was out of the question, the ICON Rapid Response Unit had wheeled large, armored speakers right up to the walls and started pumping a steady flow of heavy-metal rock at high volume into the compound. At first the younger members of the group had made a great show of dancing vigorously in front of the windows—the music was not unlike what they listened to in their free time anyway.

No one danced now. The volume had grown steadily louder with each passing day, or so it seemed. Between the incessant din of the music and the gnawing hunger, Sarah was finding it increasingly difficult to think clearly.

The tear gas attacks were still regular as clockwork. The RR unit outside was becoming quite adept at placing the canisters where they would create the most aggravation. Every three or four hours, a short burst of gunfire would signal the beginning of the attack and, moments later, two or three green cans would sail over the walls. Occasionally, one would miss its target and fall into the courtyard where it would be picked up and tossed back.

But mostly, the ICON sharpshooters were able to place the canisters just out of reach.

Occasionally, too, one of the sharpshooters would pick off a careless cult member, but this was rare. Of the 993 cult members led by Messiah Eleazar Ben Miller, who had taken over the Big Sky Regional Administration Center three months ago, a total of 687 remained. At least, that was what they were told. Sarah had seen a few of the dead bodies, but they hardly added up to the missing 306. She thought she knew what had really happened to them, but it was dangerous to say anything about it.

Two nights ago she heard a hushed commotion outside her window. The noise died down to the sound of running feet on the gravel of the forecourt, and soon after, there were shouts in the street outside the walls. Then all grew quiet again. She couldn't make out exactly what had been shouted but knew what it meant—some lucky souls had defected.

Sarah watched as a young man plugged a microphone into a large black speaker cabinet standing beside the podium. He flipped a switch that brought the speaker to life with a loud pop. After giving a few tentative taps on the microphone, he stood aside and waited. Silence descended on the crowd as all heads turned expectantly to the door leading to the administration building. They waited for The Messiah to appear.

During her time in the cult, Sarah had seen The Messiah many times. He was a big man. Six and a half feet tall, weighing two hundred and seventy-five pounds, he commanded attention by size alone. His features were outsized, too, but his hands were small and delicate, almost feminine. He wore his hair and beard long and untrimmed. He had a deep, resonant voice and a direct way of speaking that captivated his devoted audience, and an unwavering zeal seemed to burn from his dark eyes.

A minute later, The Messiah emerged from the doorway, but the man Sarah now saw shuffling up to the podium bore only a passing resemblance to the man she knew. It was as if the past six days had aged him six decades. Gone was the long, energetic, springing stride, the toothy grin poking through the dark beard, the hearty bellow of greeting. The Messiah shambled now, head down, slump-shouldered, and hesitant like a doddering old man.

Upon reaching the podium, The Messiah took the microphone in his hand and drew a deep breath. "My children . . . " he said, his voice ragged from sleepless nights. He tried clearing his throat, but to little effect. Everyone strained forward to hear him.

"My children; my sons and daughters . . . I look into the face of each one of you gathered here today, and I take strength from what I see. Your faith has made me strong. Your faith has made *you* strong. Our reward is coming soon. I can feel it.

"In these last days, I have been talking to the exalted Ruler of Heaven, our shield and defender, Jehovah, Allah, almighty maker of the heaven and the earth, sea, and sky. He is greatly pleased, my sons and daughters. He has counted you all righteous and is proud for you to be his justified and sanctified soldiers. He has promised each and every one of you a place at his own high table in the next life where we will feast on the bodies and drink the ever-flowing blood of our enemies. He has promised this to me, my children, and now I pass along this promise to you, so that you might share in my glory."

The Messiah paused to let this sink in. He stroked his scrag-

gly beard, then drew a deep breath and leaned into the microphone. "We *will* drink the *blood* of our enemies at the *Lord's* high
table in *heaven!*" he shouted with something like his former
strength.

When the spattering of applause died down, he continued.
"Our work here has not been in vain. Our glorious Lord says that
we have made a noise that even now echoes throughout the
world, shaking the mighty in their fortresses. My children, I once
shared with you the vision of the righteous fulfilling their destiny
in every corner of the globe. I imagined a virtuous army dis-
pelling the powers of darkness, dispatching them with a fist
clenched not in oppression, but in holy anger.

"I still cherish that vision, my children, but now I understand
that it will be realized in a different form. My glorious maker has
revealed that we must prepare the way for greater works by his
hand. We are his beloved firstborn. And now"—he thrust his arms
outward; his voice had been gathering strength and now boomed
off the walls of the courtyard—"it is time for us to claim our new
bodies!"

Sarah noticed a movement in the doorway behind him.

"It is time," The Messiah continued, "for us to ascend to a
higher plane of existence. By leaving our earthly bodies, we will
sublimate into the indestructible bodies the mighty maker
reserves for his heavenly host. No longer restrained by our earthly
vessels, we will be free to travel between the celestial spheres at
will—*his* will, my children. Our battle will no longer be physical,
but spiritual. We have been *chosen,* my children! Chosen to be
the first of a legion of spiritual warriors who will scour the earth
until it gleams like a fresh-cut diamond."

He paused again, looking out over the assembly. "Sons and daughters!" he cried suddenly, "let us now drink to our divinity!"

Sarah craned her neck to look through the bobbing heads of the people. It took her a moment to see that a utility wagon had appeared from behind the podium, bearing what seemed to be a number of large plastic water containers. Several men moved from behind the wagon, each of them clutching a long stack of small paper cups in one hand and a drawn sidearm in the other.

"Don't be afraid, little children," The Messiah continued as the men took up positions in front of the wagon. "Drink deeply of the sweet nectar of heaven. Drink from the cup of life! Your earthly cares are at an end—tonight you will be in the Lord's heavenly house." He cast his eyes over the gathering. "Who will be the first to demonstrate the depth of their faith?"

"Here!" came a cry, and a hand went up. "Here!"

One of the attendants moved toward the upraised hand and paused before an enfeebled woman lying on a stretcher before the podium. He offered a cup, which she took in a shaking hand and gulped down instantly.

"Yes, drink deep, my daughter," The Messiah said, his voice a soothing invitation. "Drink all of it."

Within seconds, the woman began to shudder. "Do you feel it, my *child*? Do you feel the hand of God, the spirit of the fiercest in battle, changing you? Is it not glorious, my daughter?"

The woman convulsed; a small stream of white liquid spilled from her mouth.

"Let us all sing a battle song of righteousness, my sons and daughters! Let us usher in the new age of spiritual enlightenment with great rejoicing!" bellowed The Messiah with the old fire. He started a triumphant chorus as the woman slumped back onto her bed, limbs jerking.

Sarah sang along with everyone else as the attendants moved slowly through the throng. Many crowded around the wagon, but some were too weak to stand and had to be served. Sarah watched mothers help their children press the cup to their lips and gulp down the drink. Sarah sang, her voice quivering softly while lines of people collapsed and fell like lazy domino chains.

The singing was very low when the cups finally reached the far wall where Sarah waited. There were fewer than fifty people left to take up the musical refrains. The Messiah now sat on the edge of the platform, head in hands and a gun in his lap.

When those nearest her went down, Sarah slipped down against the wall, too. And when no one was looking, she rolled herself next to a nearby body and pulled the still-warm corpse over her. To make her deception complete, she took some of the white fluid from the lips of the corpse and dabbed it around her own mouth. Then she lay back and, shutting her eyes against the horror, forced herself to remain utterly, deathly still.

When ICON forces stormed the compound nine hours later, they found only eight survivors: Sarah, and seven others in deep comas, not having taken enough poison to kill them completely. They also found four men beside the podium, each with a bullet through his head and no evidence of having drunk the poison. These particular victims were known to be upper-echelon members of the cult. The gun that fired these bullets was found in the hand of Jonathan Miller, a.k.a. The Messiah, a.k.a. Eleazar Ben Miller. He had also put a bullet into his own head.

The charred remains of almost four hundred men and women were found in a fire pit at the edge of the Regional Center's rose garden.

one

Alex Hunter stepped out of the yellow cab and into the heat-flash that bounced off the pavement. It was 10:45 A.M. He'd been in the city less than thirty minutes, and already his head was pounding. Sweat trickled down his collar and seeped into his shirt; he felt as if he were swimming inside his uniform. *Just what I need,* he thought grimly, *a September heat wave in one of the dirtiest, most crowded cities on earth.*

New York, New York—so great they named it twice. *Yeah, right,* he thought. *Probably, they just couldn't believe it the first time.*

Hunter hadn't asked for this assignment. It had been dumped on him from a great height. Smacking the heads of rabid radicals was not his idea of a good time, and besides, it was a waste of his considerable talents. *What am I doing here?* he wondered as he gazed up at the ICON tower looming over him. He had asked and answered that question a hundred times since flying in that morning. *You know what you're doing here, and you also know why.* The black-tinted windows of the tower shimmered in the sun, making the enormous building appear to sway in its own private, slow-motion earthquake.

He climbed the twenty-four steps to the entrance and placed his palm on the metal push bar. It was hot and he yanked his hand away. "Out of the frying pan," he muttered, "and into the fire." Putting his shoulder to the door, he shoved his way in.

The reception area was a box of reinforced concrete and bulletproof glass—a cramped, airless cubicle with sticky rubber matting on the floor. Hunter shook off a feeling of mild claustrophobia as he fished his ID from his pocket, waving it at the nearest of the three armed guards waiting inside the door. One of the guards motioned him through and pointed to the security booth, where a bored-looking officer sat behind an assessment screen. Hunter swiped his ID card across a magnetic pad and waited for his details to appear on the monitor. In a moment, they came up:

> Hunter, Alexander Scott
> PIC: TZY-022-567-8040-NQ
> ICON RNK: *Lieutenant, First*
> ICON CLSFCN: *Special Agent*
> SECCLR: SA Priority / Top Level
> SVC-RD: *10 yrs* Awards: 5 / Citations: 1

The duty officer yawned and pressed a button beneath the counter; two large steel doors opposite the entrance clicked open.

In a second reception area, Hunter was met by another security guard. "Morning, sir," said the guard, stepping out from behind his desk. "Gun, sir?"

"Yes," Hunter replied. "Standard issue. Nothing fancy."

"You'll have to leave it here."

"Yeah?"

"We've had a few incidents lately," the guard informed him. "You'll get it back."

Hunter unsnapped his hip holster and gave the man his sidearm, then unbuttoned the jacket of his dark blue uniform and pulled his handgun from its shoulder holster. "Take care of them," he said, handing over the two automatics. "I don't want to see them all scratched up when I come back."

"Sure thing," replied the guard as he tagged the weapons and dropped them into a metal box behind his desk.

Hunter rebuttoned his jacket and started through the metal detector in the doorway. "Have a nice day, sir," the guard called after him.

"Too late for that," said Hunter, stepping through the doorway and into the lobby. The first thing to hit him was the cool air. Hunter closed his eyes and felt the sweat chill his skin. When he opened his eyes again, he took in the gigantic scale of the room. *Mother ICON*, he thought, gazing at what seemed to be three or four acres of cool pink marble and several tons of gleaming brass, *you've outdone yourself this time.* He'd been in dozens of ICON headquarters around the world, and all were built to be imposing, but this one surely topped them all. The proportions were calculated not only to make visitors feel small and unimportant, but also irrelevant, insignificant, and impotent.

The International Confederation of Nations—known the world over as ICON, the last and greatest empire, mother to the unwashed billions—maintained its grip on power with an ever-tightening iron fist. But the world was changing; fever and ferment were everywhere; people were restless, discontented, even angry. Rebellion was becoming commonplace, part of the daily routine—heck, in some quarters it was almost a civic duty. All of which made Hunter's job more challenging. Not that he minded—it kept him in beer and bratwurst.

"Agent Hunter!" a female voice called out.

Hunter turned and was met by a pretty woman in a uniform bearing a silver supervisor's insignia. She was petite, with fine, sandy blond hair, pale skin, and a hint of peach-colored lipstick. Her appearance was immaculate—nothing wrinkled, nothing irregular, nothing out of place. Her uniform was perfectly tailored and she carried a small brown leather portfolio. She exuded a cool, official air and an aloof sexuality that Hunter found very appealing.

"I'm Janet Riley." She extended her hand and Hunter shook it. "I asked to be notified when you came in. You've got an appointment with Commissioner Steiner scheduled now. Shall we go up together?"

"Lead on."

She led him to a bank of elevators and entered the express car that ran only to the upper floors. Supervisor Riley put her ID card in a small slot underneath the call button and pressed it. A red light flashed for a second and then turned green with a ping.

The elevator took them straight to the thirty-second floor where, after a smooth and silent journey, they were delivered to a sleek waiting room with jade green carpeting and a rank of low brown leather chairs. A receptionist behind a walnut desk glanced up at them for a fraction of a second. "Go right in. The commissioner's expecting you," he said, his voice as languid as his manner. Riley stepped aside and let Hunter go first. He took a deep, silent breath, put his hand to the brass doorknob, and gave the massive paneled door a push. The door swung open quietly, and he stepped into what might have passed for a luxury airplane hangar.

Hunter's gaze swept around the room, taking in the sumptuous interior. Two walls were glass, floor to ceiling, affording an impressive view of the waterfront and Staten Island beyond; the other walls were taken up by three large paintings—postmodern paint-spattered tantrums, to Hunter's inexperienced eye. The floor was an open field of sky-blue carpet, and the ceiling was dotted with tiny spotlights that glowed like stars in a cream-colored firmament. In the center of the room a thin man sat in a tall chair behind a veritable blockade of polished granite—perhaps the largest desk Hunter had seen in his life.

"Ah, Special Agent Hunter," said the man, looking up. "Pleased to meet you."

Hunter advanced quietly across the carpet. There were no other chairs in the room. Visitors obviously weren't meant to stay here very long—at least, not comfortably.

"Commissioner Steiner," responded Hunter as he came face to face with one of the most powerful men in New York. A long, thin neck supported Steiner's round, bald head. His slightly hunched shoulders gave him the appearance of a vulture on a perch—an impression only strengthened by two keen dark eyes that watched the world from beneath dark brows. He wore the standard gray uniform of all ICON's top-level commanders.

Hunter remained at attention as the commissioner rose slowly from his chair and raised his hand in a salute, which Hunter returned with practiced precision. Supervisor Riley acknowledged her superior with a nod and took her place beside Steiner's desk, silent, her hands folded before her, waiting to be addressed. Commissioner Steiner resumed his seat and reached for one of the two yellow folders before him on the otherwise naked desktop. One of the folders bore the blue stripe of a personnel record—which Hunter assumed was his own—and the other was a red-tagged duty folder.

"We were expecting you last night, Agent."

"Please accept my apologies, sir. My flight was canceled."

"Yes, I know," replied the commissioner distractedly as he flipped open the file with the blue stripe. He read to himself for a moment, then said, "You've been an unfortunate man, Agent Hunter." He tapped Hunter's file with a finger. "Your last assignment landed you in the soup, I see."

"You could say that, sir," he replied automatically. "Due to unforeseen circumstances, there was considerable collateral damage. I took full responsibility."

"Yes," mused the commissioner, as his thin lips twitched into a smile. "I'm sure you did." He closed the file and pushed it across the granite desktop. "Don't worry, Agent. I'm not here to judge you. This isn't the first time that an officer has been stripped of his rank, and you won't be the first one to bounce back—assuming you want a second chance."

"I most certainly do, sir."

"Then you have nothing to fear from *this* quarter. We won't let a little collateral damage worry us." Steiner placed a narrow hand on his chest. "Personally, I like a man to show some initiative. Things happen in the field—I know that. All I ask, Agent

Hunter, is that you keep me informed. I want to know what my agents are up to. That way I will always know how best to help them if something . . . unfortunate should happen. Understand?"

"Perfectly, sir."

"Good. And I want you to remain in touch with Supervisor Riley here." Steiner nodded at the woman standing silently beside him.

"Yes, sir."

"Just a tiny formality, nothing more. You are more than qualified to look after yourself in the field, I know that. But it is my policy in situations like this, where an agent may be struggling," he spread his hands in a gesture of sympathetic understanding, "to keep the lines of communication open."

Hunter bristled slightly at the implication that he was damaged goods. "You can trust me, sir."

"Oh, it isn't about *trust*, Agent," replied Steiner quickly. "Don't think for a moment we don't trust you. But if you should find yourself in a position where you need someone on the other side of the fence to help you out, do not hesitate to call her." The commissioner glanced at Riley and smiled. "She's good, or she wouldn't be working for me."

"Thank you, sir. I'll remember that."

Steiner waved his hand in a dismissive gesture. "Now then, down to business." He picked up the red-edged file and handed it to Hunter. "Here's your brief—no need to read it now. You'll want to get acquainted with the city first, of course. New York is quite . . . *unique*, as they say, but very straightforward. We can of course, arrange a tour . . . " his voice trailed off.

"Thank you, sir," said Hunter, taking the hint. "As it happens,

I actually prefer making my own way around."

"I thought so." The commissioner flashed an enigmatic grin. "Great minds think alike."

Hunter waited for something more, but that seemed to be the end of the conversation. "Well, if there is nothing else, sir," he volunteered, "I'll get started."

"Good," said the commissioner, rising from his seat. "You'll keep me informed on the progress of your investigation? I want reports."

"Of course," he answered, adding, "but these things can take time."

"I understand, Agent," said Steiner affably. "Just make sure Supervisor Riley can get in touch with you at all times."

"I will do that, sir."

"Fine." The commissioner stood and raised his hand slowly. "And you'll give me reports?"

"I will, sir."

"Good man." Commissioner Steiner gave his new agent a final salute.

The interview over, Hunter tucked the folder under his arm, put his heels together, and gave a quick salute. Commissioner Steiner nodded and settled back into his great chair.

Hunter turned and started away; he had almost reached the door when he heard from behind him, "New York has its share of hotheads, rebels, and malcontents, I don't deny it; but we keep a tight rein on things in this city. Terrorism is the hot issue right now; it's the media's favorite buzzword. But we have things pretty well in hand here, you'll see."

How very reassuring, thought Hunter, and wondered yet

again why on earth he was here. He gave the commissioner a last nod and paused while Supervisor Riley opened the door for him.

"Don't take it so hard, Agent," whispered Riley as soon as they were outside. "Just get through this assignment in good shape, and you'll soon have your old rank back. I'll see to it."

"Thanks," he muttered. Then, wishing his baby-sitter a good day, he turned and walked away.

"You'll phone me?" she called after him.

two

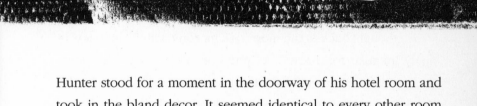

Hunter stood for a moment in the doorway of his hotel room and took in the bland decor. It seemed identical to every other room he had inhabited in his tenure as an undercover agent. The hotels, safe houses, and even the odd official residence—each was nondescript, interchangeable, and, above all, anonymous. This one, the Belvedere, was no exception. A slightly down-at-the-heels residence hotel owned by ICON through a front company and used for various operational purposes, it was just as inconspicuous as all the rest, despite its favored location in Manhattan's Upper East Side. His old instructor at the academy maintained that this studied dullness was for the agent's protection: What people didn't notice, they couldn't remember. Dullness was the cloak of invisibility the safe houses wore. Hunter knew it was also cheap, and therein lay its chief virtue.

Even so, he wondered, *would it kill anyone to paint the walls a color other than "dirty socks" beige?*

Hunter tossed the red-tagged duty folder on the low dresser and humped his bags to the empty luggage rack. He took a look in the minibar and found nothing but a frost-covered ice-cube tray and a vague, fishy smell. "Nice," he growled, slamming the door with his foot.

Toppling backward onto the bed, he decided it was, like the room, neither one thing nor the other—not hard, not soft, neither comfortable nor uncomfortable. A strictly regulation, all-purpose, medium bed. There was also a regulation TV set and the standard, rattling air-conditioning unit; both worked, however, which was more than he expected. His mood lifted slightly.

He thought back to the morning's meeting with Steiner. It was highly irregular for a low-level grunt, even an undercover low-level grunt, to be briefed by a top-level commissioner. Probably, it was just another way to keep a close watch on Hunter—to chart the path of his downfall, to further document that he alone was to blame when the trolley went off the rails. And the mission he had just been handed? Probably bogus, too. They'd most likely dug it out from under a pile of collected crank calls, petty crimes, and nuisance complaints.

And what was it with this town and the *heat*? Hunter dragged himself off the bed and switched the AC to MAX.

After a quick shower and a change to civilian clothes, he felt almost human again. Slipping the smaller of his two weapons into his front pocket, he left the room and went in search of lunch.

Outside the hotel, the heat assaulted him again with the force of a blast furnace. He looked right, looked left, and caught the spicy aroma of hot dogs from a pushcart vendor on the corner. *What the heck?* he thought, and strolled over to buy a couple of dogs and a drink from the immigrant vendor, who made change with one hand while wrapping hot dogs with the other. Hunter loaded the buns with mustard, relish, and onions, knowing he'd suffer for it later. Central Park was just a block away, so he made his way to the edge of the park, found an empty bench, and spent the next few minutes happily munching his dogs and sipping from a can of Dr. Pepper.

He polished off his meal and decided to take a walk through the park. His travel-stiffened joints and muscles needed a stretch, and he wasn't exactly eager to head back to his room to read his assignment and discover what life held in store for him over the next few weeks or, if he was really unlucky, several months. He spent the next two hours ambling around the leafy pathways, ogling girls on roller blades, and sidestepping the beggars—of which there seemed to be an inexhaustible supply.

The red-tagged duty file was waiting for him on the dresser when he returned to the Belvedere.

Right, he thought, settling himself into the bed, *let's see what bunch of twitching social misfits they have for me this time.* He tore through the seal and flipped open the bulky folder. The first page was headed: ZION INTERNATIONAL PARTY. Underneath it were the words *Known Operatives,* followed by two columns of names. The second page bore a photograph of a bearded white male, middle to late forties, wearing a small cloth hat over a mass of wildly tangled dark hair. The name under the photo read: "Michael Menahem, a.k.a. Judah Menahem, a.k.a. Father Moses (most common)."

"Well, well," Hunter murmured to himself, "glad to meet you, Moses. Let's see what you've been up to."

He scanned the next few pages quickly—summaries of surveillance reports and wiretaps, and a dossier of suspected activities collected from various field operatives. It read like a page from a revolutionary's scrapbook: conspiracy, subversion, possession of illegal firearms and explosives, robbery, several suspected homicides . . . it was all there. Father Moses had eluded police in four states and was wanted for questioning in three more. Furthermore, he had never paid a penny's worth of income tax in his entire life.

"Moses, Moses, Moses," chided Hunter, "you've been a bad monkey."

So bad, in fact, that the only thing keeping Moses out of ICON's clutches was, Hunter reckoned, the simple fact that Moses was just one small potato in a stew with bigger, more toothsome morsels to be had. And now, with the current terrorist crackdown, Mother ICON meant to have them.

Along with the fact sheet on Father Moses, there were reports on other key members of the radical group and a potted history of the cell. There were transcripts of secretly taped meetings and a few harebrained articles written by the more flamboyant spokesmen of the group. He flipped through these and the rest of the stuff, idly pulling sheet after sheet from the file, scanning each quickly before tossing it aside. This might not be a bum assignment after all.

He glanced through a couple of the wiretap transcripts and waded through the turgid text of one of Father Moses' speeches. By the time he finished, a profile of the man and a plan had crystallized in Hunter's mind.

Apparently, the Zion International Party, or ZIP as it had come to be known, aimed to bring about a new world order of brotherly love and prosperity for one and all through the establishment of the heavenly city, or Zion, here on earth. This they planned to do through violent revolution.

They believed that the systematic destruction of fundamental government structures would conclusively demonstrate the utter futility of the present world order, thereby forcing God Almighty to bring down the final curtain on history and inaugurate the eternal kingdom. True believers—those who joined ZIP and assisted in the achievement of its aims—could look forward to special perks: a palace with enemies scattered around as convenient footstools, inexhaustible wealth, life everlasting, and as many concubines as could be comfortably imagined.

Cool, thought Hunter. He skimmed the rest of the material, more of the same, and then turned to the terse assignment description stapled to the file's inside cover. The routine was, for the most part, boringly familiar. He was to infiltrate the Zion International Party, learn what he could about its membership and their connections, and then sabotage it in whatever way was most effective: fomenting internal strife, leaking secrets to the police, orchestrating the downfall of leaders, drilling holes in the bank accounts so operating funds dried up—any or all were possibilities. It would be Hunter's choice when the time was right.

Hunter reached for the remote and clicked on CNN while continuing to shuffle through the papers. The television droned in the background and Hunter's mind wandered. He might get lucky with some elementary sabotage; such things happened. But he'd also need a good plan B in case his identity was compromised or the organization was more impenetrable than he expected. In any case, he could always bail if things got too hot, and hope that the info he'd gleaned could be used in legal prosecution, or—what was more likely, owing to ICON's drive to cut down on paperwork—

he could summon a timely swoop-in by lightning raid.

Calling in the cavalry wasn't really so bad, and there was no shame in it because everyone knew it was extremely hard to bring down such an organization single-handedly—even though Hunter had done so many times himself. But each case was different, and you never knew going in how it would play. There were so many factors to consider.

Hunter preferred the safe and silent sabotage route. He liked to be miles away when the final meltdown occurred—let someone else mop up the mess afterward. In and out, extraquick— that was the key. It had the small, added advantage of reducing his overall exposure. The undercover agent's career was usually short—hang around too long, and people get to know you, your face gets recognized, and that was dangerous. Hunter knew his days as an undercover operative were numbered; he just hoped he could get his old rank back before coming in from the cold. A good outcome to this assignment might just do the trick.

Picking up the remote, he punched up the volume on the TV a couple of ticks. There was a feature about yet another Middle Eastern terrorist threat, with film of ICON troopers standing guard around a deserted and taped-off section of Times Square. Then there was a recap on the most significant terrorist activities of the past year, for the benefit of anyone who had been living under a rock since then. Hunter watched the now-familiar pictures of the explosions and twisted wreckage, and heard the latest speculations—"Are they alive? Are they dead?"—on the leaders of the headline terrorist groups. Then half a dozen suicide bombers appeared on the screen, lined up like the Brady Bunch.

But the story that the press wasn't telling, the story they

weren't allowed to tell, Hunter knew. He knew about ICON's covert mobilizations in the Middle East, the secret war that was being fought there. It wasn't for the people, or religion; and it wasn't for the land—but for what was *under* the land. . . .

He switched off the television. "Surprise, surprise," he muttered under his breath.

Restless again, he got up, stuffed a city map in his pocket, and went out to take his second stroll in New York City.

Procedure advised taking plenty of time to get a feel for location and surroundings before diving into a new case. New York, a larger city than any he had operated in, would be different, he decided. Its size actually made it easier for him in many ways. In a small town, for example, where everybody knew everybody else and nobody but *nobody* could point a toe in the wrong direction without the whole town knowing about it, he would have to spend months merely integrating himself into the fabric of local life. In big cities, however, people were used to anonymity and transience; the population ebbed and flowed continually and strangers roused no suspicion. Heck, in a place like New York, *everyone* was a stranger to everyone else and most of them preferred it that way.

Hunter made his way to the location of his assignment, labeled Carnegie Hill on his map. It was a fair distance, but he walked in order to get the lay of the land. Entering the neighborhood, he wandered around, taking his time, soaking up the ambience of the place. It was, he decided, a borderland community, a buffer zone between the businesses and brownstones of the wealthy Upper East Side and the rough-and-ready ghettos of Harlem. The place was scattered with commercial areas full of boutiques, banks, delis, cafés, and health food stores for the more well-to-do; and pawnshops, pizza parlors, video-rental shacks, and discount liquor stores for the poor. The streets were busy and teeming, but the residents bustled purposefully from place to place, and although there were plenty of wacky ethnic establishments of one sort or another—a Tibetan rug and incense store, a Latino used-record shop, a Save the Rain Forest thrift shop—there were noticeably fewer loiterers, drunks, and indigents than he'd encountered in the park. In fact, the place seemed to hum with activity, as if the eclectic mix of its residents somehow ramped up the energy.

It was, Hunter decided, exactly the sort of place he would settle down in, if he ever achieved that particular luxury: a plain, unfussy neighborhood where you could be yourself, no apologies. He felt completely at home after only a couple of casual loops through the area, and decided to forgo the formal familiarization process and dive into his assignment.

Time to visit the chief of police. The local authorities always liked to know who was playing in their patch, of course, and it was handy for the agents. It not only helped keep everyone singing off the same page, it also decreased the chances of getting hassled by some well-meaning flatfoot whose enthusiasm for law enforcement could ruin weeks, months, or even years of painstaking undercover work. Lastly, and high on Hunter's personal preference list, keeping in touch with the ICON locals helped keep special agents from getting shot by uninformed policemen when the fat hit the fan.

So, after one last ramble around the neighborhood, Hunter headed back to the hotel to give Police Chief Devlin a call.

three

ICON Police Headquarters was yet another massive, government-issue concrete bunker. Fifteen stories tall, ringed by a sharp-slatted iron fence topped with razor wire, and bristling with an array of shortwave, microwave, and satellite towers, it was an overbearing, if not downright belligerent, presence in an otherwise lackluster section of Lower Manhattan. Hunter stood across the street for a moment to study the layout. ICON police streamed in and out through any of several entrances; cars constantly shot up out of the underground garage to enter the flowing streams of traffic; the building's shiny black glass windows reflected the sun onto the pavement below.

"Let's make this quick," Hunter muttered, as he waited for the crossing light to change. He fastened his ID to his shirt and hurried across the four-lane street. He sprang up the steps and into the building where, after negotiating two preliminary checkpoints, he found himself standing before the obligatory bulletproof glass booth containing three uniformed guards, one of whom was the duty officer.

"I've come to see the chief," he announced loudly into a speaker set in the glass. "I've got an appointment."

The officer flipped through a printout on a clipboard. "Yeah, okay. Fifteenth floor, corridor D. Check in with the floor warden, he'll show you where to go," came the tinny reply.

Corridor D was, as promised, presided over by an aging policeman who sat at a small desk, reading *Sports Illustrated*. "What?" he asked as Hunter approached.

"Special Agent Alex Hunter to see Chief Devlin," he said, holding out his ID.

"Down the hall, second door on the left."

He found the door and was about to knock when he heard a voice call from inside. "Come on in, Hunter."

He stepped into a large room crammed with technical gear. Along one wall was a bank of video screens, computer monitors, and printers; a phalanx of inbuilt radio, telemetry, and radar equipment; as well as infrared scanners. A portable metal detector was propped against the other wall, and a standing hanger carried the chief's armored riot suit. A large glass cabinet contained an impressive array of weaponry, old and new: half a dozen assault rifles, assorted handguns, something that might have been—was it possible?—a hand-held, laser-guided rocket launcher. Amid all this hardware was a burly man in a high-backed leather office chair. Dressed in a crisp, dark blue uniform almost identical to Hunter's, the chief of police sat with his hands behind his head, puffing a cigarette and gazing at the projected images on the wall opposite his desk.

"Chief Devlin?" asked Hunter.

"That's me," said the big man. His hair was cut in the regulation no-nonsense ICON cut—short back and sides; but the addition of a large handlebar mustache and full-blown sideburns, which were almost completely gray, gave the chief a distinctly wolfish appearance.

"Welcome to ICON New York, Agent Hunter. Take a seat." Devlin gestured to a chair and resumed his perusal of the video screens. "I've been reviewing some operation tapes. Have a look," he said, pointing to the bank of screens, "you'll like this."

Hunter turned his attention to the central video display, which showed the front of a row house somewhere in the city. The screen just below showed the back of a house from the alley—presumably the same house—and two ICON police in full regalia edging their way toward the back door. A third monitor showed the house from above in a slightly tilted view—shot from a chopper, Hunter guessed. The fourth displayed the grainy black-and-white image of a dark room as seen through a hidden camera. There were three men with guns standing watch over another man, two women, and three children.

A speaker on the wall hissed and a voice said, "Optimum attack position attained. Waiting for go."

"All of this can be synched up real easy these days," said Devlin proudly. "Has to do with digital time-stamps and—"

Devlin was interrupted by the sound of his own voice on the tape. "Green for go. Repeat: green for go."

"I love this part," the chief said, sucking on his cigarette.

All at once there was a dry, explosive sound—though unaccompanied by the usual flash of fire and instant cloud of smoke produced by a mortar shell or incendiary device. In the same instant, the house seemed to vibrate; the windows wobbled and then burst into pulverized smithereens. It was as if the entire front of the house had been struck by a great, invisible hand. A sudden swarm of ICON police in riot gear invaded the front lawn.

Watching the grainy images in the fourth monitor, Hunter saw the three men in the dark room thrown to the floor. The hostage family immediately grabbed their heads; the children shrieked and writhed. A second later, half a dozen ICON policemen were in the room. Six seconds after that, the kidnappers were disarmed and on their bellies.

The other screens showed the arrest of four or five other men on different sides of the house—most of them clutching their heads and screaming.

It was all over in less than a minute.

Chief Devlin flicked the remote at the wall and the screens went blank. He beamed brightly at Hunter and let out a contented sigh. "All suspects apprehended and nary a shot fired in anger," he declared proudly. "That's what I call good police work."

"Very impressive," agreed Hunter. "What did you use?"

"High energy pressure wave—one of our new toys. Similar to a sonic blast or something—it's technical." He stubbed out his cigarette. "Now then, what can I do for the famous Alexander Hunter?"

Hunter was taken aback. "Sir?"

"I've studied the files of the Big Sky incident. You made some good calls."

"Thank you."

"S'alright." Devlin nodded. "I mean, you had to take that bust in rank, I understand that—it happened on your watch. But still, you done good."

Hunter collected himself. "As you probably know, I've been assigned to a case in your backyard. I just wanted to let you know about it before I got started so there won't be any crossed wires down the road."

"I hear you. And you're clear with me. In fact, I've already had a memo from the commissioner." Devlin leaned back in his chair and regarded his visitor with pale gray eyes. "So, what's up?"

"Oh, the usual—hotheads and troublemakers," Hunter said. "It's an extremist group calling itself the Zion International Party. Ever heard of it?"

"Nah. Should I have?"

"Probably not. Most of these organizations like to keep a low profile locally and perform their hijinks further afield. I don't think they've been operating very long."

"And this—what did you call them?"

"The Zion International Party—ZIP, for short."

"They're here in the city?"

"Yes, sir. They are."

"Anything you need from me?"

"Not at the moment, Chief. I'll keep you updated on the operation. When the time comes to shut these guys down, I hope it can happen with a minimum of fuss. If things go my way, they won't even know what hit them."

"And if things don't go your way?"

"Then you're the first person I call."

The chief smiled. "Glad to hear it. We're always looking for situations to field test our latest knickknacks." He stood up, signaling an end to the conversation. "Is there anything else? I'd show you around, but I've got about a million things to do right now."

"Yes, sir," replied Hunter, rising to his feet. "Thank you for your time."

"Fine," said the chief, moving toward the door. "Stop by anytime. I've got another tape or two I'd like to show you."

"I'll be in touch."

"Good luck," said the chief, closing the door.

By the time Hunter left ICON Police Headquarters, the sun had disappeared behind the high rises all around him, and the city was noticeably cooler. *It just might*, Hunter mused, *turn into a halfway pleasant evening.* The streets, he noticed, were busier; all those who had lain low during the heat of the day were stirring now. Turning a corner, he happened upon an Asian section of town. Vietnamese "dollar" stores, Chinese grocers, and Laotian laundries lined the street. Jammed between a Thai restaurant and a Malaysian funeral parlor was a tiny Korean day-care center bravely flying the flags of all nations above its door.

Kids played on well-swept front stoops and in the dirty streets; restaurant windows glowed with neon and twinkle lights. Men home from work sat on the steps and leaned on balcony railings, passing beer and cigarettes to one another; women chatted to their neighbors as they watched the children darting in and out of the slow-cruising traffic. The borough was coming to life.

A Vietnamese noodle bar, its window open directly onto the street, sent a mouth-watering aroma of stir-fried beef and spicy peanut chicken Hunter's way. Suddenly ravenous, he stopped to have a look at the menu posted below the stainless steel counter.

"Hey! Hey! Mr. Man! Whachoowant?" The proprietor, a wizened man with skin like a leather handbag, grinned at him. "You want something good?"

"Well, I—" Hunter began.

"You wait! I fix you something good. You wait right there."

"Look, I'll have—" Hunter squinted at the menu.

"No, it's okay. I fix you something good."

"All right," agreed Hunter, surrendering. "But not too hot, okay?"

"Not too hot!" hooted the noodle man. "Okay, Mr. Not-Too-Hot, okay. You want a drink? I got good Vietnam beer. I give you something nice, you bet."

"Sure. Whatever."

A cold brown bottle materialized on the counter before him; it bore a red label with a picture of a dragon and a name in an indecipherable script. He took an experimental swallow. The beer bit back with an icy nip. *This is more like it*, thought Hunter, taking another swig.

Three street kids rolled by on skateboards, dodging and weaving through the sidewalk traffic. They sped by the counter and down the street. "Hey, Mr. Man. Here you go!" cried the noodle man, placing a large, steaming bowl on the counter before him.

Hunter examined the contents; among the tangle of brown noodles were bits of black mushroom, mung beans, and shredded cabbage, along with chunks of chicken, pork, and beef. Under the smiling encouragement of the noodle man, he took a cautious spoonful into his mouth. The taste was slightly salty and peppery, with an agreeable vinegar tang; the noodles slid down like warm jelly, producing a pleasant burn in the back of his throat. "Good," allowed Hunter judiciously. "Very good."

"You right, Mr. Man!" cried the noodle man happily, on his

way to harass another customer. "Very good!"

Hunter worked his way through the bowl of noodles, watching the street life unfold around him. Eventually, the skateboarders returned. This time they slowed as they passed the noodle bar, and stopped. "Hey, mister," said one of the boys suddenly, "buy a beer for us?"

"Sure thing," said Hunter. "How old are you?"

"We got money," said a second boy, digging into his pocket.

"Great," said Hunter, "now all we need is ID."

"We're old enough," declared the first boy belligerently.

"Then it'll say so on the ID," said Hunter. "Let's see it."

"Umm . . . I think I left it in my other jeans," said the boy.

"Too bad," sympathized Hunter. "Better luck next time."

The noodle man appeared at the window just then and shouted, "Hey! You kids! Whatchoowant? Stop bothering my customers."

The boys started away to avoid the interest of the noodle man, but as soon as he turned back to his kitchen, they resumed their ineffectual petition of Hunter. Just then a fourth boy came running up. "He's back! You gotta come see him this time."

"Who?" said one of the kids.

"You know—that guy. The Water Dude! He's down at the park with his gang, by the lake. You guys *have* to see him this time. There's, like, hundreds of people an' he's gonna do something awesome!"

"Nah, don't wanna."

"You ain't got nothing better to do," said the boy who'd asked for the beer. "I heard my brother talk about him. He's thinking of hanging with him this summer. C'mon, let's check it out."

The boys raced off down the street. Hunter slurped down the last of his meal, paid, and continued on down the street, merging with the late evening crowd.

four

It was well past midnight when Zack Levinson locked the inner doors of the temple. The last worshipers were long gone, but he lingered over the necessary rituals for closing. Although he'd been a member of this temple for nearly sixty years and was a trained priest with a good reputation, he was allowed to work only two weeks of the year—so he liked to make the most of it. The other fifty weeks, he didn't do much of anything: read, watch TV, hang out at the Senior Center on 149th Street, and teach the occasional Hebrew class.

The street was dead quiet as Zack armed the building's alarm and locked the large wooden doors. He turned, took in the silence, inhaled deeply, then started down the temple steps. He was content; it had been a good day.

Upon reaching the sidewalk, he turned in the direction of home. He took only a half-dozen steps before he was stopped by a large, dark figure stepping out of the shadows. Zack gave out a cry of surprise and lurched back, clutching his chest.

"Where's your son?" asked the man, his face obscured by shadow.

Zack's shocked silence swiftly passed, and then he turned on the man who had accosted him. "Whaddya think you're doing, sonny, sneaking up on a old man like that? You crazy? I could'a died here!" He strained for a look at the man, but there wasn't enough light.

"Where is your son?" The stranger asked again, edging closer.

"My son? You want to know where my son is? Why? What business is it of yours?" Zack demanded, his anger increasing.

"Your son—John." The voice was low and menacing. "Where is John?"

The stranger took a slow step toward him. Zack inched away. "Look, you—whoever you are—I don't know where he is, okay? How should I? Do you *know* my son? He could be anywhere!"

"Tell me," the voice insisted. "He's here in the city."

"You think? Maybe, maybe not. Maybe he left, and I don't know where he was going—maybe the Yukon. Maybe Siberia. I'm an old man; what do I know?"

The figure remained motionless, then slowly turned and started down the street. Zack watched the dark stranger melting back into the shadows. "Hey!" he cried after the stranger, "Hey! You find him, you tell him to call his mother once in a while!"

Hunter spent the next day sifting through the surfeit of background information on religious cults posted on the Internet, trying to get into the mind of the radical religious activist. Then he accessed the massive ICON database in Tucson and spent several hours visiting militant web pages and chat rooms. He subscribed to several e-newsletters and even ordered a few books and T-shirts. He paid particular attention to the book lists on the sites, reading the synopses of the more intriguing selections and noting their authors and titles.

By midafternoon, he was ready to make his initial contact with ZIP. The main headquarters was believed to be above a small bookstore a half-mile or so away; the bookstore itself, called Changing Times, was thought to be owned by the group.

Hunter looked at himself hard in the mirror, searching for anything in his appearance that might mark him out as an undercover agent. He had stopped shaving and his haircut was slightly longer than regulation. He changed his posture, slumping and rounding his shoulders to ease the lightning-rod straightness favored by ICON officers. He wore an old Gap T-shirt and no-name jeans, with last year's Nikes. Pulling a worn wallet from his back pocket, he checked out his new ID: a New York driver's license, Social Security card, and credit card, all in the name of Samuel Taylor.

He locked his other ID and regulation firearm in his room safe, keeping his unregistered automatic tucked safely and discreetly away, and headed out.

It was another stinking hot day, so he couldn't tell if the sweat soaking his T-shirt was nerves or heat. Never mind. He stood across the street from Changing Times and gave it a practiced once-over. Nothing much to see. The store's upper floor windows were dark and covered with grime. No movement. Hunter took a deep breath and crossed the street.

The bookstore was like a walk-in freezer. A window unit airconditioner above the door poured cold air onto his head as he entered, drying the sweat on his neck. A man stood behind a high, poster-plastered counter, with a phone pressed to the side of his head. A big, black-bearded hulk with a face as flat as a dinner plate, he turned in lazy acknowledgment of his new customer's entrance. Hunter nodded in his direction and, assuming the guise of a man intensely interested in extremist literature, proceeded to peruse the shelves.

Even the most devoted zealot would have had to agree that Changing Times was not exactly a retail dynamo. The nearly bare wooden shelves displayed only a handful of scruffy-looking tomes, a few lonely stacks of dog-eared paperbacks, and several piles of cheap, self-published pamphlets. The books were roughly similar to those he had seen on the various radical websites. They had laborious and punctuation-laden titles like *The Next Revolution: Where Do You Stand?*; *How to Survive the Coming Apocalypse (The Do-It-Yourself Guide to Barricades, Bunkers, and Bomb Shelters)*; *Anarchy: The New Social Responsibility*; *Stop the World, I Want to Get Off: A Manifesto for Lasting Social and Cultural Change and Permanent Racial Harmony*; and *When Worlds Collide: An Examination of Political Activism*.

Hunter edged his way down to the end of the bookshelves to get within earshot of the store clerk. He picked a book off the shelf—*Seven Seconds: Everything You Need to Know About Atomic Attack*—and pretended to become deeply engrossed in the care and maintenance of urban fallout shelters, while doing his best to eavesdrop on the phone conversation. But the big clerk did more listening than talking, and his replies were so low Hunter could not make out anything he said.

Eventually, the call ended. The man behind the counter put down the phone, glanced up, and said to Hunter, "This ain't a library."

Hunter closed the book and neatly placed it back on the shelf. "Yeah, well, I was waiting for you to get off the phone." He moved to the counter. "Do you have *Reap the Whirlwind* by Archie Leech?"

"No." The bearded man gazed evenly at Hunter. Not quite hostile, his bearing was definitely far from welcoming.

"Really?"

"We can order it for you. Take a couple weeks."

Hunter rejected the idea with a frown. "Do you have anything on religious prophecy? Kabbalah, Illuminati, Sirius Connection, stuff like that?"

The man jerked his head. "Those books over there."

"I've already got most of those," Hunter lied. "What about Alan Gibbons? Anything by him?"

The large man raised his eyebrows. Hunter must have hit a live one, sufficiently obscure and radical enough to show that he wasn't just another time-wasting dabbler off the street. "Not at the moment," the man replied.

"You don't have much," Hunter commented sourly. "This *is* a bookstore, right?"

"That's what the sign says," the other returned. "We just started up a couple weeks ago," he continued, less belligerently. "Still waiting for a shipment from our main supplier."

The shop door opened just then and a stumpy young man walked in, stopped, took a quick glance around, and promptly backed out the door again with a mumbled apology between his teeth.

"Another satisfied customer," observed Hunter.

"Look," said the clerk, stepping out from behind the counter, "I'm closing now. You gotta leave."

"Oh?"

"Lunch break. I'm alone today so I gotta close the shop." He forced an unfriendly smile. "But come back anytime."

"Sure," said Hunter, moving toward the door. He took a few leaflets from an overflowing table by the doorway and flashed a grin back at the man. "I'll drop in again soon."

"You do that."

The clerk followed Hunter to the door, locked it behind him, and hung a "Closed" sign in the window. Hunter walked slowly down the street, considering his various options.

Next morning Hunter made a call to Police Chief Devlin, who was happy to provide Hunter with everything he needed: the use of a small surveillance team for a few days and a whole arsenal of video equipment. The men and their gear came tidily packed in a dented, dirty brown van with *Tully's Satellite TV* written in large black letters on the side. If the van's exterior was mud-hen plain, inside it gleamed with state-of-the-art high-tech spy toys.

The team went about its work with a cool efficiency Hunter found reassuring. And, while the Tully's crew installed tiny video cameras on the rooftops of the buildings adjacent to and across the alley from the Changing Times bookshop, Hunter sat in the air-conditioned van, sipping coffee and organizing the contents of his laptop.

"Ready, sir," said Gerald, the team leader. A slender, quiet young man only a year or two out of basic training, he had an electronic engineering degree from NYU and a computing systems design degree from Cal Tech. He climbed into the van and settled into the seat beside Hunter. "Want to inspect the installation?"

"No," replied Hunter, "just fire it up. Let's see what we've got."

Gerald pressed a small round patch above his shirt pocket and said, "Grey Ghost—we're going live." He flipped a few switches on the console before him and three screens blinked on. The monitors showed uninspired views of the alleyway, back door, and front entrance of the bookstore. With a deft movement on the keyboard, he retrained and focused one of the cameras, then turned to Hunter. "We're on. What do you think?"

"Perfect," replied Hunter.

"Okay, do you want to do the honors, or shall I?"

Hunter leaned forward, looking at the serried ranks of buttons, knobs, jog wheels, and softly glowing red, yellow, green, and blue relay switches on the console. "What do I do?"

"Just press this button here," said Gerald, indicating a red blinking light, "and that starts the recorder. Then we just sit back and wait."

"Do we have to sit right here?"

Gerald shrugged. "It's up to you. The transmitter has a two-mile radius, so we can move around."

"Good," decided Hunter, "then take me to the nearest pizza place and I'll buy you a slice."

"You're the boss," said Gerald. He tapped the patch on his shirt again and called the other two team members to return to the van. As soon as they were aboard he said, "Tom, take us to Sbarro's. Alex wants to buy lunch."

"You got it, sir."

And that, for the next three days, was that. Hunter spent each morning drinking coffee and reviewing the hard-disk camera recordings of the night before; then it was lunch at Sbarro's, or a deli, followed by the inevitable afternoon snooze, then a routine check on the equipment before calling it a day and heading back to the hotel, while Gerald's second team took over for the night shift.

By the evening of the fourth day a curious pattern of traffic into and out of the bookstore had begun to emerge. Hunter noticed two significant details: There was far more activity at the rear of the shop than the front; and some days more people entered the building during the day than left, while on other days, more left than entered.

Gerald noticed it too. "I wonder what they're up to in there" he said, watching the monitor as two men in T-shirts and coveralls entered the shop from the alley.

"Nothing good," replied Hunter. "How much you want to bet?"

"So, what's next?"

"I want to get some good photos of whoever's inside."

"You want us to go in?" asked Gerald. "We can. Just say the word."

"Not yet. I'd rather get them to come out."

"Gotcha."

Hunter smiled. "Why don't you guys call it a day. Get some sleep and meet me here tomorrow morning at—say, ten—and we'll roll the cameras." He smiled to himself as he climbed out of the van. "Don't be late now; it'll be a good show."

Hunter watched as the van drove off, then walked down the

street and turned in for a leisurely supper at the Nanking Palace.
He took in a double bill at the Bijou Discount Cinema. The movie
let out around midnight, and inexplicably hungry again, Hunter
bought a couple of jelly doughnuts and some orange juice from
a closet-sized kiosk and headed home on the subway.

five

Hunter slipped into his plastic subway seat and stared out the grimy window. The after-hours traffic was sparse and the car almost deserted. He munched his still-warm doughnuts, sipped his OJ, and watched the tunnel lights speed past as he counted down the stops to his station.

He thought about the next day's activities and sketched out a plan in his mind that made him smile with wicked anticipation. Meanwhile, the train stopped at yet another semideserted platform and opened its doors. For a moment it didn't look like anyone was getting on—until Hunter heard shouts and three young toughs jumped the turnstiles and raced toward the train. The last one made it into the car just as the doors closed and the train started to pull away.

Hunter had seen a thousand of these guys since coming to New York: hard-rolled stocking caps, spotless hooded sweat-shirts, baggy jeans, headphones with tiny silver MP3 players attached, wrap-around sunglasses, and enough gold chains, chunky rings, and fake diamond earrings to choke a pig. These particular specimens, he noted, sported pink bandannas stuffed into the rear pockets of their designer jeans—gang colors, most likely. Despite the warm evening, they wore puffy black nylon jackets and elaborately designed new Nikes with the shoelaces untied. *No doubt about it,* Hunter thought, *today's common city gangster is as fashion conscious as any catwalk supermodel.*

Laughing and shoving each other, they made their way down the aisle to seats in the middle of the car where they all huddled together to light their hand-rolled cigarettes. Soon an illegal smell drifted Hunter's way; he turned his attention back to the window.

At the next stop, just one man got on; a medium-height, medium-build, medium-looking guy in khakis and a light jean jacket. He broadcast a nervous tension that Hunter picked up instantly. Maybe it was the sight of the gang kids that set the guy on edge—Hunter could understand that, all the more so since the smell of dope smoke now filled the car. But there seemed to be something else . . . something Hunter couldn't quite put his finger on . . . something slightly oily and unpleasant.

When the man slid his hand into his open jacket and looked down the aisle to the end of the car, Hunter instinctively turned to follow the man's gaze. Another man—also of medium build, in his midthirties—had his hand in his jacket. This second man gave a slight nod to the first; both turned toward the kids and drew their guns.

Hunter hit the floor as the first shots exploded. He counted off eight rounds. There were muffled cries from the middle of the train—then two more shots . . . and silence.

As the train slowed into the next station, Hunter jumped up with his own gun drawn. He plowed straight into the shooter closest to him, throwing him against the door in a one-handed choke hold. He placed the barrel of his gun against the man's cheek.

"Drop it."

There was a dull clunk as the gun slid from the man's hand and hit the floor. From the corner of his eye, Hunter could see the second man approaching.

"Drop your weapon," Hunter shouted, "and stay where you are!"

The second man froze.

The train squealed to a halt. The car doors automatically slid open. Hunter felt his weight shift as the man in his grasp began to fall out through the gap in the doors.

With a quick sweep of his foot, Hunter threw his captive to the floor before they both fell onto the platform. The second man seized his opportunity and bolted for the open doors at the back of the train. Hunter leaped for the emergency stop cord and pulled it. It didn't do any immediate good, but at least the train wouldn't be going anywhere else for a while. Ordering his captive to stay flat on the ground, Hunter turned his attention to the other shooter, who was already escaping through the turnstiles. Hunter sprang through the doors and sprinted after him.

As Hunter bounded up the stairs to the street, he noted with grim amusement that this was his stop. He reached the top of the stairs and shouted again for the fleeing man to stop. When he didn't, Hunter fired a warning shot above his head. The effect was instantaneous and gratifying. The running man froze so fast his shoes almost skidded out from under him.

"Don't you move a muscle!" Hunter called, darting forward.

"Okay!" the man cried. "Just don't shoot!"

"Throw your gun down," Hunter commanded.

"I left it in the train," the other man replied.

Hunter slowed and approached cautiously. "Hands on your head." The man raised his hands slowly and rested them on top of his head. "Move to the wall."

The man stepped to the wall of a nearby building, where Hunter frisked him, finding nothing but a cellular phone, which he took. "Okay, now down on your knees—and keep your hands on your head."

The man very slowly, and without moving his hands from his head, dropped to his knees. "Onto your stomach," Hunter ordered, and again the man complied without hesitation. "You've done this before, haven't you?" said Hunter.

The other man snorted. Hunter gave him a kick in the ribs. "Hey!"

"Oh, is that too rough for you?" Hunter wrenched one of the man's hands off his head and twisted it around to his waist.

"Hey, man! You don't know what you're doing."

"Give it a rest." Hunter painfully twisted the other arm into place, then pinned down the man's wrists with his foot. "Why'd you kill those kids?"

When the man didn't reply, Hunter gave him a tap on the side of the head with the muzzle of his gun. "Answer me."

"I'm an agent."

"What?"

"It's true. Bronski—my badge is in my front pocket."

Hunter placed his gun to the back of the man's head and released one hand. "Dig it out—slowly. No sudden movements."

The man slid his hand to his front pocket and fished out a flat black leather wallet. Hunter swiped the wallet from him and told him to put his hand back on his head.

There was indeed an ICON badge inside the wallet. "Where'd you steal this?"

"I didn't steal it," the man said. "It's mine. Bronski, that's me."

"What's the number?"

"Badge number 466-4092-49," replied the man. "There. Happy now? Can I get up?"

"No," Hunter told him. He looked at the badge and then at the man, trying to decide what to do.

"Look, if you don't believe me," the man suggested, "call my precinct. The number's in my cell phone."

"Okay, let's do that," Hunter replied, retrieving the phone from his pocket.

He found the word *Precinct* in the phone's auto-dialer and pressed it. The other end rang twice and then was answered by a female voice.

"Who is this?" Hunter asked.

The woman on the other end gave a precinct number.

"This is Special Agent Alex Hunter," he said, and gave his PI code number. He could hear the light tapping of a keyboard as she verified his identity.

"How can I help you, Agent Hunter?"

"I need to know if you have an Agent Bronski on your books."

There was a pause and more tapping on the keyboard.

"Yes we do, Agent Hunter. May I ask—"

"Can you put me through to him?"

"I'm sorry, but that agent is on active assignment at the moment. If you want to leave a message—"

"Forget it. Who's his supervisor?"

"His immediate supervisor . . . " there was a pause and some more tapping. "Umm, that would be Captain Gregory."

There was a mumble from the ground. "Let me talk to Gregory."

"You shut up," said Hunter, giving him another tap.

"Hey!" cried the man. "Cut it out."

Ignoring him, Hunter said, "Could I speak to Captain Gregory, please? It's urgent."

"I'm sorry, the captain has left the precinct building."

"Look, just call Commissioner Steiner," whined Hunter's captive.

Hunter cut the call to the captain and scrolled to the commissioner's number, which was also in the man's cell phone directory. The line rang twice and was answered by a vaguely familiar voice that said, "Bronski. Is it done?"

"Special Agent Alex Hunter here. Is this Commissioner Steiner?"

"Hunter? Yes, this is Steiner. Where's Bronski?"

"He's here with me, sir."

"Is he all right?"

"He's fine. I caught him and a buddy of his just after I saw them shoot down three unarmed men in a subway car about ten minutes ago."

Steiner gave a weary curse and a sigh. "It's all right, Hunter; nothing to concern you. Listen; bring him in to the precinct station. I'll meet you there and explain everything. Can I talk to him?"

Hunter held the phone to Bronski's ear. Bronski listened for a few seconds and then said, "Yes sir, I understand." He nodded to Hunter that he was finished. Hunter put the phone back to his ear. The call had been terminated. "He wants you to give me back my badge and gun," said Bronski.

"Fat chance."

Thirty minutes later, Hunter was sitting in a private office with Captain Gregory, Commissioner Steiner, and the two trigger-happy agents from the subway.

"That's really all it is, Hunter, just a misunderstanding," said Captain Gregory, an amiable pudding-faced career cop with an office devoid of paper, paraphernalia, or personal effects. He perched uneasily on the edge of his chair as if he feared leaving any impression of himself.

"So what are you telling me? These guys are your private undercover assassins?"

"No, no. They're just on active assignment to—" Gregory began.

"To shoot kids?" demanded Hunter.

"Watch your mouth, Agent," said Steiner.

"Look, this is New York." The captain shrugged. "These things happen. I'm sorry you got caught in the middle of it, Hunter, but these men were just doing their jobs."

"Some job they did too—firing without warning on a public train."

"Agent Hunter, this is not your jurisdiction," said Steiner firmly. "And I will *not* have you interfering with agents in pursuit of their duties. It's none of your business, so butt out."

Hunter turned to Bronski and his partner, neither of whom had said a word throughout the proceedings. "You didn't even flash your badge. Those kids never had a chance."

"We did what we felt the situation demanded," replied Bronski smugly. "Not that I have to explain anything to you."

"No, you don't have to explain anything to me—I was there. You had the jump on those guys, and none of them was armed. Not a single weapon among them—not so much as a comb!"

Bronski sighed and looked at Gregory.

"I won't say that there might not have been a different way to handle the situation," schmoozed Gregory, "but look, there are certain pressures and demands on us right now that are having an adverse influence on our statistics. . . . "

"Statistics? Are you kidding me? Did I miss something here? Is there a bounty on high school kids? Does every cop on the street have a monthly quota of homeys to bag?"

"You're out of line—" began Gregory.

"I can put in a call to High Command and have a dozen Internal Affairs agents here tomorrow morning. What's that going to do to your departmental statistics?"

Gregory swore under his breath.

"Of all the people in this room," Steiner returned, "I think you should be the last one to point a finger at anyone else. Especially after . . . or shall I say, at this *particular* junction in your career."

Hunter leveled a cold stare at Steiner, who returned it in kind.

"You're either with us, Agent Hunter, or against us," Steiner said dryly.

Hunter broke. Suddenly he felt beaten and weary; all he

wanted was a stiff drink and a clean bed. "Fine," he said. "Whatever."

"All right, then." Steiner smiled. "Don't worry, Agent Hunter, you haven't lost today. If anything, we're all very impressed that you managed to take down two very experienced career agents all by yourself."

Gregory nodded in enthusiastic agreement.

"It might take a little while for you to get used to the way we do things around here. There's a price to be paid for peace, and that price can be high. We all know that." Steiner rose from his chair and crossed to where Hunter sat; he rested a fatherly hand on the agent's shoulder and said, "Go home, get some rest, and forget this ever happened. You've had a very long day, I'm sure."

Hunter nodded, too tired to care anymore. With a muttered apology to his superiors, he left the precinct in a daze and walked back to his hotel.

six

Tired from his late-night excitement, Hunter began the big day with a jumbo grand mocha latté and a lox-and-cream-cheese bagel the size of a VW hubcap. He crossed Fifth Avenue and found a bench in Central Park—a pleasant enough place to start what promised to be another sizzling day in this steam cooker of a city. Taking intermittent bites of bagel and gulps of coffee, he tried to interpret the events of the previous night, but try as he might, he couldn't make sense out of any of it.

After an hour of spinning his mental wheels, he gave up and turned instead to the fun and games he had planned for the staff and friends of the Changing Times bookshop. Tossing his paper cup and bagel wrapper into the nearest trash can, he walked to Lexington Avenue, caught the subway, and rode down to Chinatown. He quickly found what he needed, then sped back uptown to join his crew at the *Tully's Satellite TV* van a block from the bookstore. He rapped on the side door. "Hunter," he announced.

The door swung open and Gerald greeted him. "Chinese?" he

said, looking at the plastic bag in Hunter's hand. "You shouldn't have—at least, not this early in the morning."

"Are we ready to rock and roll?"

"Ready when you are, boss."

While the others listened in, Hunter explained his plan and what he needed from the team. "Can you do that?" he asked when he finished.

"Sure," grinned Gerald. "Just give us a few minutes to readjust the cameras, and we're good to go."

"Then let's get busy," said Hunter.

Gerald turned to his two assistants. "You heard the man."

The team set to work recalibrating their equipment, and Hunter donned a pair of gray workman's coveralls that Gerald had provided. They were a little short in the leg, but close enough. He took one of the small metal toolboxes from beneath the console and transferred the contents of his plastic bag into it, then closed the lid and sat back, smiling to himself.

"We're ready, boss," said Gerald, returning a few minutes later. The other two climbed into the van behind him and took their places before the console.

"Okay, kids," said Hunter, "keep your eyes and ears open. We'll get only one chance, and I don't want to miss a second of this."

"Got it," said Gerald. He punched a button on the console. "We're rolling."

"Back in a flash," said Hunter. Picking up the toolbox, he left the van, walked down the block, and made his way to the alley behind the Changing Times bookstore. He climbed the fire escape of the building opposite and took up a position next to a dummy satellite dish Gerald had installed on the first day of the operation. He knelt down, scattered some tools around, and pretended to be adjusting the dish.

After a few minutes of playacting, he pulled open one of the compartments of his toolbox and took out two large smoke bombs. Hunter lit the first one and gingerly lobbed it across the alley onto the roof of the bookstore. The missile landed square in the middle of the flat roof, where it fizzed nicely. Satisfied with his placement, he took up the second smoke bomb, lit it, and tossed it next to the first. He waited a moment for the smoke to get nice and thick and black, then fished out his cell phone and dialed 911. By the time he got off the roof and back to the van, he heard sirens on the way.

"Now," said Hunter, joining the others, "let's see what crawls out of the basement."

The sirens grew louder, and soon a fire truck was threading its way down the street. Those inside the bookshop heard the sirens too and as the firefighters were banging on the front door of the building, most of the occupants were escaping out the back—precisely as Hunter planned. Hunter watched with approval as Gerald and his boys tapped the remote triggers of the alleyway cameras, filming the dozen or so people who were scuttling away like rats to the races.

By the time the firefighters finished searching the building, Hunter reckoned he'd got a truckload of glossy new photographs of every single person to leave the shop—including one series that he was particularly anxious to feed into the ICON Instant ID system. For, just as the firefighters had entered the front door of the bookshop, the back door burst open and three men ran out—

two men flanking a third. The two kept their hands in their pockets, possibly clutching guns, while rushing the middle man into a dark blue SUV parked halfway down the alley. Hunter guessed they'd rousted someone pretty darn important to the ZIP gang.

"Well, the show's over, boys and girls," said Hunter, rubbing his hands with anticipation. "Let's see what we've got."

They drove the van to a secure parking lot, changed vehicles, and continued to ICON headquarters with the tapes, film, and recorded hard drives. While Gerald and the boys readied the data, Hunter checked in with Devlin, gave him an operation summary, and thanked him for the use of his surveillance team. "Did you catch any bad guys?" asked Devlin.

"I wouldn't be surprised," replied Hunter. "We'll know soon as I've had a chance to run some matches."

"Give me a ring if anything comes up I should know about," Devlin told him.

Hunter left, promising to be in touch, and made his way down into the subbasement where the intelligence division made its home. Gerald had already downloaded copies of the morning's digital pictures to Hunter's laptop and had them up life-size on a large screen. Reviewing the photos, Hunter saw that he had several nice shots of the man who had been hustled into the getaway car as well as the two thugs with him. "Crop these," Hunter instructed. "Let's have some head shots."

Gerald zoomed and cropped the images and those of all the other faces of the people fleeing the building. He then connected to the ICON Operations Center International Mainframe in London. The Antiterrorism Branch maintained a photo database of known and suspected radicals, extremists, and criminal agitators the world over. Hunter was hoping for a match or two from his morning's effort. He typed in his security code and sent the files off, then sat back to wait for a response.

Gerald fetched some bad instant tea, and Hunter flicked through the TV channels on a small desktop monitor, alternating between BBC World, the North American Broadcasting System (NABS), and CNN. He quickly grew tired of the forced jocularity and hammed-up reporting of the well-coifed hosts, but eventually the ubiquitous Middle East update started to run, and that interested him. He turned up the volume as a tired-looking man bulked out by a bulletproof vest under his heavy trench coat appeared on the screen. There was the inevitable bombed wreck of a building behind him and the usual gaggle of gawky kids with rocks in their hands and expressions as vacant as the landscape. The video feed was jerky and it sounded like the man was talking through a plastic tube.

". . . where the situation has done nothing but deteriorate," he was saying. "ICON peacekeeping forces are much in evidence— white uniformed troops stand guard on every street corner. The thirty-eight deaths from this latest attack on the one remaining medical center have sealed the fate of the tenuous peace process. It is growing increasingly difficult to see how full-scale war can be avoided."

The image changed, showing some dark-skinned men in floppy flat caps and desert camouflage working a floor-mounted machine gun. The sound was marginally better.

"Mercenaries from the surrounding areas are descending on the isolated enclave, enticed by the promise of spoils if the ICON troops can be driven back. The prospect of capturing sophisticated armaments has inspired patriots and profiteers alike, creating new allies. The mercenaries bring strengths that the local forces desperately need—weapons and experience, much of it provided, ironically, by ICON-trained forces—bolstering the tired and ill-equipped rebels."

Then it was back to the reporter outside the ruined building. "Negotiators say that a disarmament agreement is less likely with each passing day as, according to one ICON spokesman, the rebels refuse to negotiate in good faith. The rebels? They aren't saying anything. They have no spokesman, no PR machine, no interest in waging a media war—just a solid determination to protect the land they call their own. So as the third week of bombing raids continues, this is Tom Carson for NABS."

In the studio the blond anchorwoman added, "Meanwhile, terrorist activity in North America has been growing. Although solitary terrorists like the 'Subway Poisoner' and the 'Washington Anthrax Postman' have tied up investigators for months, a spokesman for ICON Central Command indicates that the biggest threat comes from radical groups already present in our main cities—such as the one that spectacularly self-destructed in the now-infamous Big Sky Suicide Siege." She flashed a pretty smile and turned to introduce the weatherman. "So, Lance, tell us, what can we expect for the start of tomorrow's Australian Open Golf Tournament?"

Hunter slumped down in his chair. He supposed most of what was being said about the Middle East conflict was true, but he could easily read between the lines. ICON didn't care about peaceful negotiations; they were just tired of the endless warring of a handful of inconsequential border countries beyond the immediate reach of ICON Europe. High Command now considered it safer and simpler to go in with force and let the pieces fall where they might. It wasn't the worst outcome. When ICON came, so would peace and stability for the region—as well as better education, health care, and technology. So, you lose a little, but you gain a lot in the end. What was so bad about that?

His thoughts were interrupted by a beep from the computer and a flashing red triangle that appeared on the screen. This warned him that the message was encrypted, so he pecked in his security codes and pressed the receive key on the keyboard. The box expanded and opened to reveal the results of his search.

The computer ranked its matches from the lowest to highest probability. It was discouraging that the first seven photos produced no matches at all. Three middle-aged women, two younger women in their twenties, and two young men—one dark-haired and the other with yellow spiky hair and multiple ear piercings— remained unidentified. Either they were not in the database or the digital information was in some way inadequate.

The next photo, of the big bearded man Hunter met behind the counter, produced two possible matches, although both were in the low 25-percent certainty range. After studying the pictures provided, Hunter decided the second was the most likely. The name given was Wilson Conroy, and his record showed an arrest and conviction for drug trafficking fifteen years ago and for small-arms smuggling seven years ago; Conroy was presumed to be living in Syria. Hunter flagged the file as a probable identification and moved on.

There was a 38-percent certainty match for Leon Ribini, a tall, blocky figure with a deeply pitted face that looked as if it had been worked over with acid and a spoon. His police record was long and consisted primarily of weapons charges of various kinds—most of which carried fines instead of prison sentences—along with several call-outs for "domestic incidents," none of which was pursued to prosecution. He was definitely one of the men piling into the SUV.

The tenth photo, with a 54-percent certainty rating, was of a woman named Ruth Lewis, thirty-four years of age. She had eleven different addresses dating back twenty-two years, some of them ranging as far afield as Paraguay, and five of them current.

The final two reports were of most interest to Hunter. There was a 66-percent certainty match for Michael Menahem, a.k.a. Judah Menahem, a.k.a. Father Moses. The report basically duplicated the information Hunter had already been given, but there were more photos of the man. Moses had obviously shaved recently, but the wild and wiry hair was harder to disguise. This was the second man in the alleyway. "Hello again, Moses," said Hunter, and moved on to the last photo.

This image was of the man in the middle, the one that Ribini and Moses had been so determined to get into the van and away from the building. The computer was 88-percent sure—as high a certainty factor as Hunter had ever seen—that the man was Isaiah Henderson, a.k.a. The Prophet.

The dossier didn't mention any previous association with the Zion International Party—which Hunter found interesting—but the suave-looking, well-dressed agitator was known to have committed serious felonies and was wanted in several states and numerous foreign countries, including Peru, Israel, Syria, and Zimbabwe. His crimes ranged from petty larceny and fraud to murder. He was last known to be associated with the Humanitarian Front of Judah, a now-defunct terrorist group that had been brought down in a very high-profile raid in the Middle East, orchestrated by one of Hunter's colleagues from three years ago. Most of the group's members had been arrested only to have their arrests quashed for lack of evidence; several stood trial, were convicted outright, and executed. Henderson, however, had given police the slip and had never been found—until today.

Hunter felt his pulse quicken. Henderson was definitely a major league player, surely one of the top ten international terrorists—a very big fish if Hunter had ever seen one. Hunter's little assignment had just turned into a huge opportunity to put the past in the deep shadow of a stellar achievement. His position in ICON and restoration of his rank—if not a promotion—awaited him if he could bring The Prophet down.

Gerald returned as he was finishing up. "Find anything interesting?" he asked, sliding in behind the desk.

"One or two possibilities," Hunter told him. "Enough to keep me going, anyway." He looked at his watch. Six o'clock. Time to eat. "Would you mind shutting things down here? I'd like to get onto these leads while they're still fresh."

"No problemo, boss."

"Thanks for your help."

"A pleasure, Agent Hunter. Anytime."

On the way back to the Belvedere, Hunter stopped for a decent dinner at Dos Amigos, then spent the next few hours in his room, reading random chapters from his new little terrorist library. It all proved mostly a much—obscure cant and rabid rant delivered in serious semiliterate prose—so, growing bored at last, he tossed the books aside and decided to take a shower and hit the sack early.

Little man, you've had a busy day, he thought as he switched off the light. He knew he'd need as much sleep as he could get before starting the next phase of action. He'd also need another hotel room.

seven

Hunter moved into Carnegie Suites, his new hotel, the next morning. It was conveniently down the street from the Belvedere. As he filled out the registration form, he told the desk clerk that he was in town on business but had to travel out from the city most days to see clients and expected he'd be gone a lot—sometimes days at a time. "Not to worry, Mr. Taylor," said the clerk as he swiped "Mr. Taylor's" credit card. "Your things will be perfectly safe with us."

In his room—a real improvement over the first, with a good desk, a comfy sofa, a sitting area, and a decent corner kitchen—he unpacked the books and some clothes he'd bought at a charity thrift shop. Anything that could associate him with ICON—his ID, assignment files, regulation sidearm, and laptop—remained in the safe in his old room at the Belvedere, and his uniform was locked in the closet. From now on, all his official research, phone calls, and correspondence would be done over there, making his new room the "clean" one. Anyone curious enough to search the suite would find no trace of his true identity.

Unpacking finished, Hunter decided to pay his chums at the

bookshop another visit. On the way out, he paused briefly to chat with the doorman—often a useful ally. "Summer stinks in this city," declared Eddie, "but I wouldn't wanna be anywhere else."

"Why's that?"

"Where else is there to go?" the doorman smiled knowingly. "Hey, listen, you need anything like, you know, baseball tickets, I can get them for you no problem. Mets, Yankees, no problem. And no one's cheaper, either. You just ask Eddie." He thumped his broad chest.

"Thanks, I'll keep that in mind."

"You new to the town? This your first time in the Empire City?"

"Yeah."

"Thought so. Can spot 'em a mile away." He grinned. An extremely short man—he couldn't have been much over five feet—Eddie the doorman had a ready smile and a never-met-a-stranger disposition. "What's your name, pal?"

"Sam," replied Hunter. "Sam Taylor."

"Listen, Mr. T.," Eddie lowered his voice and leaned closer, "you ever need some company, and I mean of the female per-suasion, you understand, look no farther. I know all the best girls."

"Well, I—"

"Or, you know, if guys are more your thing . . . I'm not judgmental, you understand—I can fix you up there too. Just say the word."

"Thanks, but no, ladies are fine with me, Eddie." Hunter gave Eddie a wink and slipped him a twenty.

"Hey, you have a nice day now."

Hunter walked to his destination and took a table at the café across from the bookstore, where he could keep an eye on it while he worked out his approach. This part of the operation was always tricky; it required all his skill and art. Extend himself too far, come across as too anxious or pushy, and he would arouse suspicion. He didn't kid himself—one mistake and a shrewd operator like The Prophet would be onto him in a second. On the other hand, if he held back too much, remained too aloof, too indifferent, the slender contact would snap and he'd be out in the cold. He had to win their confidence, put them at ease, and build a bridge to the future—all this, and only a few precious minutes to do it.

Fail this time and he could kiss any chance of promotion a fine fare-thee-well.

He gazed across at the bookstore and, taking a last fortifying bolt of bitter coffee, decided to make his move. "Here we go, ladies and gentlemen," he muttered to himself. "It's show time!"

He tossed a few coins on the table and walked as calmly as he could across the street and into the bookstore. The two men behind the counter glanced up at him. One of them, the bearded man Hunter was convinced was Wilson Conroy, leaned on the cash register, and next to him, none other than Father Moses himself. They appeared to be studying a large flyer, or poster, and were visibly annoyed at being disturbed.

"Something we can help you with?" Father Moses asked.

Hunter glanced around the store. It was exactly the same as he remembered it. "Oh, I just dropped by to see if the new shipment was in yet."

Father Moses starred blankly at him. "Shipment?"

"Uh . . . yeah," the bearded man said, "this is the guy I was telling you about—wanted the Alan Gibbons books, remember?"

Father Moses gave Hunter a quick up-and-down. "That so?"

"Yeah, I'm looking for *History Lies*. Can't seem to find it anywhere."

"I'm not surprised. A book like that," Moses shrugged dismissively, "it's not something most people would find all that interesting." The guy was definitely not local; there was a European tinge to Moses' accent—slight, but noticeable—that Hunter couldn't quite place. Maybe French, Hunter decided. Or Belgian.

"I understand," said Hunter. "But you could order it, right?"

"Maybe." Moses half-turned to Conroy, but kept his eyes glued to Hunter.

"I'd really appreciate it if you could try," he said, then leaned forward to share a confidence. "Just between you and me, I think the guy is fantastic—you know, the way he cuts through all the crap and lays it all out so clear. He's a genius, if you ask me."

Moses nodded slowly. "I know what you mean." To Conroy, he said, "Take his details and see if we can order that book."

"Sure." The bearded man stooped to retrieve a pad of paper from below the countertop.

"Thanks," said Hunter. "I really appreciate it."

"You said that already," replied Conroy, fumbling for a pencil. "So, let's have your name and address and stuff."

Hunter gave his information and allowed his glance to fall onto the flyer the two had been studying when he walked into the store. It advertised some sort of rally, and underneath it he saw a map of the city. Meanwhile, Moses stood off to one side, watching. Hunter got the feeling he was being sized up for a coffin.

When he finished taking down the information, Conroy said, "Okay, well . . . that's all we need." He glanced at Moses, who nodded. "We'll call you when the book comes in."

"Thanks," said Hunter, trying to keep his voice light and casual. He could feel the flimsy contact slipping away. "I guess that's it, then."

"Yeah, that's it."

Hunter edged toward the door. "I hope it doesn't take too long."

"We'll call you," said Moses.

"Right," said Hunter. He reached the door and put his hand to the brass push plate. "Well, see you around."

He was halfway through the door, when Moses called to him. "Say—you ever been in Pittsburgh?"

Here we go, thought Hunter. *Easy now, reel him in gently.* "Pittsburgh? Not really." He walked back to the counter, but slowly so as not to appear too eager. "I might have passed through on business once or twice, you know? Why do you ask?"

"Just wondering," said Moses. "You look like someone I might have seen."

"Yeah, I get that a lot," said Hunter with a smile. "I've got one of those faces."

"That's probably it," Moses agreed. He studied Hunter for a few seconds, then seemed to make a decision and extended his hand. "Mike Menahem," he said, by way of introduction.

Hunter took his hand and replied, "Sam Taylor."

"Tell me, Mr. Taylor, is your interest in . . . this," he waved his hand casually over the store, "merely academic? Are you a political scholar or something?"

"No such thing," Hunter shook his head. "The opposite in fact. I think there's too much talk and not enough action—if you know what I mean."

"Sure."

"I used to live in Chicago. I was friends with a guy who was into it—used to talk to me on our lunch break. He took me to a meeting and introduced me to some people. It just sorta grew from there."

"What meeting?"

"The Zelotes Brotherhood. Do you know them?"

Moses nodded; his eyes narrowed slightly. "We got meetings here, too. Maybe you'd be interested in attending a little get-together this Tuesday...." He bent down behind the counter, coming back up with a half-sheet of yellow paper printed with ink that didn't quite stick to the page. "It's just an exploratory session for like-minded people. Not as exciting as an Alan Gibbons book," he chuckled mirthlessly, "but you never know, you might find it interesting."

Hunter studied the handout, "Tuesday night, huh?"

Moses shrugged. "Just if you're interested. If you can't make it, you can't make it...."

Hunter folded the paper and stuck it in his pocket. "I'll come if I can." He stepped toward the door once more. "Well, see you around."

"We'll call you when your book comes in," Conroy said as Hunter left.

He gave a final wave and was back on the street. *So far, so good,* he thought. *In with a chance.*

eight

Hunter arrived at his appointed destination a few minutes before seven-thirty, carrying the yellow handout and a Rupert Stokes book entitled *Rules for Rebellion.* The building was a dilapidated community center on a badly lit street in TriBeCa, surrounded by weary brick apartment buildings with flaking paint and crumbling concrete steps—buildings ripe for yuppification. The community center's doors were closed but not locked, so he walked in and followed a path marked by a succession of hand-drawn arrows on day-glo yellow paper taped to the walls.

The place was dingy from overuse and haphazard cleaning, the linoleum floors pock-marked with cigarette burns, the institutional furniture scuffed and sagging; but the meeting room was brightly lit, at least, and ample sized. About thirty battered metal folding chairs were arranged in rows in the middle of the room before a low wooden riser with a microphone on a stand; only a dozen or so seats were taken, mostly by men. Three were women—serious looking, no-nonsense women with short hair, practical clothing, and sensible shoes.

Everyone seemed to know everyone else, and the idle chatter and sprinklings of laughter created a low murmur like a pan of water starting to boil. The mood was buoyant. Two men in dark shirts and khakis stood off to one side talking quietly while surveying the tidy crowd. Hunter recognized them as cult members the computer trace had failed to identify.

Hunter took a seat in the back row, opened his book and pretended to read. A few minutes later, Father Moses entered from the back with the six-foot-eight giant Hunter identified from the photo parade as Leon Ribini—size alone marked him out, but who could forget a face like that? Moses saw Hunter as he entered and they made eye contact briefly. Hunter nodded and leaned back in his chair.

At 7:45, the lights dimmed and Father Moses stepped up to the microphone; he gave it a few taps to silence the small but talkative crowd. After welcoming the attendees, he spoke briefly about the history of the Zion International Party, giving a greatly abridged and altogether softer version than Hunter had read in the ICON briefing file. Moses explained some of their ideological beliefs, which amounted to a rehash of the same tired old platitudes spouted by religious revolutionaries everywhere. But from the police records of some of the people involved, Hunter suspected ZIP had a secret—and far more violent—list of goals it shared only with its dyed-in-the-wool members.

After fifteen minutes of flim-flam and waffle, Moses finally introduced the key speaker, Isaiah Henderson, known to his followers as The Prophet.

Hunter leaned forward in his seat as the main attraction entered from a side door and strode purposefully to the microphone. He was a compact, well-dressed man in his prime who looked to be of Middle Eastern descent, with black, razor-cut hair and light olive skin. He walked lightly on the balls of his feet like a dancer or a cat burglar. His smooth jaw gleamed from a recent shave, and Hunter could almost smell the aftershave lotion from where he sat. Henderson carried himself with dignity: head erect, eyes level. He seemed in good physical condition, and his face was calm and confident as he turned his deep eyes on the paltry gathering.

Skipping the niceties, The Prophet began to speak in measured tones about the importance of conviction in the battle for ultimate liberation. It was obviously a canned speech; Hunter could tell he'd given it a hundred times before, and it left the impression of Henderson as a professional snake-oil salesman dutifully singing for his supper.

The Prophet finished twenty minutes later to a spattering of polite applause. Moses advanced to the microphone again and said, "Looks like we have time for some questions. I know some of you would like to ask The Prophet a few things. Who wants to go first?"

A weedy guy in a plaid shirt put up his hand and, after receiving the nod from Moses, said, "You wrote in your book that we're living in the Last Days, right? And you said that it's up to the True Believers to bring about the Final Cataclysm, right? So, like, what exactly did you mean by that, and how do we do it, like, practically speaking?"

Hunter expected a short, dismissive answer, but Henderson actually rose to the occasion for the first time that evening. As he stepped to the mike again, his eyes seemed to burn with new energy. He spoke with a passion and vehemence that tingled the tiny hairs on the back of Hunter's neck.

"We are indeed living in the Last Days, my friends," The Prophet said, his voice taking on luster and strength. "The Last Days of confusion, frustration, stagnation, and degeneration. We live in an age controlled by the power-mongers and a blind, bloated, ignorant government bureaucracy grown decrepit with age, existing solely to perpetuate itself and its own ineptitude. We live in an age where globe-spanning corporations dictate the fortunes of nations, where human freedom is bought and sold in the marketplace of expediency, where individual thought is controlled by a manipulative media which has become the whore of ICON, drip-feeding gobbets of juicy lies to a sensation-addicted public."

He paused and looked out at his silent audience. "Truly, my friends, these are the Last Days. Death, disease, poverty, and injustice! This is the jackal pack that stalks our sleeping camp, attacking the weak, the sick—those too powerless and defenseless to fight back.

"My friends! It is time to awaken! It is time to wrest the levers of power from the cold, dead hands of a corrupt elite that has imposed its stultifying will on the citizens of this planet far too long. It is time, my friends, to raise the cry of alarm, to wake the sleeping masses and alert them to the terrible fate that awaits them if they fail to join the fight. Those who are not for us are against us! We can no longer afford to waste time in diplomacy, in debate, in reasoned argument. From now on, talk must cease; the debate is over. From now on, we speak through the weapons of rebellion. We speak through action—for only through action will our words be heard."

Despite the dreary predictability of his words, Henderson,

The Prophet, seemed to grow into his theme, taking on stature and vigor as he spoke; his voice actually expanded to fill the room so that his words were not only heard, but also felt in the chest. He knew how to use the cadence of oratory to make fairly pedestrian concepts sound fresh and new and exciting.

"The world as we know it cannot continue. The old order is dying; but until it is dead, the new order cannot come into existence. We must help the dying order to die, my friends. We must aid the birth of the new order through joining with like-minded friends to create bodies of resistance to the status quo. We must stop listening to the lies and start thinking for ourselves. We must give aid to those who are willing to take power into their own hands for the good of all. Finally, we must . . ." here The Prophet faltered. Hunter got the idea that he was just getting warmed up to say something truly interesting, but caught himself and pulled back.

"We must all unite," The Prophet concluded, "against the tyranny of conformity which perpetuates the oppression against which we fight. We must all become soldiers in the worldwide war for freedom from the imposed constraints of a monolithic machine of government designed not to serve its citizens, but to enslave them. Truly, we must all become soldiers, my friends, or we will remain slaves forever. . . ."

Truths, half-truths, and tired old truisms were flung out indifferently, then caught and gathered together again to create emotionally compelling arguments. Henderson used every trick in the book, and it all worked.

The raw dynamism this man possessed when merely given a microphone and a soapbox was something to behold. If The Prophet's strength of will to motivate genuine violence was in any way comparable to the power he displayed in a simple workaday speech. . . . Hunter didn't want to think about it.

Moses was at the microphone again. "I guess we'll take one more question."

A man in the front row put up his hand and asked something about how to know which political organizations were worth supporting. The question was innocuous enough, but it gave The Prophet a chance to tee-off on a pet subject: his hatred of ICON.

He began with a catalog of horrors allegedly perpetrated by ICON throughout the world as a way of citing the oppressive force it wielded over the masses. He quickly went on to call for the unification of all warring religious and political factions. Strength, The Prophet insisted, was in numbers; internal conflict was a waste. He petitioned all the devoted brothers separated by ideological narrow-mindedness to put aside their differences and join together. He ticked off a list of the various groups and factions he had so far managed to unite under his banner of radical tolerance, and Hunter did his best to memorize them: The Judean League, The Freedom Reformation Coalition, The Zelotes Brotherhood, The Eastern Apocalypse, and several others.

Shortly after the international call to arms, The Prophet stopped—almost in the middle of a sentence—and thanked his crowd for listening. There was another round of brief applause as he left the podium and disappeared through the side door. No one else took the microphone, so people started to stand up and disperse. Hunter stood and found himself face to face with Father Moses.

"Mr. Taylor," he said, taking Hunter's hand. "So glad you

could make it." Hunter smiled vaguely. "I wonder if I might introduce someone to you. . . . "

Moses turned and waved over a young man in his midtwenties. Hunter recognized him from his unidentified photo taken in the alleyway: he was the one with spiky blond hair and facial piercings. He had a narrow face with clean-lined, almost feminine features, and a lanky body with the broad shoulders and narrow waist of a swimmer. But the most arresting thing about him was his eyes—as blue as chips of arctic ice and just as cold.

"This is Simon," said Moses. "Simon, this is Mr. Taylor—"

"Call me Sam," said Hunter. The two shook hands. Simon's grasp was dry and cool.

"Simon is also from Chicago," Moses continued, "and a former member of the Zelotes Brotherhood."

"Oh really?" Hunter's brain immediately switched into defense mode.

"Yeah," Simon replied, "I hear you were in a cell group there."

Hunter shrugged. "I went with a friend to a couple of meetings is all."

"Where was this?"

"In the western suburbs."

Simon's eyes narrowed. "The man who led this group—was his name Micah Bettock?"

Hunter frowned as if in thought. Every ICON undercover agent knew a good way to blow your cover was to play along too far in a bluff. "Um . . . I'm not sure. The name doesn't sound familiar, but I suppose it could have been. This was three years ago."

Simon smiled. "Before my time."

Hunter relaxed. "Well, it's nice to meet you anyway," he said.

He looked at his watch. "I gotta run." He turned again to Moses and thanked him for inviting him to the meeting. "It's given me a lot to think about. The Prophet—Henderson did you say his name was?—he's a very intelligent speaker. Has he got a book or anything?"

"Listen, why don't you come along next week," suggested Moses. "I'll introduce you to a few more people. It was quite a light crowd tonight. There will be more next week."

"Well, thanks," Hunter replied. "I'll try to make it."

When Hunter arrived back at his Belvedere hotel room, the first thing he did was fire up his computer and log on to the ICON mainframe to run a search for the organizations The Prophet had mentioned. The Freedom Reformation Coalition and Eastern Apocalypse both had ties to militaristic terrorist organizations active in the Middle East, and both had extensive report files on them. The Judean Human League also worked out of the Middle East and had ties to many other, smaller organizations—some legit, some not.

The Zelotes Brotherhood was a group Hunter had already encountered. They were fairly innocuous as far as extremist groups went and were mainly a front for another organization called, simply, Gomorrah—a group of uglies who really did mean business. That business seemed to be, more often than not, killing, trying to kill, threatening, or intimidating leaders in power. They also refused to pay taxes, but that seemed to be a given in any revolutionary gang.

Hunter clicked his way through the assembled reports in the file and read one of the more detailed entries by a female agent TIY-045-772-3318-DF who'd had to pull the plug on her mission after drawing too much suspicion. She listed the criminal activities the group had perpetrated during her time with them, the power structure—which was topped by a man named Isaiah Prophet (no picture available)—key members of the group, and so on. She indicated that members of the organization were trained to act as independent assassins called the "Sicarii," or Dagger-men. They were all given a list of political targets to memorize and orders to eliminate any they came across. A successful assassination would buy a higher position in the group, relative to that target's level of threat as perceived by the group. There was a note attached which stated that undercover agents carried a high price, and that the group claimed to have executed two agents in the field. She was unable to confirm this but considered the threat genuine.

Hunter felt his blood warm to the chase. At that moment, he felt himself more than equal to the task of bringing down ZIP and personally hauling The Prophet's butt to the nearest ICON slammer.

nine

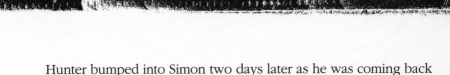

Hunter bumped into Simon two days later as he was coming back to Carnegie Suites from a long and sweaty jog in the park. He caught sight of the young man standing in the entrance, talking to Eddie the doorman.

"Simon, hi," he said, stepping under the green-striped hotel awning. He nodded to Eddie, who touched the bill of his hat in response. "What brings you here?"

"Hi, Sam, glad I caught you." He smiled, but the warmth never touched his eyes, which remained blue and cold and distant. "Moses sent me over. I've got your book here." He held up a copy of *History Lies*.

"That was quick. Want to go for some coffee?" Hunter asked. "I need to towel off and change my clothes first though." Simon seemed on the verge of rejecting the invitation. "Well, come on up, and I'll get your money anyway."

They entered the lobby of the hotel and rode up to the fourth floor. Hunter unlocked the door and let his guest in. "Hang on a sec, would you? I gotta use the can. Make yourself at home."

Hunter took his time in the bathroom, running water in the sink to splash his face and neck, lingering long enough to give Simon time to snoop around.

"That's better," Hunter said, emerging with a towel to his face. Simon was pushing an empty drawer closed with his foot. Hunter fished out a twenty from the pocket of his trousers, which were slung across the chair. "Keep the change."

"Thanks," said Simon, handing over the book.

"So, you work at the bookstore too?"

"Sometimes." Simon's eyes flicked around the room, his gaze landing on the books and pamphlets Hunter had artfully arranged on the desk.

"I'm looking forward to reading this," Hunter said, placing the book on the desk with the others. "How about that coffee? There's a Mr. Good Bean just around the corner."

"Yeah, thanks, but I better get back," replied Simon. "I told Moses I wouldn't be gone long."

Hunter smiled. "Well, maybe next time, then."

"Sure, whatever. Listen, about next Tuesday night—"

"The meeting? Yeah, I'm coming."

"We were wondering if you would like to come to a different meeting tomorrow night."

"What kind?"

"A more personal, private kind of thing. Moses said I should tell you it's for people who really want to make a difference. You know, an active difference."

"Sounds okay," Hunter replied, trying not to sound too eager.

"It'll be a chance for you to meet The Prophet personally," offered Simon, sweetening the offer.

"No kidding? Okay. Well, I'll have to see if I can change my schedule."

"Yeah, you do that," said Simon. His voice took on a subtly insinuating quality, which Hunter noted. "I mean, *if* you're really interested. Thing is, you probably won't get asked again, you know?"

"Okay, I guess I can make it," replied Hunter.

"If it's too much bother for a busy man like yourself," Simon said in his softly insinuating tone, "maybe you should forget it."

"Look, I said I'd go, all right?" replied Hunter with more exasperation than he felt. "Just tell me when and where. I'll be there."

Hunter saw the edges of Simon's mouth twitch and knew the young man was struggling to keep his cool. "It's a ways from here. I'll pick you up downstairs. Eight o'clock."

"I'll be there."

"Don't be late. I won't wait around." Simon turned abruptly and started for the door.

The guy would be dangerous if crossed. It was time to make nice. "You sure you won't change your mind about that coffee?" he asked. "They got great muffins too."

"Another time," said Simon without turning around. Hunter shut the door after him, then stood for a moment deep in thought. What he thought was that things were heating up nicely—perhaps too nicely? Impossible to say. He'd just have to play along to find out.

Hunter turned off the TV. Bored with watching the interminable news—everything else the small selection of channels had to offer was either tedious, idiotic, or both—he looked at the burgeoning collection of books piled on the bed beside him. He was rapidly growing sick of his religious nutcase research, even though he still had a lot to get through. Maybe he should go out, take a walk, get some fresh air, and then come back for a final push. Yes, that would be the best thing.

Or maybe he would just stay planted like a potato in bed and stare at the wall. It was still hot outside, and he didn't really feel like moving far from the air conditioning. He switched on the box again.

An hour later he had once again flicked off the TV, thrown the remote in the corner, and was pulling on a T-shirt and jogging shorts when the phone rang. He paused for a second. Who knew his number? Was Simon or Father Moses calling him? He answered it.

"There's a visitor for you, boss," came Eddie's cheerful voice.

"Visitor?"

"Female. Ve-e-ery nice one too, sir." Hunter could hear Eddie lick his lips. "So, shall I send her up, or physically throw her off the premises?"

"Hang on, I'll be down in a second."

A short time later, Hunter appeared in the hotel lobby where Eddie was talking to a stunning woman. Her head was tilted back, allowing her long, dark hair to spill over her bare shoulders, and she was laughing at something Eddie had said. Her laugh was throaty and low, and Hunter warmed instantly to hear it. She turned as Hunter came up and gazed at him expectantly from beneath finely arched eyebrows; her eyes were large and slightly slanted, giving her an exotic appearance.

Her skin was smooth and clean with only light makeup, perfectly applied. She was slender and willowy, with long legs, and when she moved—as she did now, walking toward him—she swayed gently, as if in a breeze. *Definitely my type*, thought Hunter.

"Mr. Taylor?" she said, her voice low.

"Yes," replied Hunter. "And you are?" He looked into her eyes and marveled at the depth of the rich brown he found there.

"Call me Rosa."

"Nice name."

She smiled, and the smile seemed perfectly suited to her generous mouth and lips; it was unforced and genuine, as was her manner when she held out her hand. Hunter took it in his, and the touch of her cool fingertips against his palm gave him a pleasant buzz. "I think you want to buy me a drink."

"You read my mind."

They found a small bar attached to a restaurant not too far from the hotel. Hunter bought them both drinks. In the golden evening light slanting through the windows, Rosa looked magnificent—definitely a cut above the women Hunter usually settled for. She had an elegance and refinement that was rare in someone of her profession. Eddie certainly knew his stuff.

"So, where are you from?"

Rosa gave a small shrug. "Does it matter? I've lived a lot of places—both coasts and in between. What about you?"

"Chicago."

"Were you born there?"

Hunter felt an almost compelling need to be honest with her, but quickly reminded himself that he was Sam Taylor 24/7, not just when with the Zipsters. "No, I was born in St. Louis, but we moved when I was really young."

"St. Louis, huh?" A sparkle appeared in Rosa's eye. "So tell me, Mr. Taylor . . . "

"Call me Sam."

"Sam? That's funny . . . you don't look like a Sam."

Hunter shrugged. "You don't look like a Rosa."

"Touché." She laughed, charming Hunter to his socks. "So tell me, Sam, what's the most exciting place you've ever been?"

Hunter's brow creased in thought. "Hmm. Good question, well, let's see now . . . " Hunter had been to lots of places: Cairo and Madrid stood out. But he settled on something more prosaic. "Cleveland," he said at last. "Definitely Cleveland. Or Cincinnati."

"You're kidding."

"Yes." He smiled. "Actually, I don't travel that much. Born and raised in the Midwest. So far, New York is the most interesting place I've been in a long time. It's big and intricate. Like a colossal beehive. There's always something happening."

"That's true. And why are you here in the Big Beehive, Mr. Sam Taylor?"

"Business—it's as boring as that. How about you? What's the most exciting place you've been?"

"I was in France once. Paris. I was young—eight or nine, I think—and my parents took me. I still remember the Louvre, though. To me it was like a country in itself. So big! Whenever I see a picture of it, I try to look away so that it doesn't spoil my memory. It's always much grander when I see it in my mind."

Hunter gazed at her, smitten. She drained her drink and then raised her eyes to meet his. Setting aside her glass, she leaned forward on her arms. Tilting her head upward, extending her long, graceful neck, she smiled. "Shall we go?"

Even though he knew what was coming next—and was looking forward to it—Hunter was enjoying sitting across from this beauty and wanted the moment to last. He raised his hand to call the barmaid. "There's no hurry. Let's have another drink first."

He ordered two more drinks and then turned back to Rosa. "Next question," she said. "If you had all the money in the world . . . "

Hunter found Rosa fully as intoxicating as the drinks and was walking tall on the way back to the hotel. He pressed a twenty into Eddie's hand as he passed and led his companion to the elevators and up to his room.

Thursday was the last day of Zack's work in the temple. It had been two weeks since the dark prowler had accosted him, and he was now extra cautious when locking up. Each night he scanned the streets from the inside windows before leaving through the large double doors.

This night felt different from the previous nights. As his back was turned to place the key in the lock, he felt a curious tension rising up through his spine—as if cold eyes were watching him. He took a deep breath and then turned around quickly, preparing himself for what he would find, which was . . .

Nothing.

Old Zack let a sigh of relief escape his lips. It was then he reminded himself that *every* night felt different. Every night he felt sure that he would meet his shadowed visitor again, and every night he was disappointed. A happy disappointment though, he thought, and chuckled to himself as he descended the stairs.

Halfway down, and he heard a swift movement behind him. Could it be? Yes. The same man as before. "Hold it right there, Zack," the stranger said.

"What do you want this time?" The old man asked, his voice weaker and thinner than he would have liked.

"Where is your son?"

"That again?"

"Your son—where is he?" demanded the stranger, moving closer.

"Listen to me. How can I tell you what I don't know?" the old man made to push past the shadowed figure. "And, tell me, how is it you don't know where he is when he walks around every day with five hundred of his closest friends? Give me a break!"

With a swift, efficient movement, the inquisitor lunged for Zack, seized his neck between two strong hands, and lifted the old man so that his feet dangled, weak legs flailing.

"Where is your son?"

Zack could not answer; the pressure on his throat was too tight. He gasped for air and felt the hands ease off slightly—just long enough for him to draw a deep breath and then answer, "Catskills! I th—caghk! I think he's in the Catskills!"

The pressure on the old man's throat tightened again. His vision grew hazy and every blood vessel in his head felt as if it would explode.

Then, suddenly, he was released. The dark man's hands left his throat and Zack felt himself fall; he hit the stairs and rolled down to the sidewalk where he lay panting, trying to catch his breath sufficiently to scream for help. Just as he was drawing air to cry out, the stranger swooped once more and took his head between his strong hands, gripping him like a vise.

The dark man twisted sideways and up, snapping the elderly priest's neck and tearing his trachea. With a mewing whimper, he slumped into a heap.

The black figure straightened himself and then briskly crossed the street and vanished into the shadows.

ten

Eight o'clock the next evening, Hunter was standing outside the Carnegie Suites hotel watching a dark blue SUV roll slowly past: the same one he'd seen in the alley of the bookstore. It proceeded down the block and stopped, double-parking in traffic. The passenger door opened. Simon stepped out and motioned for him to come.

Hunter hustled down the block. "Get in," said Simon.

He climbed in the back, and Simon got in beside him and slammed the door. "Who's your friend?" asked Hunter as the car pulled away.

"Oh, yeah," said Simon, "Sam, meet Leon Walsh." Simon gestured to the driver, known to Hunter as the crater-faced Leon Ribini; he made a mental note to update the man's aliases on his file.

"Hi, there," Hunter said. The big man just grunted and nodded at him through the rearview mirror.

"So," said Simon, settling back in his seat, "did you manage to get a look at that book?"

"Yeah, I read a couple chapters last night. . . . "

They talked about *History Lies* while the car made its crosstown journey. Hunter was prepared to have a serious conversation about Alan Gibbons, The Prophet's political theories, or the price of tea in Tibet—anything to take the chill off Simon. But the cooler-than-cool young man didn't seem interested; he was just killing time, making small talk.

The SUV crossed the East River and headed out on the expressway toward Jackson Heights and into Queens. After a while, Leon turned off the expressway onto a near-deserted street in an upscale neighborhood. They cruised a few more blocks. Leon pulled into a parking garage underneath a sleek office building and nosed into a reserved parking space right next to the elevator.

"Must be an exclusive meeting," observed Hunter as he got out.

"Yeah, I guess," said Simon. He pushed open the door. "Like I said, this is different from the regular Tuesday thing."

Leon pressed a button on the elevator, the doors slid open, and they rode to one of the upper floors. They got out and walked down an empty corridor to a door marked "Conference Room," where Leon knocked twice, waited, then knocked once more. A moment later there came a click as the lock was released from the other side.

"After you," said Leon, pushing open the door.

Hunter stepped through, suddenly very aware that no one had seen him go into the building, and he hadn't filed any reports with Supervisor Riley stating his intentions to attend the short-notice meeting. Sloppy. If there was plastic sheeting laid out on the conference room floor, he was going to hightail it out of there.

The room was empty except for stacks of wood-and-chrome chairs in one corner; a man in a dark suit stood directly in front of Hunter. The man looked past him at Simon, nodded, and said, "They're in the back."

Leon led them across the room to another door, opened it, and ushered Hunter through. Inside this second room were a dozen men of varying ages. All were well dressed in smart casual shirts and trousers; some had on ties, and one or two wore blazers. They were helping themselves to a cold-cut buffet laid out on folding tables. They talked quietly, hardly bothering to glance around as the newcomers joined them.

"You hungry?" asked Simon, indicating the buffet. It was the first thing approaching real warmth Hunter detected in the young man. "We can get something if you want."

"Sure, why not?" replied Hunter.

Following the others' example, Hunter joined the line at the buffet, picked up a paper plate, and began loading it with meat, cheese, bread, and pickles. He was spooning on potato salad when he caught sight of the man himself: Henderson, The Prophet, was standing by a floor-to-ceiling window, holding the vertical blinds to one side and looking down onto the street below.

Leon approached Henderson; the two exchanged a few words and then Leon beckoned Simon and Hunter over. Hunter put his plate down and followed Simon, who introduced him, saying, "This is the guy I was telling you about."

"Hello—ah, Mr. Taylor, is it?" said The Prophet. "I'm happy you could join us." His voice was softer and deeper than three nights ago, and he looked tired. But as before, he was immaculately groomed. His face still glowed from the shave, and this time

Hunter could smell a heavy application of Davidoff aftershave.

"It's a privilege to meet you, sir."

"Welcome." The Prophet did not extend his hand. "It was good of you to come at such short notice."

"Not at all," Hunter said. "The pleasure's mine, um . . . Mr. Prophet."

The Prophet laughed, a deep-throated chuckle. "Please, call me Isaiah." The smile quickly vanished, however, and Hunter found himself under hard scrutiny. "I understand you've been getting to know Simon here." He put a fatherly hand on the young man's shoulder.

"Yes, a little." Hunter turned to observe the aloof young man as he spoke. "It seems we share an interest in Alan Gibbons."

"As do we all, I should hope." The Prophet allowed himself a thin smile and opened his arms as if to embrace the others in the room. "I think you'll find that all of us here tonight are like-minded. That is why this has been arranged." Turning once more to his scrutiny of the newcomer, Henderson said, "What is it you do for a living, Mr. Taylor, if I may be so bold?"

"Call me Sam," said Hunter. "As it happens, I'm a risk asses-sor for an industrial insurance company. I'm in New York work-ing up a report on one of our larger clients, and also to make a few new contacts. For many of our clients, it makes a lot of sense to self-insure, but there are pitfalls if you—"

"I see," Henderson interrupted. "How very interesting. Well, perhaps we can help. Our organization has many useful . . . " he paused and looked Hunter in the eye before adding, "contacts." Shifting his gaze to Simon, he continued, "We are a group that knows how to take care of its own."

Hunter felt some sort of message pass between the two men, and then The Prophet turned away abruptly. "Would you like a drink? Leon here will get you a beer." He gave a nod to the hulking giant, who lumbered away. "Now then, Mr. Taylor—Sam—I was wondering if you'd be interested in helping me with a special errand."

"Could be," Hunter allowed amiably. "What sort of errand?"

"There is a certain religious group meeting up in the Catskills this weekend. Simon's going up on a fact-finding mission. If you're not too busy, I thought you might accompany him."

"Sounds okay. What would I have to do?"

"Nothing much. You'll be attending some talks, gaining some impressions. It's information gathering. If we find a few like-minded people, we might open a dialogue with them, 'build a bridge' so to speak. There is strength in unity." He smiled. "What do you say?"

Before Hunter could answer, Leon returned. "Ah, here's your beer," said Henderson.

"Thanks." Hunter accepted the lukewarm bottle. "Well, it sounds interesting. I don't know, though. I'm supposed to go over a stack of old worker's comp claims with my client to include in—"

"Well, think about it," said The Prophet. "Talk it over with Simon. Now, if you'll excuse me." He started moving away. "Perhaps we can chat again later."

When The Prophet had gone, Hunter and Simon retrieved their plates, found chairs, and sat down to eat. "So," said Hunter after a moment, "what's this errand thing all about?"

"There's this traveling mystic," replied Simon. "Fantastic orator, from what I've heard. People flock to him like flies on a cow pie. He stalks the woods and wilderness areas mainly. Camps out in state parks. He likes to get everybody all excited, and lately he's been touching a nerve with a lot of activists like ourselves. His views are starting to coincide with some of our own about immediate progressive political reunification. Doesn't put it quite like that, of course. Has a way of chopping it up, helping people understand. He could be a great resource if we can bring him alongside our organization because, as I say, people are eating this stuff up."

Hunter raised his eyebrows slightly as Simon took a swig of his beer.

Simon turned his icy gaze on Hunter, his expression flat. "If nothing else, it's a weekend in the Catskills. What do you say?"

"Sure," Hunter replied. "Why not?"

They continued eating while The Prophet made the rounds, cozying up to his guests, none of whom was introduced to Hunter. As he was finishing his sandwich, Henderson came back and said, "Well, Sam, have you decided?"

"I was just telling Simon that I'd be happy to go."

"Good! Good!" The Prophet clapped his hand to Hunter's shoulder and kneaded the muscles gently. Suddenly enthusiastic and friendly, he said, "I am so encouraged. It is beautiful up there—have you been? No? You will fall in love with the place, I guarantee it. Simon will make the arrangements, and he'll pick you up at your hotel."

Henderson stuck out his hand. "I'm very glad we had this chance to talk, Sam." He glanced at his watch, then said, "Plans have changed slightly and I've got to run, but you and Simon feel free to stay and take advantage of the buffet." The Prophet smiled and walked away. He paused to talk to a group of men at the door, then left the room.

Simon turned to Hunter. "I'll take you home so you can get ready. It's camping out, so I wouldn't bring anything fancy."

"Fine with me," said Hunter. "It'll be good to get out of the city for a few days."

"Okay, then, I'll pick you up at ten o'clock tomorrow morning."

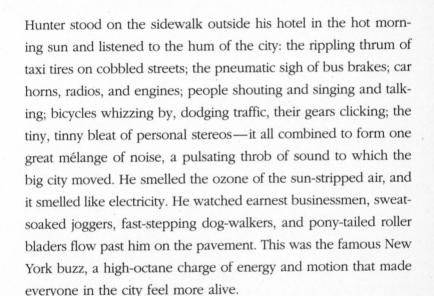

eleven

Hunter stood on the sidewalk outside his hotel in the hot morning sun and listened to the hum of the city: the rippling thrum of taxi tires on cobbled streets; the pneumatic sigh of bus brakes; car horns, radios, and engines; people shouting and singing and talking; bicycles whizzing by, dodging traffic, their gears clicking; the tiny, tinny bleat of personal stereos—it all combined to form one great mélange of noise, a pulsating throb of sound to which the big city moved. He smelled the ozone of the sun-stripped air, and it smelled like electricity. He watched earnest businessmen, sweat-soaked joggers, fast-stepping dog-walkers, and pony-tailed roller bladers flow past him on the pavement. This was the famous New York buzz, a high-octane charge of energy and motion that made everyone in the city feel more alive.

Or maybe it was just the coffee. Hunter glanced down at the tall brown paper cup in his hand; it was his second cup of Mr. Good Bean that morning. *Might account for the slight edgy, tingly feeling in my stomach. That, and the thrill of the chase.*

He was carrying only one weapon, and that made him nervous.

Concealing one gun was a problem—especially in a T-shirt and jeans—but two was next to impossible. Be that as it may, he regretted leaving the other behind and was only slightly comforted by the other precautions he'd taken, such as putting Devlin's number on speed-dial under "Mother."

He'd sent a report to Central Command last night outlining all he had discovered so far: not much, but it was a start. He'd informed them of the trip to the Catskills, and he would look for a chance to buy something with his credit card as soon as they reached their destination. All undercover agents carried special credit cards that, when used, put up an electronic flag and forwarded their details to Central Command.

He was as ready as he could be, but on the other hand, he realized that if The Prophet was planning for a suspected ICON agent to drop off the face of the earth, he couldn't have orchestrated a better setup.

The blue SUV pulled up right on time. Hunter tossed in his nylon gym bag containing a change of clothes, his Alan Gibbons book, towel and toothbrush and whatnot, then climbed in after it. He greeted Simon and the driver, a man he hadn't seen before. They drove the few blocks to Grand Central Station, mostly in silence.

Whatever was on Simon's mind, he apparently didn't want to talk about it, so after a few halfhearted attempts to draw him out, Hunter gave up, sat back, and enjoyed the short ride to the train. Tickets in hand and carrying a green backpack, Simon strolled onto the platform. The two of them boarded the first-class coach to Kingston. The train was nearly empty so they took two seats across the aisle from one another.

The taciturn Simon immediately closed his eyes and went to sleep. Hunter didn't really want a midmorning nap, so he sat back and watched the traffic on the platform until he felt the train start to move, then got up to look for yet another cup of coffee.

Walking on unsteady legs through the swaying cars, he finally located the restaurant car. There were a few passengers already at the tables, so he took a stool at the bar, where he sat staring at a bad, overheated instant cappuccino. He was thinking through possible strategies he might use to warm up the ever-frosty Simon when a great scruffy bear of a backpacker settled on the stool next to him.

The man smiled at him through a tangle of beard that reached to his beer-belly and, in a voice that sounded like gravel in a bucket, asked, "So, goin' up to see the Washer?"

"The Washer?" said Hunter.

"Yeah, Washer John."

"A friend of mine is looking for this traveling mystic," Hunter replied, deciding to go with the truth and see where it got him.

"Traveling mystic—yeah, that's him. That's Washer John."

"Well, I'm just along for the ride."

"Can always spot 'em," declared the man with satisfaction. "Can also tell you ain't never seen him before, neither."

"Yeah? How can you tell?"

"Ain't got the light in the eyes—know what I mean? All you got is questions." The man widened his own faded brown orbs until they virtually bulged out of their sockets, pointing to them with a tobacco-stained finger. Turning to the bartender, he hollered, "Hey! Whattaya gotta do to get a beer around here?"

While the barman rustled in the refrigerator for the beer, Hunter leaned back to study the aging hippie next to him. Hidden in the gray wisps of beard were several talismans that Hunter was reasonably sure had once been love beads. A chubby Buddha squinted cheerfully at Hunter from a chain dangling below the man's ear, while Vishnu bobbed up and down on a string below his chin.

The fellow's faded army jacket was a patchwork of tattered badges and obscure emblems. There was a Star of David on one side of his chest and a decrepit "peace" sign on the other— together with half a dozen other insignias of a wild-and-woolly past: some advertised actual, geographical locations; a few made oblique political statements; and some newer-looking badges were of subverted corporate logos with cleverly selected obscenities worked into the design. Hunter spied the ever-popular "ICONoclast" patch on the man's arm.

The barman placed a paper doily on the counter and set a sweating bottle on it. "Hey, I'm Robert, by the way," said the hippie. "People call me Bob." He raised his bottle in salute and took a big swig.

"Glad to meet you," Hunter told him. "You've seen this Washer John?"

"Sure, couple of times. Amazing guy. Just went down south to bury a friend—sad case . . . homeless, vet, the whole nine yards. Anyway, I'm just heading back now and hope to chill with the heads for a spell. He's the real deal, Washer John."

"So, tell me about him. What's he like?"

"All right—tell you what though, you got a cigarette?"

Hunter said that he didn't; Bob shrugged and produced a tobacco pouch and papers. Hunter offered to buy him another beer instead.

"You got yourself a deal." Hunter ordered the beer and the hippie swiveled around in his seat. "Well, some people think Washer John's a prophet. A lot of people think so, actually. Anyway, he wanders around with this *huge* entourage, you know, usually about a hundred or so, but once this summer it must have been over a thousand. It gets out of control sometimes, to be honest."

Bob paused to light up the cigarette he had just rolled and then went on, "Now, your garden variety prophet will often be militant, talking about how the common man got to rise up and unite and overthrow the wicked overlords, and usually that's because he just wants to be an overlord himself, you know? But this Washer John fellah ain't like that. He don't talk out against anyone, or hit up his followers for money or anything like that. He just wanders around in the hills, calling on folk to repent and get right with God 'cause, he says, the fat's going to hit the fire real soon."

"Seems harmless enough."

"Sh-yeah, harmless he ain't," replied Bob. "No way. Not if you've heard him talk. You think forgiveness is a simple, straight-forward concept, right? Man, you should hear him go. He'll have you feeling sorry for every ant you ever accidentally squashed, and what you said to your mother twenty years ago. All the same he puts the most complicated ideas the most simplest way, and it's like . . . a kind of poetry, you know? But with attitude. Dude'll blow your mind. You gotta see him to believe him. I mean, plus this guy's built like an ox—okay? So anyway, all these hundreds of people follow him like he's the actual messiah or something. So what I like—"

"Wait a second," Hunter interrupted. "This messiah thing—what's that? I mean, I keep hearing the word, but what is it exactly?"

The hippie took a long drag on his cigarette, "Yeah, well, messiah is just another word for leader. Jewish, I think. Yeah. It actually sort of means, like, champion or deliverer, but sort of military-like, you know? One sent by God. The Jews got only one god you know, but there's been hundreds of messiahs over the years and they usually have an agenda, right? They want to have their own country, or destroy the established power, or kill the tribe over the river, whatever. Usually they die a pretty sticky death, though—at which point they say that the guy wasn't *really* the messiah after all, just another messed-up dude. Whatever. Anyway, there's this rumor going around that when the real, actual, *true* messiah appears the whole world will end."

Bob made an exploding gesture with his hands that sent cigarette ash drifting into his beard. He swigged on his beer and plunged ahead. "Anyway, this John guy, he's wandering around the woods and mountains and stuff, preaching to whoever listens. He also does this—and this is why they call him *Washer* John—he does this thing where every once in a while when he comes across a river or a lake or something and he finds a shallow part—I actually saw this happen in Minnesota about a year ago, where the Mississippi is just a trickle in the bushes, anyway . . . " he put the cigarette in his mouth so he could better gesture with his hands.

"Okay, anyway, he tromps on out into the river and people line up and wade out to him. He puts his hands on their heads and starts pushing everybody under the water. Boosh! Then the next one, Boosh! One after the other, like dunking watermelons. And it changes people, you know! I can't explain it. I hope he does it when we're there, 'cause you really should see it. He did it to me once, and I haven't been the same since. It's not something I can describe . . . the feeling is just like . . . "

The ancient hippie trailed off and leaned back in his seat. After a lengthy pause, he turned to Hunter again. "Do you know what they say he eats?"

"No, what?"

"Grasshoppers."

"Get outta here!"

"I'm not kidding. This is what he does, okay? Pay attention, you might need to know this—it's a survivalist thing. The first thing you do is get some honey. Now, that's not as hard as it might sound—all you have to do is to find a bee and follow it back to where it lives. Simple. Next you take a little honeycomb from the bees. I don't know how you do that. Maybe you smoke them out or sneak up on them from behind or something. Anyway, you take this honeycomb and haul it to the nearest meadow or pasture or whatever. You put it on some leaves and leave it there for a few hours, or overnight, sticky side up, and when you come back, you have a plate full of grasshoppers and whatnot. They smell the honey and wander over to take a look, and—Hey, presto! Instant protein and sugar hit!" Bob laughed and rolled on his stool.

"Huh," Hunter sat back with a bemused smile on his face.

They sat in silence for a moment. Then the older man edged his stool closer to Hunter, leaned in, and said, "But that's not the strangest story I heard about Washer John."

Hunter raised his eyebrows with interest.

"There's a story going around about what happened when Washer John was born." He extinguished his cigarette. "Do you know what a angel is?"

Hunter shook his head.

"It's sort of like a ghost—only with muscles. The idea is that when God made everything—there's only one Jewish god remember—well, he also made these, like, giant spirits to help him out. And he called 'em angels."

Bob stubbed out his cigarette and continued, "Well, the story is—and I'm telling it to you like it was told to me—is that John's old man and his wife couldn't have kids. And this was a real shame, because in their culture it's really terrible not to have kids. It's like you've done something to offend the Big Guy and he's getting back at you, and letting everybody else know it, too.

"So, the years pass, and eventually it gets to the point where the two of them are so old it don't matter anymore. His wife's gone through, you know, The Change. So here's the old guy working in the temple—he's a priest by the way—and one day he gets chosen to go to the altar to burn incense for a special offering. Very important, big deal this—you maybe get chosen once in your life *if* you're lucky. So he goes inside to burn incense while everyone else is standin' around prayin' outside.

"It takes a while to get the incense goin', right, and, I don't know, maybe he's thinking about children and why it is he can't have any, or whatever. . . . But he turns around and suddenly there's this big fellah standing there—and I mean *big!* He's eight foot tall if he's a inch, and he's wearing a kind of shining armor with a flaming sword and a twenty foot *wing*span, man, and—"

"Wingspan?" asked Hunter, chalking up the story to too many bad drugs for Hippie Bob.

"Yeah, angels got wings—didn't I say that? Well, they do. Anyway, he's just standing there, looking around. Needless to say, a fellah like this creeping up on him, the old man just about jumps out of his skin.

"The big fellah up and says to him, 'Don't be afraid, little guy, your prayer's been answered.'" Bob raised his hands in a gesture of amazement and wonder. "So now the old guy is wracking his brain, trying to remember what the heck this fellah's talking about, when the angel goes, 'Your wife is gonna give you a son, man. Ain't that great?' And he starts in listing things about this kid: 'You gonna call him John. He can't drink wine, but he's gonna be filled with a spirit anyway—the Holy Spirit, yeah? And he's gonna bring back all the lost children of the world.' And it goes on like this, see?

"Now, once the angel gets finished recitin' all these prophecies, the man, he clears his throat and says, 'How do I know what you're saying is true? My wife is really old, you know? And I'm even older. I think maybe it's just a *little* too late for this kid thing.'

"Well, the angel stands there and looks him up and down and says, 'Look, you know I'm a angel, right? My name's *Gabriel.* I live with *God,* see? Talk to him every day! Man, look at me, this ain't *Candid Camera*! Here I am, giving you some *great* news, directly from *God* the *Almighty,* right? News that anyone else in your position would be doin' cartwheels over, and do I hear a simple thank-you? No way! Not you! You act like I got the wrong house! Look at you, what do you know about anything?' The angel is really ticked, you know.

"'Okay, so now,' says Gabe, 'you think you're so smart, you know what? Since you can't say thank you, you're not going to say *anything* for a while. In fact, you're going to be absolutely tongue-tied until your son is born. Think about that! Teach you not to believe a angel when he brings you good news.' So Gabe flies off, muttering, 'And it wouldn't kill you to kneel the next time you meet a member of the Heavenly Host. Man, the stuff I put up with. . . . '

"Meanwhile, everybody's outside wondering what the old guy's up to. He's been in there a long time, but no one can go in and check up on him 'cause that's the rule. Eventually he comes out and they ask him what happened, because just lookin' at him they know that *something* must have happened, but all he can do is point and grunt and stuff, but no one can understand him, or if they do, they don't really believe him.

"So the days go by and dad can't talk, but he does what he can at the temple. The temple managers are thinking of firing him because when the old man finally writes down what happened, they thought he'd let his marbles roll into the traffic, you know? So the months are passing, and pretty soon his wife stops leaving the house. They know she's still there though because a few friends go in to see her, and word starts gettin' around that the old gal's pregnant. Everyone's going, 'Whoa, no way! She's probably just bingein' out on doughnuts and ice cream or something,' but then, sure enough, about nine months after the angel incident, she pops into the hospital and comes out with a kid. A son."

"Imagine that," mused Hunter.

"Hey, but that's not the end, right? Everyone's floored by this. I mean, old man Levinson kept trying to make them understand, but they just wouldn't believe him. And he still can't talk, so now he's wondering, 'Why can't I talk? The angel said I would be able to talk when the kid is born, so what's up?'

"Anyhow, they all go off to the temple to perform the rituals

for when a kid is born—believe me, you don't wanna know!—
and then it comes time to name him and they naturally ask the
mother what she wants to call him. She says 'John,' and they look
at her and say, 'Are you nuts? What kind of name is that? Name
him after your father, or uncle, or something. Give him a family
name.' Apparently, it's against tradition to create new names. So,
they say, like, 'Are you sure?' She nods her head, 'Yeah, I'm sure.'
Then they try to persuade her again, and so now daddy stands up.

"He jumps to his feet, and everybody looks at him, and
they're thinkin', 'Whoa, what's got into the old dude now?'

"Finally, he opens his mouth, and says, 'Look, fool, his name
is *John*, get it right!' And then, because he's so happy that he's
finally talking again, he starts dancing around and singing this little song. It's incredible! It's hours before they can calm him down
enough to go on with the ritual."

The aged hippie leaned back and lit another cigarette, "That's
it." A smile spread across his face. "That's the way it happened."

Hunter let the story digest for a few seconds. "Nice fairy tale,"
he allowed. "But I don't think it'll play at the box office."

"Hey, man, make up your own mind. I just pass it on like it
was told to me." Bob swirled the last of the beer in his bottle and
downed it in a gulp, then stood up. "You can take it for what it's
worth. But like I said, this guy is the real deal."

Hunter finished his coffee and said goodbye to Bob. "Yeah,
see you 'round," he said. On returning to his compartment he
found someone in his seat. It was the great ugly brute, Leon Ribini.

Hunter forced a smile and greeted the brooding giant as if
pleasantly surprised to see him. However, nothing could have
been further from the truth. That one of The Prophet's closest

assistants, a man who appeared to be a personal bodyguard, would show up unannounced on an errand like this was definitely not a good sign.

That Simon didn't tell him about it made it even worse.

He considered Simon an intellectual threat, but Leon was a physical one. Right now, Hunter honestly didn't know which was the greater.

twelve

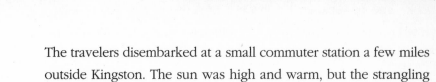

The travelers disembarked at a small commuter station a few miles outside Kingston. The sun was high and warm, but the strangling heat of the city was gone and the air was fresh. Hunter said good-bye to Bob and wished him well.

"Who was that?" Simon wanted to know.

"Some guy I met in the bar," replied Hunter. "Why?"

"Come on." Simon struck off to a little car-rental shack and told the others to wait outside while he went in and collected the keys. Hunter looked around for a newspaper stand or a hot-dog stand—anyplace where he might buy something with his card. He saw an ice cream shop across the parking lot. "I'm thirsty," he said to Leon as he started off. "Want a Coke or anything?"

"No," said Leon, "and you better stay put. Simon said to wait here."

"Don't worry. I won't be a minute."

Before the big man could stop him, he turned and made a bee-line to the kiosk, where he took his time selecting a half-liter Coke and a newspaper to read in the car. He gave the girl behind the counter his card, and signed the slip as a silver-gray Mazda pulled up. "Have a real nice day," said the girl as Hunter rejoined the others. He climbed in the rear, where he had the back seat all to himself. "Are we getting lunch anytime soon?" he asked as the car zoomed off.

"It's a ways yet. Let's get some miles behind us before we stop," Simon replied, shifting gears and tromping on the pedal. "We'll get something along the way."

"Whatever you say, Chief," said Hunter, settling back with his Coke and newspaper. He made a pretense of being very interested in the *New York Times*, but remained alert and made a mental record of their route.

Simon sped along Highway 28, heading roughly northwest toward the town of Phoenicia, where they stopped for a quick burger before turning off the main road and heading up into the hills. They came to the town of Lanesville, a small, orderly tourist trap whose single main street was lined with outdoor outfitters—with names like Grizzly Adams Mountain Gear, and River Forest Kayaks—and trendy, ultrachic boutiques selling everything from Prada handbags to gourmet garlic presses. A few miles beyond the town, they arrived at the entrance to the West Kill Wild Forest Parking Area—an immense parking lot crammed with cars and camper vans. "We walk from here," Simon told them. "It's still a ways to go."

And walk they did. The Diamond Notch trail began at the end of the parking lot and snaked its way up into the West Kill Wild Forest. The three men followed the well-marked trail deeper and deeper into the forest. No one spoke, and Hunter didn't mind the silence; after the heat and stink of the city, and the long car ride, he enjoyed the exercise and the clean pine-scented air.

The trail rose gradually toward the mountain pass called Diamond Notch. Occasionally, they passed camping areas occupied by tents and campers; Simon ignored these and kept on walking. By the time they stopped a few hours later, the sun had drifted behind Wild Kill Mountain and a chill had begun creeping into the air.

The shadow of the mountain soon cast everything in deep gloom, although the sky remained light. Simon slowed his relentless pace and eventually stopped. A sign on the trail proclaimed a camping area called Peekamoose Point. The pine wood wasn't too dense, but Hunter couldn't see any campsite—only a few large rocks and boulders scattered among the tall trees.

"Yeah, Lonnie, where are you, man?" blurted Simon suddenly.

Hunter turned to see Simon with a cell phone to his ear. "Okay, got it." He started off into the rocky forest. "This way," he called to Hunter and Leon; the two fell into step behind him.

As his eyes became better adjusted to the deep-shadowed woodland, he saw that some of the larger rocks were, in fact, well-camouflaged tents. They walked on, and the campsites became more numerous. People were moving around the woods, and here and there campfires flickered in the early evening gloom. He smelled smoke and the tangy aroma of bacon.

After a few minutes' walk, they stopped again. Simon took out the phone. "We're here, but I can't see anything," he said to the person on the other end of the line. "Give us a signal."

They waited, and a few moments later, Hunter caught the glint of a light flashing through the trees in the near distance, bobbing from side to side.

"There," said Simon. "That's the signal."

Their beacon turned out to be a large Maglite waved in the air by a skinny kid in baggy paramilitary gear.

"Hi, man," said the boy—Lonnie, a thin-faced young man of eighteen or nineteen. Simon and Leon greeted him in turn, and then there was the very brief introduction of Hunter—along the lines of "It's okay, he's with us."

"Cool," said Lonnie. "You can bed down in here with me. Simon, I set you guys up next door." He indicated another tent a few yards away. "I only got two tents 'cause I wasn't sure how many were coming."

"No problem," said Simon. "Got anything to eat?"

"Beans and weenies," replied Lonnie. "There's bread, too, and I can make some tea."

"Do it," said Simon. "We're starving."

While Lonnie dumped beans into an aluminum pot, Hunter tossed his bag into the tent and satisfied himself with the sleeping arrangements. Then he found a stump nearby, rolled it up near the fire, and sat down. Simon and Leon sat across from him, arms on knees, staring into the flames—two city guys looking very out of place in the wilderness. Every now and then, Leon slapped at a mosquito and muttered a curse; other than that, neither said a word.

"Cheer up," said Hunter. "It may never happen."

"What?" said Simon, raising his eyes from the flames.

"Whatever has you wound up so tight," he replied, smiling expansively. "Relax. We've got the weekend in the great outdoors, and nothing to worry about. Enjoy!"

Simon gazed at him with cold eyes for a moment, then

nodded slowly. "Yeah, you're right. We're here; we might as well enjoy it."

He became more talkative then. Over their simple meal, he told a story about growing up on the Southside of Chicago, where every year as a kid he had been promised a camping trip to the Catskills by an uncle. "I had an uncle like that once too," said Hunter, working hard to keep the conversation going. "So, where'd you go?"

"We didn't," replied Simon. "We somehow never got around to it." He shrugged. "It doesn't matter."

Hunter nodded. "Well, you're here now."

"Yeah," Simon agreed, look around the campsite in the dark. Then, turning his eyes to the campfire, he added, "I didn't miss much."

They finished the meal and lingered over tin cups of Lonnie's weak tea. Then, the conversation having ground to a halt, Simon stood up. "I'm going to bed." He dashed the contents of his cup into the fire and glanced at Hunter, who imagined he sensed a slight thaw in his icy attitude. "See you in the morning."

Leon remained a silent, unmoving lump. He sat hunched on his log with his knees under his chin, clutching his cup in both hands as he stared at the fire. "You ever been camping, Leon?" asked Hunter.

The big man raised his pockmarked face and stared at Hunter as if he were a bug he'd like to squash. Then he shook his head.

"It's great," said Hunter. "You'll like it."

Leon slapped the side of his neck where another mosquito had just given him a jab. "Hate these buzzards," he growled. He gulped down the rest of his tea, threw down his cup, and stood. "G'night," he grunted, and stumbled off to the tent.

Hunter and Lonnie sat up for a while, listening to the low murmur of conversations from the other campers scattered round about. Gradually these sounds died away, leaving only the swish of the breeze in the tall pines. "Well, I guess I'll turn in," said Hunter.

"Me too," said Lonnie. Hunter followed him into the tent and lay down on his sleeping bag without bothering to take off his clothes. Lonnie flopped onto his sleeping bag and promptly went to sleep. Hunter slipped his hand into his pocket, withdrew his gun, and checked it surreptitiously. Satisfied, he replaced it. He rested his hand on that pocket and allowed himself to drift into a light sleep.

Hunter awoke the next morning to the clatter of a forest full of campers trying to get breakfast together. Lonnie had snuck out, so he took a moment to recheck his gun and return it to the inner compartment of his bag before going out to see who his fellow campers might be.

They were all young, most in their midtwenties, he judged; a few slightly older, into their thirties. Only a few, like Hippie Bob, were over forty.

Many seemed ill at ease in their camping environment; they were dressed in city clothes and city shoes and had the rumpled, slightly dazed look of people who were beginning to realize they had packed unwisely. Some had come slightly better prepared; these, like Lonnie, were given to quasi-military gear—camouflage-pattern baggy trousers and jackets with multiple pockets and zippers everywhere, high-laced boots, and floppy khaki shirts with roll-up tabs on the sleeves. Several of the more survivalist types sported big, chunky knives you could skin a mature buffalo with.

Lonnie was sitting cross-legged on a ground sheet outside the tent, his hair wild, his clothes hard-creased. He grinned and offered cereal as Hunter joined him, pulling a jug of milk from a big plastic cooler. Hunter poured himself a bowl and sat down beside the lanky young man. "So, how do you know Simon?" Hunter asked, lifting a spoonful of cornflakes to his mouth.

"Same way you do, through the Brotherhood."

"Yeah," said Hunter. "To be honest, I'm new to all this. Simon hasn't said too much. How about you—have you been in it long?"

"Nah, I'm new, too."

"What about Washer John—ever seen him?"

"Oh, yeah—but just to keep tabs on him for Isaiah and the Brotherhood," Lonnie answered, adding, "Washer John can be a hard guy to find when you need to. I just hope he doesn't take off into the bush again like he did a couple weeks ago. Sometimes I think he just forgets we're here and disappears without telling anyone. Then we all up stakes and start searching wherever we can."

"What's he doing all the way up here, anyway?"

"Simon didn't tell you?"

"Like I said, he didn't say much."

"Well, you never actually know *what* John's going to do," said Lonnie. He tipped the bowl into his mouth and slurped down the sugary milk. "He wanders around, shouting mostly. He does that water thing sometimes. You hear about the water thing?"

"Yeah."

"Well, he does that too. That's all really. It's mostly talking, but he'll surprise you sometimes with the things he says. Today is supposed to be an important day for some reason."

"Oh?"

"Yeah. Not like a holy day or anything, but something he was looking forward to." Lonnie ended with a shrug, and spooned up some more cereal. "You never know with that guy."

Hunter munched his cornflakes and listened to the neighboring campers as they prepared for the day. He looked over to the tent where Simon and Leon had slept. "They up?"

"Up and gone already. Said they'd be back later. Just hang loose."

So Hunter did. He hung around loosely most of the morning, but the two didn't return. He used the time to explore his immediate surroundings and get a better idea of the lay of the land. The campsite was located in a slightly inclined hollow with high hills on every side. The trees were mature hardwoods with some pine, spruce, and fir; a rock-strewn gully ran along one side of the hollow with a small stream gurgling through it. The gully was lined with ferns and clouds of mosquitoes that kept Hunter from exploring it too closely.

The main trail cut across one end of the hollow, and he followed it a little way to see where it went. Other trails branched off to the right and left, and these had names like Sugar Bush, Bear Trap, Logger's Slide, Mink Hollow, and Hemlock Gulch. He met day hikers along the trail and greeted them, establishing his presence in the area just in case. He walked along the chipped-bark path, drawing the air deep into his lungs and letting the tension of the last few days drain away. The day was good, the sky clear and clean and cloud-less; Hunter felt more and more like a frontiersman as the morning went by.

Around noon, Hunter returned to camp. A rumor had started: Washer John was getting ready to talk.

thirteen

The campsite was on the move. People were streaming into the woods. "Hurry, man," called Lonnie as Hunter came strolling up. "You don't want to miss this!"

"What's going on?" he asked, watching the campers in their calm, controlled haste beating a path into the forest.

"He's going to talk," Lonnie told him, starting off. "Come on!"

They followed the crowd, walking with quiet urgency through the woods for close to half an hour before the ground started to rise sharply toward a ridge that seemed to be the place everyone was heading—and then Hunter saw why: The ridge was the rising back of a shallow, fern-covered ravine, at the bottom of which ran a wide, rocky stream.

Off to the left, a crowd lined an old logging bridge over the ravine. "This way!" said Lonnie. They threaded their way across the jam-packed bridge and made for the far side of the gulch, which was less crowded. People were seated all up and down the bank like students in a lecture theater, and Hunter and Lonnie picked their way among them until they found a place at the top of the ravine where they could get a good view of what was happening below.

Washer John stood at the very bottom of the gully, perched on an enormous, round rock forming a natural dam in the middle of the stream. He was a very large and impressive black man with a long, full-featured face and great, dark, intelligent eyes glinting beneath the ledge of a heavy brow—the perfect model for a heroic statue: Hercules unchained, perhaps, or Poseidon, god of rivers and earthquakes. Thick-muscled through the chest and arms, with hands that could palm basketballs, he stood with his sturdy legs wide apart, arms upraised, head tilted back with his eyes wide open as if searching the sky for a sign.

He was wearing something Hunter couldn't quite identify, but could almost smell: the shirt, or vest, or whatever it was, looked to be some kind of raw animal skin—goat or deer. This he wore on top of a very ragged pair of cut-off jeans. His hair was matted and dull and bound in a dozen massive dreadlocks that hung down his back; a wild, bushy beard spread over his neck and chest.

Hunter's first impression of Washer John was of a man both utterly confident and utterly unkempt. He seemed so completely oblivious to his own appearance that he had not made even the minimum effort to remedy his woefully disheveled state. Ironically, it seemed as if Washer John himself stood in desperate need of a bath.

As Hunter and Lonnie settled on the slope of the ravine, Washer John lowered one arm and with the other took in the assembled crowd with a long, slow sweep, his index finger extended. The accusing finger stopped at a group of people on the opposite bank. "You family of snakes!" John boomed in a voice capable, it would seem, of shaking huge boulders from the hills nearby. "Who told you to slither away?"

All eyes turned to the offending group. They weren't actually doing anything; in fact, they seemed to be frozen by his words. A row of men, all smartly dressed in black slacks and, despite the heat, long-sleeved white shirts with button-down collars and skinny black ties. Something about their pensive expressions gave them an academic appearance.

"Who told you to flee the heavenly rage about to rain down on you like burning hailstones?" John demanded.

Turning his gaze from the shocked group to address the rest of the crowd, he cried, "Listen up! No one will escape the fire! The best you can do—the *only* thing that'll save you—is to grow repentance within you like fruit! Hear me now! Hang repentance all over you, friends! Sink yourself down into it like a pig in muck. Wallow in it until you are covered head to toe—and maybe even then it probably won't be enough." He paused to flash a wide, mocking smile. "But, who knows? It might help."

Washer John turned to address those on the other side of the ravine, and continued, "All of you need to get down on your knees and beg your Daddy's forgiveness. Cry *Mercy!* at the top of your lungs. It's no good for you," here he indicated the academics again, "saying 'I don't need no dang forgiveness,' saying 'My people were chosen by God Almighty himself,' saying 'I don't need this; *I* am a child of *Abraham!*'" John glared around defiantly, then raised his voice in a roar. "Don't you know Abraham's children are as common as sand? Common as dirt! This rock," he gave the rock he was standing on a couple of thumps with his bare foot, "is more a child of Abraham than *any* of you. You don't know Abraham—you don't know Jack!"

Washer John squatted down on his rock, lowered a hand to the water, drew out a handful and splashed it on his face. "The axman is coming," he said when he stood again. "And you all are going to be laid low. 'Cause if you don't have fruit of *any* kind, you ain't no use to anyone—you're gonna be cut down for firewood. What else is a dry tree good for? Firewood and kindling, nothing else."

"So what should we do?" someone yelled from the crowd.

"*Repent!*" Washer John shouted back at him. "Ain't you all listening to a word I say? Repent for all you're worth! Repent your fool heads off!"

"What else?" called another voice. "What do we do until the axman comes?"

Washer John stroked his beard, then shouted so everyone could hear: "Get rid of everything that holds you back! Get rid of the excess baggage. If you have two shirts, and you see someone walking around without no shirt, you give him one of yours."

"Just shirts?" came from somewhere else in the crowd. A few people laughed.

"'Course not just shirts, dummy. The same goes for shoes, cars, money, food—everything!"

"Including women?" the heckler wanted to know.

John gazed up at the ring of faces, a wry grin creeping across his face, "Yes, including women!" He exploded into a loud laugh, and a chuckle coursed through the crowd. "Brother, if you got two, that's one more than any man needs, and two more than any man can handle."

Turning around, John pointed to those on the bridge. "And you guys up there ... " Everyone craned their necks to see exactly who he was pointing to. "You ICON guys ... " Hunter looked and saw a group of policemen leaning on the rail along with the others. "You can stop taking bribes and beatin' on people what don't deserve it. I know how much money you guys make, and trust me, it's enough. It's more than *I* make."

Again he exploded into laughter. Hunter suddenly felt anxious on Washer John's behalf, but the cops merely shook their heads good-naturedly and walked off.

Washer John grinned from ear to ear, showing off a set of very large, white teeth. "Now!" he shouted. One big leap carried him off the rock and into the small pool below. Water lapped around his knees. "Who wants John to wash their souls?"

People immediately stood up and started going down to the stream. John began to shepherd them into a line, trying to maintain order. "Whoa! Slow down! Ain't no one gonna get their souls washed if they can't line up and wait their turn!"

Then someone called down from one of the slopes, "John! Are you the Messiah?"

Washer John wheeled around. "Who said that? Which one of you jokers said that?"

The speaker wouldn't identify himself. Prickly silence descended over the crowd. All jostling at the water's edge ceased. Hunter, scanning the throng, glanced at the group of academics; they were leaning forward with pinched expressions on their faces.

"I am *not* the Messiah!" roared John in vigorous denial. "Let me say it again so there's no mistake: I am *not* the *Messiah!* When the Messiah gets here, I won't even be fit to flick the mud off of his sneakers. You hear that?"

He gazed around at his audience. "Listen, you call me Washer John, 'cause I splash a little water over you. But when the Messiah comes, he will wash you with *fire!* He's gonna melt your sorry souls and remake them into something new. Right this very minute, he's making a broom out of fire to sweep this country clean from end to end. He's going to sweep up anything he can use from off the streets, and everything else is going into the furnace to feed the flames!"

The same uneasy silence preceding the answer also followed it as the crowd turned his words over in their heads.

Lonnie nudged Hunter. "Come on, I see Simon over there."

Simon and Leon were on the opposite side of the bank, making their way down to the stream. Hunter and Lonnie crossed over to join them and stood at the water's edge as Washer John dealt with each of the people in the line. Hunter was in an ideal position to hear him each time he "washed" someone; and all of them were just like the first one Hunter observed. A man came forward and John laid his big hands on him, one hand on the head and one on a shoulder, John leaning close and asking, "Are you sorry? Are you *really* sorry?" The victim, of course, nodded and Washer John pushed him under the water. The man stayed down as long as John held him under—in the washings to follow it was sometimes suspiciously long, Hunter thought—then, up the man came, splashing and spluttering, yanked into the sunlight by John's big, muscled arms.

Some of the newly washed would then wander away by themselves, looking either more or less relaxed, or terrified, than when they went in; some would shout for joy and splash off to join their friends. Most often they just came up gasping, happy to draw breath once more. Several times the newly washed came up crying, or even shrieking, in which case they'd go under again until they stopped. Some of the victims were shaking like junkies when they came to John, and others were shaking when they left.

In the end, only a small portion of the crowd went down to the river; almost everyone else headed back to the campsite once John started the dunking. Even so, it was over an hour before John was finished. Simon, Leon, Hunter, and Lonnie hung back until the last person had received the washing, and then Leon stood up.

"Excuse me, John," he said loudly.

Washer John turned to face them. His brow furrowed violently. "Well, look what we have here," he boomed. "*Another* family of snakes!"

"Could we talk with you?"

"But these serpents all have two heads! Except the little brother here," he pointed to Lonnie, "ain't got no head. And my, oh my, but they're all eager to gobble each other up. You better be careful, son. You're liable to get swallowed by accident."

He grinned and looked at Hunter. "Oh, now, this here snake is a tricksy one, you bet. What's with you, man? You come out all this way to see something and you see it, but you don't know what you're lookin' at." He laughed. "Open your eyes, man! You ain't going to find anything with your eyes closed."

A weird, queasy feeling rippled through Hunter's intestines. He wondered how well Simon could read between the lines. Washer John was dangerously close to blowing his cover. He fixed an unworried smile to his face and hoped Simon wasn't paying attention.

Washer John laughed again and started walking away. Leon cast a sideways glance at Simon, who urged him on with a sharp nod. "John, we'd like a word," said Leon, raising his voice.

The preacher's head whipped around. "Don't you talk to me like we's family. I got nothin' to say to you." With that, he turned his massive back on them and waded to the other side of the stream.

"Let him go," Simon said, starting back up the ravine. "We'll try again later."

They climbed the bank and crossed the bridge to return to camp. Hunter was the last to reach the top; he paused to look back and saw Washer John splashing toward someone standing on the bank, his arms flung wide.

"Cousin!" came the bellow from the ravine. John raced to where another young black man was standing; he grabbed the newcomer and lifted him in a strong bear hug. The young man did his very best to withstand the crunch, playfully pounding John on the back. Hunter smiled in spite of himself at this intimate scene, then turned and hurried to catch up with the others.

The four men walked back to the camp in silence. Hunter wondered what could have caused Washer John to call Simon and the others—himself as well—two-headed snakes. The two heads, or two faces, could easily apply to Hunter; did it apply to the others as well? Was this even more reason to be suspicious of Simon and Leon?

As they walked along, Simon started up a light but strained

conversation which the others, apart from the closed-mouth Leon, joined in gratefully. It soon became clear, though, that Lonnie was extremely nervous; he kept laughing out loud at the least provocation and craning his neck all the time as if he were looking for someone, or expecting something to happen.

fourteen

Simon and Leon went off again soon after reaching camp, leaving Hunter and Lonnie to fend for themselves. Lonnie produced two large cans of baked beans and some bacon, which he cooked up on a small portable stove. Hunter opened a bag of potato chips and sat down to a late lunch.

"What do you think he meant?" Lonnie asked, as Hunter, balancing his plate on his knees, dug in. "I mean, about the snake thing? Being gobbled up and all that? He was talking about us."

"I seriously doubt it," Hunter lied. "He's a nutball—probably eaten one too many grasshoppers."

"I'm not so sure anymore, man. I've heard stories that say, like, this guy knows stuff—secret stuff, about people. You know, he's, like, a prophet."

"So, okay, he's a prophet. But do you think Simon and Leon are two-headed snakes?"

"I don't know," replied Lonnie, shoveling a spoonful of beans into his mouth. "I mean, there's a lot of things about Simon I don't understand."

"Like what?"

"Like now, man. Where is he?"

"You don't know?"

He shook his head. "Do you?"

Hunter shrugged.

"Simon's, like, real mysterious," Lonnie continued thoughtfully. "I mean, I know he used to be an ICON guy, so he's got all these connections and stuff but—"

Hunter's heart nearly stopped. It was all he could do to hang onto his plate of beans while his thoughts flew off in every direction at once. Simon? With ICON? Could it be possible? Could he know about Hunter? Had Simon rumbled him? Was that why they had dragged him out into this blasted, god-forsaken, mosquito-infested wilderness of a forest without backup?

"You okay, man?" asked Lonnie. "You look like somebody just walked over your grave."

"Beans," said Hunter, giving himself a thump on the chest. "Went down the wrong way." He cleared his throat, then said, "I didn't know about the ICON thing. What did he use to do?"

"I heard he was an undercover guy. They say he was on some sort of top secret assignment, infiltrating The Lions of Judah or whatever, and he got turned."

"Lions of Judah? Is that like the Brotherhood or ZIP?"

"Yeah," Lonnie replied. "They do a lot of stuff in the East, but he was assigned to a cell that they set up over here. California, I think it was. And these guys were hard-core, they were into all sort of heavy stuff. They'd plan bombings and stuff. Assassinations."

"Tough crowd," mused Hunter.

"Yeah, so anyway," Lonnie went on, "while Simon was there, he met The Prophet and the story is that Simon worked his way into the organization, undercover-like, and then one day he made an appointment with The Prophet and told him that he'd come to spy on him, but that now he wanted to join them. You know, join the movement."

"And The Prophet believed him?" said Hunter. "That's pretty hard to swallow."

"No, see, there's more," Lonnie insisted. "To prove he was serious, he handed over all the details of his ICON assignment and stuff."

"Like what?" asked Hunter.

"You know, like the names of undercover agents working in the field, who his contacts were, what they knew, what they don't know—all that stuff. The Prophet rolls out the red carpet and welcomes him with open arms. Simon's been one of The Prophet's best men ever since."

Lonnie took another couple bites of beans.

"Is that it?" Hunter asked eventually.

"Yep. That's all I heard." Lonnie put his empty bowl and spoon on the ground. "That's what I think Washer John meant when he said that the snake had two heads—he was talking about Simon." He held up his hand with two fingers extended. "ICON and Zion. It makes sense."

"Could be," Hunter replied, and continued eating. Lonnie finished and went to fetch water to rinse off his bowl. Hunter lingered over his meal, his mind spinning feverishly. *How could this have happened? There should have been something in the files about an agent who turned. I should have been warned.*

Next, he wondered if his picture and file were in the package that Simon handed over to The Prophet? No. Impossible. He'd been given the assignment well after Simon had turned traitor. They couldn't possibly have anything on him. *Don't let it rattle you*, he told himself. *Get a grip*.

Still, he wondered, and wondering made him uneasy.

Hunter quickly decided he had the following options: One, he could cut his losses and hitch a ride back to the city, run home to Mother ICON. That would do absolutely nothing to improve his career prospects, however. It would be another black mark by his name, and his next assignment would be rounding up stray dogs.

Or, two, bring in Simon and Leon on whatever he could make stick—weapons charges, perhaps—and see if Devlin and the boys could crack them. Penetrating a terrorist organization and arresting key members after only two weeks in the field might go down a little better with High Command. It was well within his objective's parameters, enough to call the mission a partial success, at least.

But who was he kidding? Arrest Simon and Leon, and The Prophet would run so fast and so far it would be years before they caught up with him again. And who knew how much damage he could do in the meantime?

Three, he could dig himself deeper into the hole he was now in, and, by doing so, hope somehow to come out the other side. The Prophet seemed to have warmed to him slightly. He could use that and try to worm his way into the trusted inner circle. This assumed, of course, that The Prophet did not suspect Hunter's ICON status—which there was really no way of knowing. The downside of this option was . . . best not considered.

Hunter weighed the possibilities in his head and, as he mopped the last of the bean sauce with a folded piece of bread, came to a conclusion. From that, he quickly formulated a plan of action.

"Hey, Lonnie," he called, "come over here. There's something I want to show you before the others get back."

fifteen

Hunter sat outside the tent, alone, waiting for Simon and Leon to appear. The sun had dropped behind Wild Kill Mountain by the time they returned. As they approached the campsite, Hunter stuck his hand in his pocket and pressed the "send" button on his cell phone. Simon came to stand before him, looked around the camp, and asked where Lonnie was.

"I don't know. He took off about an hour ago. He said he'd only be gone a little while—but, like I said, that was an hour ago. I was going to go look for him, but you guys hadn't come back yet, so I figured somebody should stay here just in case."

"You did the right thing," Simon said. He checked his watch.

"You guys want something to eat?" Hunter asked. "I could heat up some beans for you."

Simon shook his head, "No. We—" he was cut off by the ringing of his cell phone.

"Leon? Something to eat?"

Leon shook his head, gazing at Hunter, his lumpy face arranged in an expression of bored distaste.

"Hello? Yeah, where are you?" Simon caught Leon's eye. "It's Lonnie."

"Where is he?" Leon asked.

"Are you sure?" Simon said to the phone. "Okay. No, just stay where you are. We'll be there in a few minutes." Simon put the phone back in his pocket. "Lonnie said he's with Washer John and he's ready to talk to us."

"Where?"

"In the forest somewhere. I got directions. Sam, I want you to stay here and keep an eye on things. Sorry, I'd take you with us if I could, but . . . "

"Fine," said Hunter. "No problem."

"What about that other thing we were supposed to do today?" Leon asked Simon.

"It'll to have to wait until tomorrow, I guess. C'mon—let's go."

The two left Hunter alone again. As soon as they were out of sight and earshot, he hit the speed dial on his phone, and then followed the path they had taken. "Hurry up . . . answer it," breathed Hunter, making his way quickly and quietly through the trees. He caught a glimpse of Simon and Leon from time to time, all the while keeping the ringing phone pressed to his ear.

He was jogging along, trying to keep the other two in sight when, finally, someone picked up. "Special Agent Alex Hunter calling for Chief Devlin. He's expecting my call."

Hunter slowed his pace. He took out his gun and checked it over. The metal parts slid against each other smoothly and silently, and the magazine was full. Flicking off the safety, he dashed for a large culvert that formed a tunnel beneath Highway 214; the tunnel allowed the hiking trail to continue without crossing the road.

He heard a car passing above him as he scrambled up the steep slope beside the tunnel to the road. He scanned the road both ways and located the brown sedan waiting on the hard shoulder a few dozen paces away, in the shadow of some tall pines. It was an unmarked police car containing two ICON plainclothes officers: his backup.

Two guys—that's all? wondered Hunter. *I call for backup and that's all they send?*

Hunter hurried along the road to a screen of bushes growing alongside the highway above the entrance to the tunnel. Here he could see the trail directly below without being seen. He hunkered down to wait.

He didn't have to wait long. In a few seconds, he heard the soft, crunching sound of shoes on dry gravel, and then the empty, hollow echo of footsteps in the tunnel. Hunter took a breath and rose. Quickly and quietly, he slid down the steep-sloping bank once more and ran to the tunnel entrance.

Both Leon and Simon had entered the tunnel. Simon, slightly ahead, was halfway through, but Leon was still near the entrance. Neither seemed to have heard Hunter; four running strides carried him to Leon. Just as the big thug was turning to look behind him, Hunter swung the butt of his gun smartly into the base of the man's skull. It made contact with a solid, meaty thwack. Leon gave out a groan and dropped to his knees—dazed, but not unconscious.

Hearing the sound behind him, Simon turned around to see Hunter with Leon in a choke hold, the big man on his knees, his body forming a shield. "Stay where you are, Simon!" Hunter shouted, his voice pinging inside the tunnel.

Simon froze, but not before he pulled out his own gun, which Hunter recognized as ICON-issue. "I said to hold it right there!" shouted Hunter. Rather than aim at Simon, he pressed the muzzle of his gun to Leon's head. He would later reflect that this was his first mistake.

"Well, well, isn't this just a dandy surprise, Agent Hunter," Simon drawled mockingly. "Decided to break cover at last?"

"We both know how this is going to turn out, Simon. Give yourself up and save Leon, too. ICON's shutting it all down as we speak. Right now everyone connected to The Prophet is being hauled into custody. It's over, Simon."

"You really think so?"

"Put the gun down. Even if you shoot me, you won't get away. ICON will find you."

"I'm not afraid of ICON anymore. My eyes are open. I'm changing things for the better. You can kill me and a hundred others like me, but we won't stop until ICON is just a bad memory. So don't tell *me* what's over. ICON's over!"

"Simon, I'm warning you . . . "

"Our numbers are greater than you can imagine. So go ahead and shoot," Simon spread his arms. "I serve a higher purpose now."

An armed idealist—Hunter didn't like it at all. "Put the gun down," Hunter ordered. Leon was starting to squirm. Hunter hoped his groggy hostage realized that a gun was being held to his head and chose to remain calm.

"Where's Lonnie?" Simon said, still holding the gun easily at his side. "Did you kill him already?"

"Lonnie's in custody." Hunter answered.

"So, how does it work now, Special Agent? I turn myself in and admit every dark deed I've ever done, get my buddies put away, and walk free with a grateful nation's thanks?"

"It could be like that," Hunter allowed. "You're smart; you know how the system works. You'll be able to cut a deal."

Simon didn't answer right away, which Hunter took as a good sign. If Simon was considering the future and the consequences of his actions, it would be best for all of them. But Leon seemed to be growing more aware and restless, and that made Hunter nervous. He doubted he could hold the big man much longer. "Well?" said Hunter. "What's it going to be?"

Simon gave a cold chuckle. "I can only imagine your disappointment, Agent," he said. With that, he calmly raised his weapon, aimed directly at Hunter, and fired.

The first bullet sang by Hunter's ear. The second and third slammed into Leon's chest and spun him backward into Hunter, driving them both against the culvert wall. Hunter lost his aim, but held onto his gun. He struggled to push Leon away and whipped his gun hand around as a fourth bullet ripped into his right arm. He felt the impact as an electric jolt and watched his gun fly from his hand.

Hunter heard two more shots as he went down, smacking his head on the ribbed-steel wall of the culvert.

He awoke later to the sour sweat smell of the dead man on top of him. He pushed Leon off and glanced quickly around for Simon, who was nowhere in sight. Dragging himself to his knees, he tried to get up but found himself slipping in blood— his own and Leon's. His right arm was a mass of flame, the fiery epicenter of which was located just below the shoulder in the meaty part of the upper arm. His right hand was numb and wooden. His side throbbed with a dull, ugly insistence, and he was gritting his teeth so hard the pain in his jaw rivaled the pain in his arm.

Hunter didn't bother checking Leon's pulse—the big man was awash in blood, his mouth open, tongue hanging out, his eyes bulging almost literally out of their sockets. Turning from the body, he retrieved his gun with his left hand, and then hurried to the opposite end of the tunnel, where he paused and looked around before venturing out onto the trail.

He climbed up the bank to the highway. *Where's my backup?* he wondered, looking for the officers who had positioned themselves on the road.

The instant he saw the brown sedan with its doors standing open, Hunter knew there would be no backup. Lightheaded from his climb, he started for the car, tripped and fell over the legs of a man half-concealed in the bushes beside the road.

Holding back bile, Hunter dragged himself up and stepped over the first dead agent, continuing cautiously toward the car. Both the windshield and rear window had been shot out. Through the open door, he could see the body of the second agent slumped down in his seat, probably the first to go. A camper van slowed as it came up; the driver rubbernecked but did not stop. Hunter looked up and down the road for Simon, but saw no trace of him.

The last of his strength was going. Standing there, looking at the dead officers, Hunter felt a black mist gathering in his brain and suddenly all he wanted to do was sleep. Three men dead, and himself wounded. His gun slipped from his hand; he heard it clatter on the pavement. He looked down at himself. One side was completely caked with blood. He hoped that most of it wasn't his own.

With that thought in mind, he dropped down on all fours and vomited.

As he crouched there, spitting into the dirt, he shoved his left hand into his pocket and pulled out his cell phone. Somehow his thumb found the pad and pressed the necessary buttons. He heard it ring as he raised it to his ear. Someone picked up. "Hello?"

"This is Hunter." He choked back bile, gagged, and gasped for breath.

"Are you all right, Agent?"

"Get an ambulance out here right away."

"Where are you?"

Hunter let the phone drop from his hands.

"Agent! Where are you?"

Hunter rolled forward onto the ground with an all-consuming desire for . . . sleep.

sixteen

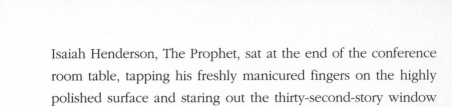

Isaiah Henderson, The Prophet, sat at the end of the conference room table, tapping his freshly manicured fingers on the highly polished surface and staring out the thirty-second-story window over a smoggy Lower Manhattan. He wasn't a man accustomed to waiting; it was he who usually made others wait, and for the same reason that he was waiting now: a tactic in the tug-of-war power game that some people liked to play. He understood, but he didn't like it.

Fifteen minutes after the agreed time, the door opened and his contact—along with his ridiculously overblown entourage— stepped into the room. Henderson couldn't help himself in rising to meet them.

"Isaiah, old man, how are you?" his contact asked with a careless smile and a faux-English accent. He was a young man, relaxed, impeccably dressed, exuding low-grade charm. His handshake was warm and firm. He unbuttoned his hand-tailored Italian jacket and handed it to one of his aides, with instructions not to wrinkle it. The two men sat down while the entourage took up places behind them near the windows.

"So, I understand you wanted to see me?" The man clapped his hands together and gleefully rubbed them together. "What can I do for you?"

Henderson resented the insinuation that he was the one begging a favor. "Pardon me, Mr. Archelon," he began, "but—"

"Antony, please. My friends call me Anty."

"Antony, then," amended The Prophet primly. "You gave instructions we were to contact you when we obtained the merchandise."

"Yes, so what can you tell me?"

"The package is here, awaiting delivery."

"You brought him here?" said Archelon, and Henderson noticed the English accent slide toward Russian.

"Where else?"

"I don't know, but . . . " Archelon looked around at his men lined up against the window, "I'm not so sure that was such a good idea."

"Why not? The package is wrapped up safe and sound; we were careful not to bruise it too much." Henderson smiled. "Will you take delivery, or shall I put the package back where I found it?"

"No, no," said Archelon quickly. "I'll take it, sure. Just give me a second to think."

Henderson smiled again. Obviously, Antony Archelon was not half as sophisticated as he pretended to be, nor half as smart. "Perhaps one or two of your men could go down to the underground garage," suggested The Prophet, "and arrange to take possession of it."

"Good idea," agreed Archelon. He turned and, with a gesture, sent three men out of the room to perform the errand. When they had gone, Archelon turned to his guest. "Now then, about this other business . . . "

"Yes." Henderson folded his hands upon the table. "I do hope there has been no difficulty."

"Well, that's what I wanted to tell you," Archelon said.

"Yes?" Henderson's voice went flat. "What sort of difficulties, exactly?"

"It's just taking a little longer than we thought to get all of the items together," Archelon told him. "There were so many that we've had to arrange delivery from many different sources, and what with ICON cracking down right and left—well to cut a long story short, it's going to take us another few weeks to get everything ready."

The Prophet's eyes narrowed. "How many weeks?"

"Six or seven," replied Archelon, who could almost feel the heat of the other man's rage as he spoke. "Look, if that doesn't suit, maybe you could take your business somewhere else. I really don't mind."

The Prophet studied Antony's boyish, round face. "Yes, fine," he said, swallowing his anger. "I can wait a few more weeks if I have to, but no longer than that. I will, of course, accept whatever you can give me now, and take the rest later."

"Of course!" Archelon leaned back, grinning with relief. "I wouldn't have it any other way."

The Prophet rose. "Now, if we are finished, I have another appointment, and I am running late."

"This won't take but a moment. I would like to ask you a

question, if you don't mind, Mr. Prophet." Antony Archelon gestured for him to sit back down. "Please. It won't take a moment."

"Very well," said The Prophet. "What is the question?"

"Now, let's be candid with each other. I know who you are and what you do, and we both know you're asking me for more than just weapons. You are asking me for the tools to create more than just a little inconvenience for ICON." He smiled. "You want to hit them where it hurts. You want to light the fire of revolution. Am I right?"

When Henderson hesitated, Archelon said, "Don't worry. This is between friends, right? A friendly discussion between two business associates who might be able to help one another out—to the mutual benefit of both. And we can all use a little help now and then—am I right?"

"Suppose, purely for the sake of argument, you are right," said The Prophet. "What then?"

"As it happens, I've been thinking about what an operation like yours might possibly require to make it run more smoothly, and I have some ideas that I'd like to share with you." Archelon paused and looked for some reaction from The Prophet. There was no spark of interest, however tiny. He plunged on regardless.

"You know my family—am I right? Well, over the years we've become quite well established and have made many powerful friends and contacts—especially within ICON."

The Prophet raised an eyebrow. Archelon allowed himself another grin. "I thought that might interest you. As it happens, many of these friends and contacts are forward-looking, progressive thinkers who could be . . . inspired, shall we say, by a man of your particular vision."

The Prophet thought for a moment and then, placing his fingertips together, touched his lips briefly and said, "I think I begin to see what you mean."

"I thought you would," said Archelon with a smile. "Why don't I have some lunch brought in and we can discuss it properly?"

seventeen

The next two weeks are a blur—scattered moments of semiconsciousness separated by periods of The Black: a timeless, textureless state of warm and cold, comfortable and uncomfortable, curiously fascinating and monumentally tedious.

He remembers movement. Swift, jerky movement—upward, sideways, down—and then waking up in the hospital. Harsh lights, green walls, the pungent tang of disinfectant . . . people talking. Two voices speak at once, his body resonates with pain, and then The Black. Peaceful, dreadful, all-embracing, smothering darkness.

Waking up in the hospital again, he looks around. Another room? Another hospital? His mouth and lips are dry. The light is too bright; it makes him sick. His stomach heaves, but there is nothing to throw up. There is a faint buzz in his ear—someone is talking. Talking to him? His head throbs in time to the ache in his side. He retreats into The Black.

Later the same day . . . or another day. The lights are dimmer now. His head is thumping like a broken and badly beaten snare drum; his throat is a sun-blasted desert. He tries to call out, but can manage only a ragged whisper. He tries to move his limbs, but they are frozen and unresponsive. He tries to lift his head, but the effort required is beyond him. Exhausted, out of breath, he closes his eyes, drifting wearily once more into The Black.

Later still—maybe a long time later—a man is standing on the other side of the room. Hunter knows this, although he cannot see him. The man is in the shadows beyond the foot of the bed, half hidden. He knows, somehow, that the man is him— shot and broken. His clothes are bloody and torn, his arms and legs smashed, his face battered beyond human recognition.

No, no, it is not him. It can't be; he was never in such terrible condition. It must be someone else. The broken man takes a step forward on his broken legs—how is he standing?—almost stepping out of the shadows, but his face is still hidden.

Delirium. The stranger's face starts to glimmer, spots of light move around it, but the features remain obscured. The lights gather and combine, growing stronger. Soon, the man's face is shining like a signal flare. The Black retreats from him; it races along the walls, trying to get as far away from the stranger as possible. The darkness is driven to the corners and lurks there cowering; it hides behind Hunter himself as he raises his head and tries to make out the stranger's face.

Hunter's own face starts to burn, and then, all at once, The Black gathers strength and attacks the room, attacks the stranger, and extinguishes the white-hot brilliance shining above the man's shoulders. This time the stranger is consumed by The Black; but just before he is devoured, Hunter glimpses the stranger's face.

Who is this man? Does it matter? No, he is delirious from the heavy drugs pumping through his damaged and weakened system. In the next few days he will forget this fantasy.

He does forget.

Now a doctor is standing over him, saying something. There are words, and Hunter tries to force them together, but they keep coming apart, flying around his head, buzzing like flies in his face. Questions. Hunter shakes his head in response to the meaningless gibbering.

It comes to him that he is being told about his injuries. He has a fractured upper arm in a thick plaster cast from shoulder to elbow; the bullet knocked a chunk out of the bone and cracked it, but the bone held and the cast will come off in a few weeks. Worse, he is told, far worse is the nasty hole in his side where the second bullet entered and exited him, puncturing both pancreas and spleen. There was also a severe concussion where he hit the steel culvert; thanks to his hard head, there is no fracture. He is still critical, but stable now.

A nurse is there, holding a cup to his lips. Hunter tries to drink but spills most of it down his chin and onto his pale green gown. He closes his eyes, but The Black does not return; the edge has worn off. Now it feels more . . . gray.

A ferocious and unrelenting tedium sets in. Eventually Hunter can shuffle around the hospital. He tries to move as fast as he can without inducing a skull-shattering migraine. His body feels ancient, dried out—like a long-neglected sponge, even though he has just taken his first shower in a month. His legs are pathetic, weak, and the nurse has to take him back to his bed in a wheel-chair. He tries to build his strength with the hospital dinners, eating as much protein as possible. It isn't easy.

He settles into a stultifying routine of waking, eating, shuffling, sleeping. One morning he sits in the garden and stares at the plants and insects. He does this twice. The third time, two men come to talk to him; his colleagues, they say. They ask him questions and he tries to answer. He talks about what happened to him after he filed his last report, after he left New York. He talks of these events in the abstract—as if none of it happened to him, but to someone else, someone far less fortunate than himself.

After a while Hunter sees all the events from a distance, and it seems like a deluge of calamity raining down upon this unfortunate *other* person. As for Hunter himself, his arm and side ache constantly now, trying to make him remember that it was Hunter, and not someone else, who was shot and left for dead.

Over the next few days the men come back. They ask him the same questions over and over. Hunter knows why. He gives them the same answers time and again, his voice dead, his emotions dead too. This makes the men happy, and then they leave him alone with the tedium, which, frankly, Hunter prefers to remembering.

The day finally comes when they tell him that he is well enough to leave. He puts some clothes on, but not his own, which were destroyed. He is careful with his cast, which is heavy and awkward and makes his arm itch terribly. He stands up too fast, making his head swim. He leans on the bed for a few seconds to let his vision clear, and then tries to straighten his back, slowly. The stitches in his side pull against the skin, the stiff muscles clench and grab, but he stretches anyway, and then walks as steadily as he can from the room.

The nurse at the desk has his personal items. There are still bloodstains on his wallet. He puts on his cold watch, gathers his cold keys and dead cell phone, and leaves the building. Squinting in the sunlight, he looks at his watch. How much time has passed? Six weeks? Eight? Who knows?

Out on the street an ICON police car is waiting for him. He walks to it and gets in. Just sit back and relax, the driver tells him, they will soon be back in New York.

So, they're taking him back to New York. The trees blur past the window—dead leaves flutter from skeletal branches. He has missed autumn. The near-naked trees move farther away as the small two-lane road they are on becomes a tributary for a larger river of highway that widens and widens into a flood of concrete and traffic with hardly any trees in sight. A mountain of buildings looms ahead, dark against the early evening sky.

Hunter spends the night in one of the rooms at ICON headquarters, a room not unlike his last hotel room. Television gives him a headache so he scours the drawers and shelves for something to read, but can't find anything. He knows it would be useless to try to leave the building, so he goes to the commissary for food instead. Hunter reflects on the future of his career as he eats, eventually deciding that it isn't too cheery. In fact, he wonders if he still has a job at all. He has nothing to look forward to except (if he's very, very lucky) a job sharpening pencils in some remote outer province.

The next day he dresses in a new ICON uniform—the first

time he has worn one since the day he arrived in the city. He carefully rips apart the seam of the right sleeve to accommodate his cast-encased arm, and then fastens the sleeve back together with a neat row of safety pins. He sizes himself up in the mirror to make sure his uniform is straight and the creases immaculate. His appearance is all he has control over anymore, the last fluttering shred of his ragged self-esteem; they'll have to strip it from his cold, dead body before he gives it up.

Hunter sits all day at a small table in a large room. Three High Command investigators are questioning him on all the things he would rather forget. He answers the investigators in the same detached way he has answered all the questions put to him in the last few weeks. This time, however, his colleagues want to know more about the two agents who were shot. One of the men suggests that perhaps it was Hunter himself who shot the two agents, that he was helping Simon to escape. Citing their own ballistics report, Hunter patiently explains why this could not possibly be the case. At five o'clock everyone goes home.

Hunter repeats the process again the next day. This time the questioning ends at three. Hunter is advised not to leave the city and is told to appear again before the board on Thursday for a review of his special-agent status. Hunter nods. He spends most of the remainder of the day in the bath, his cast resting on a dry towel on the rim of the tub.

Over the weekend, Hunter watches the Carnegie Suites hotel. He wears a muffler over the lower half of his face and stares at the entrance and windows over the top of his *New York Times*; he observes the street traffic; he watches the people come and go while he eats hot dogs and drinks sodas on a bus bench, or sips bottomless cups of coffee in the café across the street. On Sunday evening he decides it is safe enough to enter. He greets Eddie the doorman, who is surprised and pleased to see him again. Hunter gives a short explanation of his disappearance but can't endure the pretence of doing anything more strenuous, like smiling. Eddie says they haven't touched his room, because he has continued to pay his bill. Has he? Thank you, Mother ICON. It must be Supervisor Riley covering his tracks. Hunter tips Eddie and takes the elevator up to his floor.

Everything is exactly as he left it—the memories are thick in the room like dust, and almost physically painful. It seems like such a long time ago he was in here. He packs his clothes and belongings into his duffel bag and tries not to look at the books piled up on the night table and desk. When he has collected everything, he goes downstairs and asks the clerk if there is anything he owes. He doesn't.

He passes Eddie on his way out; he asks if it might be possible to get in touch with Rosa again. "Who?" Eddie asks. Hunter explains. Eddie remembers, but denies procuring her for Hunter. Sure he remembers Rosa, a good-looking woman like that. But he doesn't know where she might have come from or where she might be. Hunter catches a glimpse of the hotel manager over Eddie's shoulder, notes his strained expression, and nods in understanding. He leaves. He wants to go back to his ICON room and cocoon himself in his sheets and fall asleep, but instead forces himself to go by the Belvedere for his papers, old uniform, and laptop.

On Monday, Hunter buys a big, thick, coverless book from a street trader: *Last Tango in Baghdad*. The blurb proclaims it a stupendous best-seller. He sits in the ICON headquarters' atrium, not so much reading it as counting the pages until the end. He notices no one and no one notices him.

On Wednesday afternoon while waiting for the doctor to remove the cast, Hunter finishes the blockbuster book. The thrilling climax leaves a sour aftertaste, so he goes out to a small Italian bistro to have dinner. He celebrates his renewed dexterity with a half bottle of the house red and reflects that, in all probability, it is his last supper as a special agent. He returns early and makes sure his uniform is ready for tomorrow.

The next day Hunter arrives as before. The abstracted indifference he has perfected in speaking about his past is now skillfully applied to his future. He has given up. He will accept whatever is handed out to him; he is determined not to argue, not to complain, not to show any emotion whatever. He feels like an old guard dog about to be put down.

He enters the room expecting an official tribunal but there is only one man in a civilian suit. There have been some new developments, the man says; Hunter is to come back tomorrow for a full briefing.

Hunter returns to his room, unsure what to do. He walks down to a small movie theatre and sees two films, but is unable to recall a single detail from either of them as soon as he steps back outside. One of them might have had subtitles and the other was black-and-white, at least in places. He spoils himself with fast food and ice cream.

The next day, Hunter returns to the room as instructed. Two men are there now, Commissioner Steiner and the man in the suit from yesterday. The man is not introduced and never says a word; he just sits there, staring at Hunter. Steiner has a folder containing what Hunter recognizes as his statement of the events of his previous mission. The commissioner also has a coroner's report file in front of him. He allows Hunter to take a seat.

Steiner asks Hunter a series of perfunctory questions about some random details contained in his statement. Hunter answers them. Steiner then commences outlining the details of a case involving a decapitated corpse that was hauled out of the Hudson River two days ago, a corpse that has now been identified.

The commissioner's aide hands Steiner a red-tagged duty folder. It appears the headless body is that of John Levinson, also known as Washer John. As the only agent familiar with the victim, having met and, perhaps, talked to possibly one or more of those involved in his death, it is Hunter's job to find and arrest those responsible. Successful completion of this mission might restore Hunter to his previous rank, maybe even gain him a promotion.

Steiner extends the duty folder and holds it in front of Hunter. Hunter stares at it; Steiner's words fade into an incoherent babble. He hears his name called. He stares up at Steiner's sharp features, now pinched with a stern severity.

"Hunter! Alex! Snap out of it. Agent, you're being put back on active assignment!"

eighteen

The uniformed guard stood aside as Hunter swiped his ID card through the digital reader. The door buzzed and she pushed it open.

Hunter followed his escort through the bowels of ICON's Virginia headquarters, a complex warren of high-security cells and interrogation rooms. The cool white concrete walls and fluorescent lighting allowed no sign of the passage of time in this place. There were no shadows here. The air itself was the flat, sterile, all-purpose regulation sort—standard issue for all government buildings.

Hunter paused for a moment outside Room 15 and glanced through the one-way glass set in the wall next to the door. There was Lonnie, chained to his chair, looking bored and pitiful. He was hunched over a metal table that contained nothing but a small digital recording device. Hunter removed his sling and let his still-tender arm hang down. After testing his bandaged side and straightening his crisp uniform jacket he signaled to the security officer to open the door.

Lonnie looked up at Hunter and the guard as they entered. It took a second for recognition to register in his eyes, but eventually he made the mental leap between the clean-cut Agent Hunter before him and the scruffy, unshaven Samuel Taylor who he had met in the woods. Then his eyes dulled once more and he let out a small sigh. There was no defiance, no sneer, no hollow posturing; this was going to be quick and easy.

"Thanks, I'll take it from here," Hunter said, dismissing the guard. He eased himself into a chair across the table from Lonnie and tried to make eye contact, but Lonnie didn't even glance up. Hunter opened the file he was carrying and made a show of reading through it, shuffling the papers around. Eventually he addressed his cowed and compliant prisoner.

"Well, Lonnie, it looks like your buddies dropped you in the porcelain punch bowl."

Lonnie pressed his mouth into a hard line.

"Conspiracy, subversion, possession of an illegal weapon . . . what does that add up to? Eight years? Ten? Eight years is a long time, Lonnie—and that's *if* the judge decides to go easy on you."

Hunter paused, regarding his prisoner far more sternly than he felt. "Do you understand what I'm telling you?"

"Look," said Lonnie, lifting his head slightly. "What do you want, ah . . . " Lonnie squinted at the laminated ID card clipped to Hunter's jacket pocket. "Special Agent Alexander Hunter? You come here to taunt me, or . . . or what?"

It was an attempt at aggression, but it failed miserably. Hunter smiled. "I came here to see if I could help you."

"Oh, yeah?" Lonnie meant it as a sneer of defiance, but he could not keep the note of hope out of his voice. Hunter heard it and softened his approach.

"Yeah. But first I need to see a little cooperation."

"What—uh, so what do you want?"

"Information."

"Like what? I told everybody everything already."

"Well, it seems that a mutual friend of ours has had a pretty bad accident. You remember Washer John?"

Lonnie's eyes shot up to meet Hunter's, his eyebrows high in surprise. His entire face framed a question he didn't even have to open his mouth to ask. The young man's shock and concern were genuine, and Hunter felt a pang of pity. "What happened to him?" Lonnie asked.

Hunter held Lonnie's gaze for a few seconds and then looked down into his folder. He turned over a sheet of paper. "The body of John Levinson, a.k.a. Washer John, was pulled from the Hudson River on the twenty-seventh of November. He had been dead for an estimated period of five to ten days and was found . . . " Hunter looked up to meet Lonnie's stricken expression once more, "without his head."

Lonnie's mouth twisted into a grimace. Then he lowered his head and slumped his shoulders. "Aww . . . man! Why'd you tell me that?"

"What do you say, Lonnie? You think you might know who's behind this?"

"What?" Lonnie looked up again quickly. "No! No way! Aw, man, that's terrible. Why'd you tell me that? Who the—who would *do* something like that?"

"That's what I'm asking *you*."

Lonnie's eyes went wide. "Hey, now look—I don't know nothing about this. I liked the guy myself. Everyone did. There's nobody I know who'd want to see him dead."

"Someone did," suggested Hunter. "And I know the kind of company you keep, so tell me, what were you and your friends supposed to be doing up there?"

"Talking," insisted Lonnie. "We just went up there to talk to him."

"I don't believe you. What was the real reason?"

"That *is* the real reason." Lonnie shook his head sadly. "Oh, man. . . . " he sighed.

Hunter took a moment to study Lonnie. The young man seemed to be telling the truth, at least as far it had been told to *him*.

"Come on, Lonnie, I know you're not as clueless as all that. What happened to the chatty, informative guy I met up in the Catskills?"

Lonnie regarded him reproachfully. "I already told you, I don't know nothing."

"Oh, I think you do," Hunter told him. "In fact, I think you've pretty much worked it out. They might not have told you everything, but I think you put together a fairly accurate picture of what was really going on up there."

"Hey, look at me! I'm no one! I am officially out of the loop, always have been. I'm the grunt, the guy they don't care about, the dishrag they hang out to dry. I'm scum."

"Now, don't be modest. You keep your ears open, you pick up stuff."

"Oh, yeah? So how much did they tell *you?*"

"Wake up, Lonnie. I'm tossing you a rope. But, if you don't want to be my friend, you'll have plenty of time to make new pals in the lockup." Hunter gathered his papers and pushed back his chair.

"Hope you can weather it. A lot of guys get pretty lonely in—"

"Wait," said Lonnie.

Hunter stopped. "Yes?"

"Okay, listen, this is all I know," Lonnie blurted. He shrugged and added, "Really it's not that much—but don't blame me if it's not what you want, okay?"

Hunter drew up his chair once more. He leaned in, all ears. "Give."

"Washer John's got family in New York, a mother—"

"What do you think this is?" Hunter snapped. "Morons Anonymous? Don't waste my time. We know all about his mother."

"No, wait! Listen. I seriously didn't hear anything about The Prophet wanting Washer John dead and that's a true fact. He's not like that—I mean that guy has a hundred ways of destroying a man without even getting near him. Anyway, it's not his style." Lonnie paused and swallowed. His face looked washed out, and his brow was shining with sweat. "But, you know, there are . . . others."

"What others?"

"There's this group called . . . the Kadesh."

"The Kadesh?"

"Yeah. They might have something to do with it."

Hunter leaned back in his seat. "Explain."

"Well, Washer John used to say things about them, insulting things. These are guys you don't want to make mad, you know? They're like this secret society. They, you know, protect people and stuff. But they're sort of, what's the word? Semireligious? You know, like—"

"Skip to the end."

"Well, one of the leaders of the Kadesh—some fancy big shot, you know?—well, his wife used to be married to his brother. Who cares, right? Except the Kadesh dudes are supposed to be against that kind of thing. Like I said, they're semire—no, quasi, that's what I meant to say. Quasi-religious. Anyway, they're tied in with the temple somehow, and they . . . "

Hunter opened his mouth in an exaggerated yawn.

"Okay," said Lonnie. "So, anyway, I think they did it."

Hunter stared at Lonnie. "That's it?" he asked after a moment. Lonnie lowered his head. "That's all?"

"That's everything, man!" whined Lonnie.

"I thought you actually might *know* something. What are you giving me here?" demanded Hunter. "Washer John said some bad things about some mean people. That's your big secret? What did you do—steal a Mario Puzo book off someone in the holding pen? I thought I was going to get a story, or at the very least a name—"

"I *gave* you a name! The Kadesh leader! He's—"

"That's not a name! If y—"

"It's all I can say!" Shouted Lonnie hysterically. "Don't you—"

"Lonnie."

"*Know* what they would—"

"Lonnie."

"Dead meat, man! Roadkill! That's what!"

"*Lonnie!*" Hunter shouted, slamming his palm down on the table.

"What?!"

"Look at me, Lonnie. Look at me right here," Hunter raised a finger to his eye, "and tell me."

Hunter lowered his voice, holding Lonnie's wide, watery eyes with his own. "*What* is his *name?*"

Lonnie's jaw muscles worked, but his mouth stayed firmly shut.

"Just give me a name and we can call it a day."

Lonnie held Hunter's gaze for an instant, then lowered his head in resignation.

"I don't need to be yanked around by you, I got a hundred . . . " Hunter snatched up his files with his left hand. "I should have known better than to come down here. Thanks for nothing."

"Hey, you going to help me out or what?"

"Yeah, I'll help." Hunter pushed back his chair and stood. "The minute you get ready to give me something that isn't a complete bucket of crap, give me a call." He turned and started for the door. "Have a nice life, Lonnie."

"Up yours, *Special Agent!*"

Hunter left the room without another word or backward glance. He listened to Lonnie yell at him until the soundproof door closed behind him.

Hunter stared into the room through the window again. Lonnie had stopped shouting but was still scared and angry, shaking. Hunter decided he would let his prisoner go and relax in his cell. He'd try again to extract a name he could use, before his late-afternoon flight back to New York. He glanced at his watch. Time for lunch.

Hunter collapsed into an uncomfortable chair with a pained sigh. The day had been more than he was up to physically *and* emotionally. Lonnie had refused to give him even one more word of information, so his entire trip was a waste of time. His muscles were so knotted from the flight back that he felt like a pretzel. He had done his best to relax, but even now there was a stiffness in his neck that he couldn't shake. His arm felt like a dead weight suspended from his shoulder, and his side ached, radiating pain with every movement. While he tried to stretch out the kinks, he looked around the room—a small, window-less briefing room on the third floor of ICON HQ New York. There were a dozen molded plastic chairs with little foldaway desktops in case their occupants wished to take notes.

He watched the clock above the presentation screen as the minutes ticked past seven o'clock, impatient and annoyed but grateful for the chance to rest. He flipped open the notebook before him and looked through a small stack of printouts of e-mails that Supervisor Riley had written to him. Even though he had been reassigned, she was still keeping tabs on him. So far he'd managed to maintain only minimal contact, and he won-dered how long he could get away with that. It probably wasn't the best way to handle her—an irate supervisor could create a lot of problems—but he didn't care. Hunter found himself sur-prised at the growing number of things he didn't care about these days. Some supervisor: she didn't even visit him in the hospital when he got shot.

At five past seven, the door burst open and an energetic young man flew into the room, his arms full of briefing folders and loose bits of paper. He stepped quickly over to Hunter and, as his laptop tilted across his arms like a ship on a stormy sea, tried to shake Hunter's hand. "Hi there, Agent Hunter; I'm Clyde!"

"You're late," he replied, watching Clyde sail over to the presentation stand and begin connecting the computer to various outlets.

"This will take a couple seconds to warm up, but you can have these now." Clyde strode across the room and dumped half of the files he was carrying in front of Hunter, then picked up several of them again and replaced them with others. After gazing thoughtfully at them for a second he nodded to himself and returned to the stand. Hunter stifled a yawn. He had come back to work much too soon for this kind of dog-and-pony show.

"Okay, here we go," Clyde began, once he had hooked up his computer to the console built into the presentation stand. "So, you want to know about the Kadesh." He looked to Hunter for approval, but when he didn't get it he continued anyway. "Okay, so. Most of this is in the files, which you can read later, but here's the boiled-down version." Clyde clicked a button and the first slide came up on the screen. When he saw it, Hunter's first impulse was to stand up and walk straight out of the room. The image was a giant question mark.

"We have more questions about the Kadesh than answers," Clyde declared. "We know they're an organization that claims to go back hundreds of years, maybe thousands. They are thought to rule the Jewish community through various means—mostly tradition and intimidation."

Clyde clicked the button again and a picture of a dusty red mountain appeared behind him, making Hunter blink. "Why 'Kadesh'?" asked Clyde. "Well, the name comes from a place where Moses, one of the major heroes from the Jewish history and religious books, stopped to rest with the Jewish people when they were wandering in the desert following a liberation of some sort. . . . " Clyde glanced down, but failed to find the reference in his notes; his eye found something else instead. "Oh, yeah, the Kadesh rulers—there's apparently more than one—claim that they are descended from the kings of Israel, and also claim to have documents to prove it. Of course, no one's ever seen these documents."

Clyde looked up at his audience of one. "With me so far?"

"Get on with it," growled Hunter.

"Right," replied Clyde, sailing on. "Well, the Jewish community thrived during the centuries after the Dark Ages, amassing power in the Middle East until they were driven north and west into Europe by the Moors, a violent branch of Muslims. The Jews scattered everywhere. It's said that the Kadesh led and facilitated the escape of Jews into Europe at this time. However, it is highly unlikely that they were the antecedents of those who currently hold that distinction."

Hunter stared blandly at Clyde. Ancient history. He wondered when he would hear something he could use.

"Uh," said Clyde, failing to register his audience's fading interest, "during the religious wars in Europe in the late 1600s it was said that the Kadesh, fearing discovery and persecution, left Europe, came to America, and have secretly influenced the country's development and politics ever since. But that's pure legend; I wouldn't bet the farm on it," Clyde looked up from his notes and offered Hunter a cheesy grin. "There are any number of conspiracy theories about the Kadesh's involvement in various organizations both inside and outside the government. One of the most outlandish is that the Kadesh is actually a race of seven-foot-tall shape-changing space lizards. You would probably be shocked to know how popular that one is."

Hunter regarded Clyde with weary eyes. He needed a good cup of coffee, or a brandy. Or both. "What are the facts, Clyde?"

Clyde came out from behind the lectern and perched on the edge of the table beside Hunter. He put on a serious and businesslike expression. "So far as we can tell, the Kadesh exists as an informal ruling body for a dispossessed and constantly persecuted race. Two things are for certain: They do exist, and they do seem to possess influence in circles that are antagonistic to the overall aims of ICON. The threat has not, in the past, been felt to be of sufficient strength to warrant attention."

"What's their game?"

"They do favors for people who can do favors for them."

Hunter considered this. "That's it?"

"For example, if you've got a problem no one else takes seriously, the Kadesh might take an interest and solve it for you. Then, next time *they* need something, they come to you. The Kadesh is really a holdover from some ancient form of tribalism that has survived since before written history, created by a race that has been dumped on in every way imaginable. These days, though, the Kadesh is pretty much a toothless old dog."

Clyde turned, switched off his computer, and began pulling it free of the wires and plugs. "If you want my advice, you should look elsewhere for your smoking gun, Agent Hunter. It seems far more likely that one or two crazies dusted this Washer guy than him being marked for execution by an ancient secret society—a society whose best interest has always been to make as few and as small waves as possible."

"Anything else?" asked Hunter.

"That's all I have. Thank you for your time." Clyde decided not to risk his laptop in another handshake attempt so he gathered up his papers and bustled from the room, leaving Hunter alone with his thoughts.

He sat staring at the folders Clyde had left behind, before deciding to at least glance through them. It took him about thirty seconds to discover what he had suspected, which was that he had been handed a pile of stale garbage. He thought about consigning the papers to the circular file, but left them instead, and decided to walk down to the commissary for another in a steadily lengthening series of mediocre suppers.

As he ambled down the seemingly endless corridors, Hunter wondered at Clyde's last comment about his mission. Briefers were very rarely told anything about the assignments they were providing information for, in case it clouded what they decided to pass on. Hunter certainly hadn't told him anything about it. He shrugged. He was too hungry and tired to wonder if it meant anything.

nineteen

Hunter checked the address on the crumpled slip of paper and quickly stuffed it back into his pocket. It started to rain as he walked up the stoop to the front door and pushed the doorbell for apartment 3J.

"Yes? Who is it?" came the static-filled reply from a battered speaker by the doorbell.

"Mrs. Levinson? This is ICON Special Agent Alex Hunter. May I speak to you, please?" The door buzzed in reply. Hunter made his way inside.

As he mounted the stairs to the third floor, he met the gaze of people who came to their front doors to glare at him. These were poor folk, most of them black or Hispanic, who lived in a borough that, over the years, had become more war zone than neighborhood. Burned-out wrecks of cars lined the streets, uncollected garbage blocked the sidewalks, the lower windows of most buildings and houses were broken or boarded up, and every wall was defaced by spray-painted gang slogans and crude graffiti. Hunter felt as if he was a solitary recruit in a one-person army that had mistakenly invaded a foreign country, his uniform displaying enemy colors. He smiled at those he met and tried to show that he was a friendly soldier.

He reached apartment 3J and rapped on the door. It was promptly opened by a tiny old woman in a prim black dress. She had chocolate-colored skin, and a halo of white frizzy hair framed her delicate doll-like features. She stood bolt upright, her back straight, unlike many women of her years—which, if Hunter's records could be trusted—were close to ninety. Yet, her eyes were quick and intelligent, and her manner direct. Old age suited her very well.

"Elizabeth Levinson?"

"Yes. Come in, Mr. Hunter," she said and held the door open for him. "But do call me Bess."

Hunter entered a cozy, nicely decorated four-room apartment that completely reversed the impression of the building that he had formed while walking up the stairs. A comforting smell of baking bread wafted from the kitchen. In the living room, every knickknack and doily was neatly arranged. In fact, the only things out of place were the stacks of cardboard boxes piled on the dining table and by the door. Two of the boxes were open: one contained books; another was full of men's clothing.

The old woman closed the door behind him. "Please, won't you have a seat?" She indicated a pink, slip-covered couch. A white cloth with black edging and long, fringed tassels lay over the back of the couch; Bess retrieved it and folded it over her arm. "My husband's prayer shawl," she said, stroking the cloth absently. "I keep it close by these days—then he doesn't seem so far away."

Hunter didn't know what to say to this, so he just stood and watched her. Presently, she came to herself once more. "Can I offer you a drink? Coffee? Tea? How about some nice hot cocoa?"

The question unbalanced Hunter; he had not expected such a pleasant welcome. He thought for a moment. "Sure, I'd like that," he said, then added, "please." She bustled off to the kitchen.

"I was wondering when another one of you boys would be callin'," Bess said from the other room. "You're lucky to catch me today. I've been run off my feet with company all week."

"Do you know why I'm here?"

"Oh, I can guess," she replied. "Feel free to take a look around. I won't be a minute."

Hunter rose from the couch and examined the items on the bookshelf against one wall. There was a curious seven-tined candelabra in silver with exotic characters carved into the base, and a small round cap in white satin with tiny blue beads around the edge. Next to the cap was a postcard from Jerusalem.

On another shelf stood a row of gilt-framed photographs. In one, a young woman in a wedding dress gazed happily back at him; it took him a couple of seconds to realize it was Bess herself, and she was young and gorgeous. In the next picture she was standing arm in arm with a tall black man in a tuxedo—her husband, Hunter assumed. There were several school photos of their son at various ages, of Bess and a younger woman—her sister perhaps?—in a park, each with a young child on her knee; of a beefy teenage John with his arm draped around a skinny younger boy—both were wearing football uniforms, both had helmets tucked under their arms, and both were covered in mud. Even given the differences in the boys' statures, the resemblance between the two was striking. They shared the same bright smile, dark, sparkling eyes, and high forehead. Next to that was a photo of both boys dressed up in dark suits, those little round white caps, and long white prayer shawls; behind them, a homemade sign read "Happy Bar Mitzvah!"

Bess Levinson came back into the room, and Hunter returned to the couch. She placed a tray with two mismatched mugs and a loaf of intricately braided bread fresh from the oven on the table in front of them.

"Now then, Mr. Hunter, how can I help you?" She handed him one of the mugs and a paper napkin, then cut him a slice of bread. "There's plenty more challah if you want it," she told him. "Today's my baking day."

Hunter was slightly wrong-footed by this almost aggressive show of hospitality. "Mrs. Levinson, I'm here—"

"I wish you'd call me Bess. I'm not one for formalities," she said. Picking up a small, round sugar bowl, she offered it to him along with a spoon and confided, "I always like my cocoa a little sweeter."

Hunter smiled and accepted the spoon. "I'm here to talk to you about the deaths of your husband and son," he said, tipping a spoonful of sugar into his mug.

Instantly, the old woman's brow furrowed slightly and her mouth twitched downward. She set her mug on the table. "Oh, yes," she sighed, a shadow moving over her face, "I keep thinking it's all a terrible mistake." She turned sad eyes to Hunter. "But I don't guess it is a mistake, is it?"

"No, ma'am," replied Hunter, matching her mood. "I'm sorry." He blew on his hot chocolate, giving the old woman a moment to collect herself. "When was the last time you saw your son?"

"The last time I saw John was the day before he went up to the mountains." She smiled wistfully. "He dearly loved those mountains. I guess for a city boy they were real special."

"Was he worried about anything? Was anything bothering him?"

"If there was," replied Bess thoughtfully, "he didn't tell me—not that he would. He never liked to worry me, but I know he had enemies."

Again, Hunter was disconcerted by such a frank and forthright reply. "Ma'am?"

"Well, my John wasn't much of what they call a people person. He had strong opinions and some folk resented that. He didn't see any need to let sleeping dogs lie. He was always stirring things up—even when he didn't need to. He just wouldn't leave well enough alone, never could."

That fit with the little Hunter knew of the man. "What about his friends?"

"John didn't make many friends," she said; the sadness in her voice tugged at Hunter's heart. "Of course, the few friends he did make, he made for life. 'Grappled them unto his soul with hoops of steel,' as the poet said. That was John." She took a sip of cocoa and Hunter steeled himself for the next question.

"Ma'am," he said, smiled, and corrected himself, "I mean, Bess; it seems to me that the deaths of your son and husband are connected in some way."

She nodded, staring straight ahead. "I suppose that's so. But I don't know who could have hated them both so much. I really don't." There were tears in her eyes when she turned to look at Hunter again. "We lived our whole life without hurting anybody, without making trouble for anybody, and helping our friends and neighbors whenever we could." She sighed and dabbed her eyes. "They killed him on the steps of our own temple, can you imagine that? We've been going there for fifty years—and my husband even longer. Now this. What's this world coming to, Mr. Hunter? What's this world coming to?"

Hunter could think of no meaningful reply. He offered a muttered, "I wish I knew."

She seemed not to have heard. "I miss them both terribly. My husband, Zack—he was so handsome. And holy, to boot. And John was just like him. Not only that, but righteous as well—have you ever met a righteous man, Mr. Hunter? A man burning with desire for the truth? You can see where John got his *fire* from. My, but they were fine and handsome men," she declared with a defiant thrust of her chin. "To see them together was to see why God made fathers and sons. There was no one that John admired more, nor my husband Zack, for that matter." She held up two thin fingers. "They were that close."

An image flashed before Hunter's mind: two big black men standing side by side, a father and son, their faces ablaze with holy zeal.

"Do you have any other children?" he found himself asking.

The old woman modestly smiled, "No, Mr. Hunter, I don't. We only had John, and we were lucky to get him."

"Then the other boy in those photos?" Hunter waved a hand at the picture shelf.

"Why, John's cousin, Josh." Hunter made a note of the name. "Second cousin, really. Good boy. Cast from the same mold as John, as they say."

Hunter nodded. A fragment of what Hunter was told on the train all those months ago came to his mind. "How old were you when he was born?"

The old lady looked slightly offended but recomposed herself. "Why, I was nearly sixty, if you must know."

Hunter considered how best to phrase the next natural question, but Bess Levinson delivered him from his awkwardness.

"We didn't use any modern techniques," she confided. "No science, no drugs, no doctors, no nothing. John was a gift to us, and that's a fact."

So, the story of John's birth that the old hippie had told him had a grain of truth in it. *Interesting.* "I see," he said.

She turned her gaze to him and Hunter noted again the astonishing clarity and acuity of her eyes. Now it was he himself under scrutiny, as Bess looked him up and down. She examined his face, taking in every line, reading the set of his eyes, the fix of his jaw, studying his forehead. Then she smiled and the motherly kindness eased back into her face. "You aren't a religious man, are you, Mr. Hunter?"

It was a strange question. Most all of the major religions required you to be born into them; the others Hunter knew about weren't so fussy, but were also mostly just astrological claptrap and pseudo-mystical mumbo jumbo. As for the rest, Hunter had studied the ancient religions in school—the Roman and Greek myths, the Norse stories, which were his favorites—but no one took any of that seriously anymore, not in the bright spotlight of scientific reason. The old lady might as well have asked Hunter if he came from the moon.

Despite his bemusement over the question, he found himself

answering in a slightly defensive tone. "No ma'am, not really."

"Then I don't suppose you'll find the answers you're looking for, either."

"Are you saying you believe the murders were religiously motivated?" This was what Hunter thought, too, but had been careful not to suggest.

"Mr. Hunter, did you ever meet my son?" It was an innocent, rhetorical question. "He would have said th—"

"Actually," Hunter interrupted, "I did meet your son, ma'am."

This made her draw back slightly. "Really?"

"I met him a few weeks before his death."

"Then you know what he was like. How powerful he was. And I'm not just talking about physically strong. John could see *through* people."

Hunter recalled the image of the large, slightly deranged man standing in water to his knees, berating his audience with fearless, even reckless confidence.

"My boy was more than a match for any five regular men," she said with a mother's fierce devotion. "No, my boy was killed by something bigger, something jealous of the righteous power my son possessed. Something that was able to sneak up from behind and snatch him up."

"Mrs. Levinson—Bess," Hunter found his heart beating fast in his chest, "have you ever heard of the Kadesh?"

Once again, the shadow passed over the old woman's face. "I'm sure I haven't," she said crisply. "John never went in for that sort of thing, and neither do I."

"What sort of thing, ma'am?"

Elizabeth pouted. Hunter held his tongue and waited; he

didn't want to push her, but he would if she refused to answer.

"There's a lot of hateful people in the world, Mr. Hunter," she said at last, her mouth held in a firm frown of reproof, "and when those hateful people get together, the hate just grows and grows. My son loved—he loved life, loved people, loved truth—with a fierce and violent passion. It was a pure and true love, Mr. Hunter, and it was a wonderful thing to behold."

The simple assertion on the lips of the old woman was touching, and it made Hunter wish he'd got to know Washer John a little better.

"Hate reached out and slapped him down, Mr. Hunter," she announced. "That's what happened. I won't say more than that."

She paused and drank some hot chocolate, then leveled her keen black eyes on him once more. "I can see you're a good person, Mr. Hunter, and you're fighting the right fight. This is what you're up against. Just so's you know." She returned her mug to the tray.

"Now, I can't give you any information on the Kadesh," she said. "Don't know nothing about them."

Hunter didn't pursue the line any further. He thanked her again, then stood and made his way to the door. She followed him. "Was your son close to anyone?" he asked as he prepared to leave. "A relative, or a girl perhaps?"

"No, sir. He wasn't," she replied with a smile. "John wasn't close to women. Didn't have many friends either, as I say."

"Do you think I could have the name and address of his cousin—Josh, was that his name?"

"Oh, yes, of course," she said. "It'd definitely be good for you to look him up. *Very* intelligent boy. *Very* spiritual. He's from

Pennsylvania, but last I heard he was in town staying with some friends over in Harlem. You might find him there." She turned away. "I think I have an address somewhere."

She gave him the address from her book, and Hunter said, "I'll leave you now, Bess. Thank you for your time, and the hot cocoa. You've been a big help." As he walked back down the stairs a couple stray thoughts flitted around the edges of his mind. The first was the face and name of a man who looked familiar but that he couldn't remember ever meeting. The second was some crazy blather about two-headed snakes.

Having just spoken to his mother, however, Hunter now considered Washer John far less mad than most people. Was it possible to be *so* sane, *so* rational and clearheaded that you almost came out of the other side of the spectrum and appeared crazy to a normal person? Was there such a thing as stark-raving sanity?

twenty

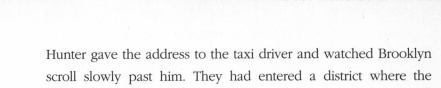

Hunter gave the address to the taxi driver and watched Brooklyn scroll slowly past him. They had entered a district where the houses ranged from cheap multi-occupancy tenements to iron-gated semi-detached mansions, many marked with the six-pointed Star of David.

He reviewed his conversation with Bess Levinson and decided that of all the possible solutions to the riddle of who killed Washer John and his father, two explanations rose to the top—and both theories hinged on who or what Washer John actually was. If John was just a raving lunatic, it was difficult to see anyone actually caring enough about what he said to make an issue of it.

But, if John was a genuine prophet—if what he said had the power of truth behind it—then he might well have provoked someone enough to get himself killed. He must have been per-ceived as dangerous to someone—but dangerous how? Washer John was a guy out in the woods talking to the trees and anyone who would listen. He seemed to be about as much a threat as a wild dog in the desert barking at the moon. What kind of threat was that to anyone?

Then there was the business with the Kadesh. Just the mention of the name and Bess Levinson, a sweet old lady, clammed up. When asked if she had heard of them she forcefully denied it, saying she didn't go in for that sort of thing.

Her reply, of course, begged the question: If she had never heard of them, how did she know whether she went in for whatever it was they did?

And then she had launched into an impassioned speech about love and hate. What was he to make of that? What was it about the Kadesh that could provoke that sort of reaction?

He thought about this as the yellow cab slid through the rain-slick streets. They arrived at the address Bess had indicated, which turned out to be a low-rent high-rise apartment building in central Harlem. He paid the cabbie and entered a lobby littered with fast-food wrappers and cast-off clothing; three treadless car tires were stacked in one corner, and a TV set with a shot-out picture tube occupied another. A sign on the elevator door said it was out of service, so he took a deep breath and started the hike up the stairwell to the eighth floor. His side ached more and more with each floor he passed so that by the time he reached the eighth floor he had to lean against the wall for a minute to catch his breath. Luckily there wasn't anyone around to see an ICON officer, head down, puffing against the wall, one arm in a sling and the other clutching his side in pain. Eventually, Hunter pulled himself together and walked down the hall to the apartment number he had been given.

Removing his sling, he gave the door a few raps and waited

for it to be opened. The door was answered by a little girl in over-size canvas sneakers. Hunter asked if Joshua Jones was there.

"No," said the little girl, "he went out. They all did."

"You wouldn't know where he was going?"

The little girl shook her head.

"It's pretty important," Hunter told her, trying to make himself appear warm and friendly. "I have to talk to him."

The little girl shook her head again, and Hunter was about to ask if anyone else was home, when an older girl appeared. "Get inside, Tamala," the girl said, scooting the other one out of the way. Turning to Hunter, she said, "You lookin' for Josh?"

"Please, if you could tell me where he is. I have a few questions for him," Hunter said. Taking in the girl's dubious expression, he quickly added, "He's not in trouble or anything. I just need to talk to him."

"They went to a wedding down the street."

"Will he be back later?"

"I don't know."

"Does he live here?"

"I don't know."

"Well, do *you* live here?"

"Sometimes."

Normally, Hunter would have pressured the girl a little bit for better information, but he was tired and, quite frankly, couldn't be bothered. All he really wanted was to get back to his room at ICON headquarters and soak in the tub for an hour or two. Even so, the thought of dragging his aching carcass back out here to Harlem tomorrow made his head hurt. He decided to push on through. "Could you give me the address where Joshua went?" he asked.

The girl shook her head. "I don't know the address," she said.

Hunter sighed and was about to admit defeat when the girl said, "But I can take you there."

The building was just down the street and over a couple blocks, but the difference was a world away from the high rise he had just been in. It was the ground floor of a large brownstone that stood on the corner of the street like a fat and prosperous colossus. Lights streamed from the open windows and the sounds of raucous partying poured out onto the streets. Hunter thanked the girl for showing him the way and gave her five dollars for her trouble.

It was late in the afternoon. The rain had stopped, and the clouds were quickly scattering. The sun had disappeared behind the buildings, leaving an early twilight sky behind; the air was chilly and damp in a freshening wind. It would be a cold night. Hunter hoped he could get this over with quickly.

After several more jabs at the bell, the door was eventually thrown open by a jubilant, well-dressed black man in his fifties. He was laughing at something funny, until he saw a man in an ICON uniform standing on the doorstep. "Why, hello there," he said. "And what can I do for you, sir? Don't tell me we're making too much noise."

Hunter asked if there was anyone named Joshua Jones in the house, and to his great relief, the man nodded. "I think he's still here. But, hey, officer, it's my daughter's wedding reception. Certainly whatever it is you want with him can wait until tomorrow?

Say," he smiled suddenly, "why don't you join us? You look like you could use a drink."

Hunter declined, saying that he had only a few questions and it wouldn't take long, so if his host would be so kind as to find the gentleman in question he would get on with his job and then be on his way. Although he spoke politely and with a smile, Hunter's tone left little doubt that it was *not* a social call. "Well, then," said the man, "I guess you better come inside."

When Hunter had closed the door behind him, he found that the father of the bride had disappeared into the crowd spilling out into the hallway from the living room. Hunter waited patiently, trying to look aloof and unaffected by the festivities around him. He could not help but notice, however, that these people knew how to have a good time. He was on the point of envying them their celebration, when a young woman in a strapless red sheath dress noticed him standing by himself and advanced, took his good hand in hers, and declared, "You should be dancing."

"I don't dance, Miss," Hunter replied as she drew him away. Indicating his uniform, he said, "Anyway, I'm on duty." His protest was lost amid the thunder of the great throbbing beat that started up just then.

Hunter was pulled into a maelstrom of ear-bursting sound and wildly gyrating bodies. Luckily for him, there were so many people jammed into the room he could hardly move, let alone dance. The young woman seemed blithely oblivious to the fact that Hunter's feet remained firmly planted in one place while he swiveled his head this way and that hoping to catch sight of Joshua Jones, or at least the father of the bride.

Eventually, the older man returned with a young man in tow. Hunter recognized him instantly as John Levinson's cousin. "Are you Joshua?" shouted Hunter, trying to make himself heard above the thunderous music.

The young man smiled and said something Hunter couldn't hear. "This way," Hunter said, and abandoning his dancing partner, he led the young man from the room and went in search of a quieter, more private place where they could talk.

They ended up in the kitchen, which once the door was closed, proved quiet enough. A busy crew of caterers clattered in the background but paid them no attention. Hunter drew up a stool beside the counter and took a moment to size up the young man in front of him.

His age was hard to peg—it could have been anywhere between twenty and thirty. Hunter remembered that Joshua and John had been of a similar age and so decided he must be closer to thirty, but there was a youthful air about him. He was of average height and in good shape with an athletic build, well groomed, and smartly dressed in a black shirt, which he wore untucked, and black dress trousers. His hair was braided in thick strands gathered at the back.

Although he lacked his cousin's heavy build, his features bore a distinct family resemblance with a strong chin and jaw, and high, smooth brow. His skin was a rich java brown, his eyes deep, dark, and expressive; his smile was quick and never far from his lips. Oddly, for Hunter had just met the man and had no real way of knowing, he seemed to be completely and transparently open, without pretense or artifice of any kind.

"What can I do for you, officer?" he asked in a pleasant, low tone. He helped himself to a glass of wine from a fully laden tray, and offered one to Hunter.

"Thanks, no, I'm on duty," Hunter said. "I'm sorry to drag you away from the party, but I have to ask you a few questions."

"It's okay, officer . . . ah, um . . . "

"Hunter," he said. "Special Agent Alex Hunter."

"I really don't mind, Agent Hunter." He flashed a toothy smile and snatched a crescent roll from a basket on the counter beside them. "You're here and I'm here, so what's on your mind?" he asked, chewing on the roll.

Hunter explained that he was investigating the murder of his cousin John. Hunter asked the usual questions—the young man's age, occupation, address, and the like—and then asked about his relationship with the deceased.

"Well, we were cousins," Jones replied with a grin. Receiving no encouragement for his humor, he became slightly more serious. He and his cousin John had been close—more like brothers, though they had lived most of their lives in different cities. They hadn't seen much of each other in recent years. Hunter asked him about the last time he saw John.

The young man took a sip of wine, then answered, "It was a few months ago—late September. I went to see him in the Catskills."

Hunter stared. That was around the time Hunter was doing target practice with Simon. The memory of that encounter made Hunter anxious and cold. "I was up there around that time. Tell me, did we meet?"

"I don't think so."

Sound flooded into the kitchen; the father of the bride swept into the room, a caterer in a tall white hat and apron trotting close behind. They both looked agitated. Behind them came another fellow who, judging from his dinner jacket and manner, appeared to be in charge of the reception. All three men engaged in a heated discussion.

Hunter turned back to Joshua Jones once more. Weary—his arm, side, and head all aching—he longed to wrap this up. "Why did you go up there to see him?"

"The same reason as everyone else. I went there to be washed," the young man said, then asked, "Why did *you* go to see him?" He finished his wine and placed the glass on the counter.

Hunter felt his uniform was sufficient answer to this sort of question, so offered no reply. Instead, he asked, "Do you know of a reason why anyone would have wanted John dead?"

"There are lots of reasons why people want to kill each other," Jones replied. Voices rose across the room as the host and caterers became more impassioned about whatever it was they were discussing.

"Yes, but can you think of any—ah!" Hunter broke off with a gasp. He doubled over and instantly grasped his side, his wound suddenly a sharp, red-hot stabbing pain.

Jones was instantly at Hunter's elbow. "Are you okay?"

Hunter nodded and explained it was a recent injury that he had strained today. Jones helped him straighten up, and as he leaned against the counter, the younger man put his hand to Hunter's side, probing the injured area gently.

"Would you like me to help you?" Joshua Jones asked, his voice low, almost a whisper.

It was an odd question and Hunter didn't understand. "What do you mean?"

"Do you *believe* that I can help you?"

Hunter gave him a puzzled stare. "Are you a doctor? Have you had any medical training?"

Jones shook his head.

"Then I doubt you can do much for me."

The young man looked as if he was going to say something else, but he stopped himself and took his hand away. A middle-aged woman in a blue silk dress appeared just then and, after giving a nod to Hunter, said to the young man, "Son, is everything okay?"

The young man looked at Hunter as if he should answer the question, and Hunter found that he was saying, "Yes, everything's fine. I was just leaving." To Jones, he said, "I'll let you folks get back to the celebration, but I'd like to continue this conversation. Where can I find you tomorrow?"

"Come by the synagogue on Fifth Avenue. It's the Sabbath. I'll be there most of the day."

Hunter shook hands with Jones, pushed through the kitchen doors, and made his way to the front hall. He heard the mother address her son behind him as he left the kitchen. "There's a problem, son. I told them you could help."

"Wait a minute, Mama."

The young man caught up with Hunter in the hallway. "Hey, you don't look so good. Sit down for a minute. No one will mind if you rest here for awhile."

Weary with the rigors of the day, Hunter's natural reluctance melted away and he let himself ease onto a padded bench in the hallway. Jones stood over him for a moment, an expression of pity on his open, good-natured face. He did not speak, but

Hunter felt immeasurably comforted by the look alone. "Thanks," he said, "you can go back to the party. I'll be all right."

Without a word the young man turned back to his mother, who was waiting at the kitchen door, and they both disappeared into the kitchen once more.

The party was still in full swing, the music pounding, people shouting, laughing. Lacking the energy to chase down another cab, Hunter took out his cell phone and dialed up ICON transport and requested a car. He was told it would be a twenty-minute wait, so he leaned his head against the wall and closed his eyes.

The next thing he knew, he was being shaken by an exuberant wedding guest. The man's face was glowing with rosy inebriation. He had a comb-over that had become unhinged and swung loosely in a sideways U over his right ear. He wore his shoes around his neck and held a brimful glass of wine in his none-too-steady hand. Ignoring his new friend, Hunter glanced down at his watch. Fifteen minutes had passed since he sat down. He leaned forward to stand up.

"Hey," the guest exclaimed, "you gotta try this!" The wine glass was thrust under Hunter's nose.

"No, thanks," Hunter said, brushing both man and glass aside. He stood and stepped toward the door.

"Come on, man, you gotta!" Once more the glass was offered. "It would be a . . . a *crime* to leave without at least *tasting* this stuff. It's fabulous!"

"And so are you," Hunter murmured under his breath. To rid himself of his pest, he accepted the glass and took an exploratory sip. It was very good, surprisingly good—rich, earthy, sweet, and tasting of the light and air of a sun-drenched Mediterranean hillside.

Even Hunter, who had never cultivated a taste for fine wine, could tell it was very expensive. He raised the glass again for another mouthful and let the divine nectar roll around his tongue for a moment before swallowing.

The wine produced a pleasant warmth that soothed him all the way down. He could feel it spreading through him with a delicious radiance—as if he'd swallowed liquid sunshine.

"Yeah," said the party-goer knowingly. "Now you're gettin' the idea."

"Thanks," said Hunter, handing back the glass. "You're right, it's great stuff."

"Keep it," said the man, moving off at last. "There's plenty more where that came from."

Hunter sat back down to drink his wine; and when he rose a few minutes later he felt more relaxed and refreshed than he had in days, or even weeks. He placed the empty glass on the side table next to him, and closing the door to the party behind him, he stepped out into a fresh, rain-rinsed evening. The rain had stopped, leaving behind a sky streaked with the crimson and gold of a fiery sunset. He stood for a moment, gazing up at the swift-moving clouds and breathing in the sweet, cool air, then walked down the steps to his waiting car.

twenty-one

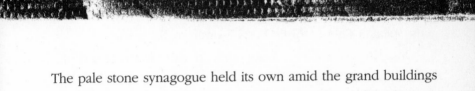

The pale stone synagogue held its own amid the grand buildings of Fifth Avenue, and that was saying something in Manhattan's extravagant Upper Midtown. Hunter was aware, as never before, just how much religious imagery was salted away among the towering monuments to commerce and consumerism. Walking through Rockefeller Center, Hunter paused to admire golden Prometheus frozen in midflight, clutching a ball of fire. An art deco Zeus stretched out a hand to apprehend the gilded thief from above the doors of the nearby GE Building, while a somewhat preoccupied Mars and Venus cavorted across the courtyard. A statue of Atlas supporting the world on his mighty shoulders toiled silently away on his pedestal outside the Time & Life Building, and several semiclad Fates danced in a bronze frieze along the building's exterior.

Against the ambitious angularity of the thrusting towers, the rounded prominence of the synagogue was much more inviting. The sand-colored stone was carved with splendidly intricate tracings, giving the building a peculiar texture, while the curving mounds of its several enormous domes made it look like a living thing against the flat-planed concrete and glass giants surrounding it.

On the way in, Hunter passed bronze plaques depicting the distinctive six-pointed star, the vine leaves with bunches of grapes, and the strange symbols that looked like wobbly Greek letters.

It was Saturday, and the place was packed. Hunter had over-slept, to his great annoyance—he blamed the painkillers he'd taken the night before—so the service was already in progress as he stepped through the door. A sign in the entryway advertised guest speaker Rabbi Moishe Ben Hyam from Tel Aviv.

Once inside, Hunter's heart sank. Several hundred people were milling about in a wide vestibule. Men wore hats or the lit-tle round skullcaps, and many were wrapped in the tasseled prayer shawls. Women eyed Hunter from under headscarves of various kinds. It would be next to impossible to spot Joshua Jones in this crowd.

Hunter stood straight in his freshly pressed uniform, ignor-ing hostile glances from worshipers who apparently resented a uniformed ICON officer at their religious service. Two ushers approached to inquire whether he wanted to be seated—their manner suggested that in his own best interest Hunter really ought to decline the offer and beat a hasty retreat. But Hunter held his ground, and the ushers retired to watch him from a short distance away.

He turned his attention to the throng. Every size, shape, color, and social standing seemed to be on revolving display. Judging by dress and demeanor alone, there must have been six or eight different ethnic groups represented. The diversity sur-prised him: Who'd have thought so many otherwise ordinary-looking people should hold to such ancient superstitions?

At the other end of the great vestibule stood a series of huge double doors made of glass. Through these, Hunter could see the arena-like main auditorium with a semicircular stage, on which stood a red, satin-draped screen. Before the screen was a veritable waterfall of cascading baskets of yellow and white flowers. And in front of the flowers was an ornate golden stand that supported an enormous scroll. Wound around spindles of gleaming gold, it was partially unrolled to reveal a section of curious squiggly letters.

In the center of the stage, an elderly rabbi was leading the service. Speakers above the doors allowed those in the vestibule to follow what was happening on the other side of the glass. The old rabbi—head raised, face tilted upward, and hands out-stretched in a gesture of praise—intoned a warbly chant in a language that Hunter did not recognize, but which he assumed to be Hebrew. The old fellow droned on in his odd singsong while worshipers stood rocking gently, like grass in a breeze.

At last the chant ended, the worshipers sat, and the rabbi introduced the special guest speaker, Rabbi Moishe Ben Hyam.

A small souvenir kiosk next to the door created an annoying distraction as a noisy cash register churned out receipts to chattering tourists. Irritated by the constant hubbub, Hunter moved to the nearest door and slipped silently into the auditorium for a better look. The speaker mounted the stage to a clatter of enthusiastic applause. He was a short, smooth-faced fireplug of a man with a full head of long hair, lovingly curled and oiled until it gleamed. His jet-black suit was hand tailored. Rabbi Hyam gave the impression of being not only extremely wealthy and powerful, but also insincerely humble. Hunter disliked him instantly.

Oozing an oily charisma, the rabbi, all smiles and winks, thanked the head rabbi and others who had invited him to New York. He said how wonderful it was to be in the city, and in this beautiful synagogue once again. He dropped the names of prominent members of the local Jewish community and said how glorious it was to be among God's righteous people, people whom the Lord had blessed with such impressive material well-being so that the world might envy them and turn from its wicked ways and embrace God. Through finance, he said, the Lord had favored his own and brought shame upon those who scorned his chosen people.

And then he started to laugh.

It was not a joyful, hearty laugh, or even a good-natured chortle but a disgusting, sinister giggle. And Hunter wasn't the only one to recoil from it; judging by the commotion coursing through the congregation, this weird laugh confused and upset a lot of listeners. Shaking his head and stamping his feet, the rabbi clutched his sides and doubled over in obscene laughter. Elders, seated on the platform behind the speaker, shot nervous glances at one another; they clearly weren't expecting this unsavory outburst either.

Then Rabbi Hyam straightened up. Arching his broad back and throwing a hand out in front of him, he pointed toward the rear of the sanctuary near the place Hunter was standing. Hyam kept laughing and pointing so that everyone turned around to see what had provoked the man's twisted mirth. Many of those seated nearby took one look at Hunter's ICON uniform and assumed *he* was the object of the rabbi's attention. But from where he stood, Hunter could see that the finger wasn't pointing directly at him, but slightly to his left, at the doorway behind him. He turned.

And there was Joshua Jones, standing in the doorway a few feet away. His mother was with him, as was the elderly Bess Levinson. There were also a few younger folks, teenagers some of them, who bore the strong family resemblance. They were all standing stock-still, transfixed by the rabbi's bizarre behavior. Joshua lifted his hand slightly and motioned for the others with him to remain where they were. Then he headed down the aisle, stopping in the middle of the sanctuary.

Hyam was laughing so hard now he could hardly breathe. His insane guffaws boomed out over the loudspeaker system and reverberated throughout the enormous auditorium, splitting the air like the pealing of a cracked bell.

The congregation squirmed in discomfort; some were leaving their seats and making their way to the exits. Two elders fled the stage. After a particularly draining burst of laughter, which degenerated into a rattling, gasping gurgle, the rabbi leaned into the lectern and grabbed the microphone, holding it tight to his mouth. His snarl made everyone jump.

"What are you doing here?" Hyam shouted in a roar distorted by the overtaxed PA speakers. Before Joshua could answer, he shouted again. "Son of Mary, Son of God, Son of Man, Son of a—!"

"Rabbi Hyam!" cried one of the seated elders, leaping to his feet, his jowls trembling. "Please! Control yourself."

Ignoring him, the visiting rabbi darted from behind the lectern. Grotesque, his face contorted in an ugly sneer, he jabbed a stubby finger in the direction of Joshua Jones and screamed again, "What are you doing here?"

Jones remained unmoved. Arms folded, confident and

unafraid—and, Hunter thought, much taller and more muscular than he remembered—Joshua seemed an entirely different person than the one he had met the previous evening.

"Have you come to *destroy* us?" cried the hysterical rabbi. The question was hissed, rather than spoken, and an odd trick of the sound system or the acoustics made it sound like several people speaking at once.

Calmly and with an air of restrained power—like a coiled steel spring—Jones waited, his eyes glinting with fierce defiance.

"*We* know who you are, even if these idiots, these groveling morons don't!" Rabbi Hyam thrust his arm clumsily forward, nearly toppling from the stage in his attempt to indicate the entire congregation. "This is a war you cannot win! We can lose time and time again, but you . . . You! Should *you* slip up even *once* then it would be better if you had never been born!"

Hunter braced himself. As an ICON officer, it would fall to him to maintain order. He moved his hand to his shoulder holster.

"Oh yes, we know who *you* are! The Holy One of God!" Hyam cried. He laughed insanely and began spitting at people in the front rows.

"Silence!" Joshua shouted, and it was the clear, resonant sound of a trumpet blast. The single word echoed off the walls and filled every corner of the immense room. Moishe Ben Hyam looked suddenly shocked—as if he had been struck in the face. His mouth closed with an audible snap, and he seemed to shrink into himself; he stepped behind the lectern and stood cowering.

Jones strode a few more paces toward the stage, stopped, and raised his hand. "You! Come out of him!"

An odd thing to say, thought Hunter, but the effect was

instantaneous. Hyam knocked the lectern aside with a mighty sweep of his arm and let out a high, piercing shriek. It lasted for several seconds, but to everyone in the auditorium who clamped their hands to their ears, it seemed an eternity. As the scream trailed away, the rabbi sank to his knees. He broke off with a shattered whimper, leaned forward, and tumbled off the low platform onto the carpeted floor below.

Those closest to the stage rushed forward, mobbing the fallen rabbi. Joshua Jones merely turned and started walking back up the aisle toward his family. Hunter was preparing to intercept the young man when a woman grabbed his sore arm and said, "Hey, you're a policeman—aren't you going to do something?"

She pointed to the people crowding the area where Rabbi Hyam fell. "Well," she demanded, "what are you waiting for?"

Hunter frowned and made his way down the aisle; his eyes met those of Jones going the opposite direction. Hunter threw out a hand and said, "Don't leave!" then moved into the commotion around the platform. Soon he was shoving his way through the mob, loudly declaring his name and ICON status.

Pushing into the center of the crowd, he knelt alongside the inert body and ordered those around him to stand back and give him room to work.

At first glance, the stricken rabbi seemed none the worse for his dramatics. He was breathing deeply and steadily, and didn't appear to be in pain or distress. In fact, Rabbi Moishe Ben Hyam seemed to be asleep, or perhaps unconscious from the shock of . . . whatever it was that had just happened. A mental breakdown, perhaps?

Over the heads of the crowd, Hunter glimpsed Jones and his

family departing through the glass doors across the room. He clenched his teeth; murder investigation or no, he still had to stay there and play ICON officer until the paramedics arrived.

By the time the ambulance team was wheeling a gurney down the aisle, Hyam was awake and sitting with his back against the stage. He didn't say a word, but it was clear that he was aware, if more than a little dazed. He apparently comprehended the paramedic's instructions but remained silent until, under questioning, he suddenly rejoined reality. He lowered his head and began gently weeping into his hands.

twenty-two

The short winter day was fading fast. *Time to pack it in,* Hunter thought. He decided to cut through the park and check the zoo, then hit the synagogue one last time on his way back to ICON HQ. A light fog was rising as the shadows deepened, and the air was cold and damp.

As Hunter approached the Central Park Zoo where, according to Jones' mother, Joshua often liked to hang out after services, he mulled over the exceedingly strange scene he had witnessed in the temple that morning. It seemed, on the face of it, to be an elaborate and stagey performance—certainly rehearsed, perhaps for the benefit of the congregation. To what purpose, though, he couldn't guess; he was entering unknown territory now. He knew where he stood with anarchists and revolutionaries, but spiritual hucksters? That was a whole different ball of worms. Nothing was ever straightforward and logical, but subject to weird beliefs that in turn made people behave in strange and irrational ways—and if he didn't know it before, he knew it now.

It didn't matter, he decided firmly. He wasn't really interested in these things; what the Jews did in their own synagogue concerned him not one tiny iota. He just wanted some information about Washer John's death. He hoped to close this case quickly and move on to the next one.

As he approached the zoo, Hunter found his way obstructed by a knot of people in the path. They were huddled together at the bottom of the steps leading up to the jogging track, and Hunter's first thought was that they were watching a street performer. He skirted the crowd, but in passing he heard a voice he recognized emanating from the center of the close-packed cluster. The people laughed when the voice finished.

Carefully picking his way among the people, Hunter found that they were all standing around an ordinary park bench on which two men sat: an old man, plainly dressed, and beside him, Joshua Jones. The two were deep in discussion, virtually oblivious to the crowd surrounding them. Nevertheless, their speech was loud and clear, easily heard and followed by the onlookers. Although some wore wary frowns, most seemed to be eating it up with a spoon.

The older man was talking now, with a gentle smile on his face. "My friend," he said respectfully, "we know that you are a great teacher. We've heard you talk on numerous subjects and your lessons are, shall we say, interesting."

"Please!" laughed Josh, holding up his hands. "Your flattery is overwhelming."

"I mean it," protested the elder gentleman mildly. "I am always interested in what you have to say. Maybe you don't know it, but you speak like no other rabbi I ever heard—and I've heard them all, let me tell you." He paused and glanced at the crowd.

"Am I right? Of course I'm right!" To Jones, he said, "So, tell us, our people have been longing for the kingdom of God for centuries. You say it's near at hand. Why?"

At the word *kingdom*, Hunter held his breath. Was Jones a revolutionary too?

"You want to know about the kingdom?" wondered Jones. There were nods and murmurs of agreement all around. "Don't be so quick to ask," Jones warned. "Just knowing about it carries a cost. It could be more than you care to pay."

Now the older man was frowning. "Try me."

"Okay," replied Jones, "it's like this." He closed his eyes and drew a hand over his face, as if erasing all expression. When he opened his eyes again, he said, "There was a famine in a far country. An aid worker took a truck full of rice into a border village where the people were desperate for food.

"As he drove into the center of the village, all the people saw him coming and ran to meet the truck. He parked in the town square, climbed into the back of the truck, and began tossing down bags of rice to the hungry people.

"Well, there was a lot of pushing and shoving; everybody was jostling everyone else to be first in line to get the food they needed.

"Some of the bags of rice went to some little children who couldn't carry them. The children tripped and fell, and the grain was spilled on the ground, where it got trampled into the dirt.

"Other bags went to the old women of the village. But some young men, too lazy to stand in line, hid in the alleys and waited until the old women passed by. Then they jumped out, grabbed the bags of rice, and ran away.

"Some of the rice bags went to a local merchant who

carried them to his shop and locked them in the storeroom to sell later. Other bags fell to the town mayor, who went around dispensing rice to anyone who would vote for him in the next election. But some of the food went to good, honest people who carried it home to feed their hungry families. The families ate and grew strong and healthy, and they were saved from the famine."

Jones finished to uneasy silence. Hunter could almost hear the mental gears grinding in the heads of those around him, trying to work out what Jones was talking about. Hunter himself hadn't a clue. It didn't sound like politics. Probably it was some kind of intellectual game and he didn't know the rules.

The elder gentleman shook his head. "I hate to say it, Rabbi Joshua, but you lost me with that one. Would you like to tell us what your little story means?"

"Nick, my man," chided Jones gently, "your eyes are open, but you're not seeing. You're listening, but you're not hearing a word I say." Turning his face to the crowd, he said, "Wake up, everyone! Think long and hard about what I'm saying because if you get it, then you'll get more. But if you fail to get it, then you'll lose even the tiny bit you think you have."

Nick shook his head again. The young man smiled and patted his friend on the back. "We've been talking here a long time. It's getting late, and I've given you all plenty to think about until next time. Let's call it a day."

There were groans from the crowd and, Hunter noticed, some griping from those who felt they'd been tricked by the smooth-talking Jones. As the two men stood up, Hunter stepped forward through the quickly dispersing throng.

"Interesting speech," he said. "Remember me? I wanted to have a word with you today."

A man from the crowd grabbed Hunter by his good arm. "Listen, pal, he doesn't have to speak to you if he doesn't want to."

Some of the others started berating Hunter too. "Yeah, show a little respect, why don't ya?" said one. Another popped up with, "What's ICON got to do with this? Leave him alone—he hasn't done anything!"

Help came from Joshua himself. "It's okay, guys. I know this man. I'm happy to talk to him."

"What?" demanded the man who had first grabbed Hunter. He turned on the young rabbi. "Don't tell me you answer to ICON. They jerk your chain and you follow?"

"He's a man—like you. And that's how I meet everyone in the end, as simply themselves, alone."

This seemed to satisfy the onlookers, or at least confuse them sufficiently to let Hunter go. They started to disperse once more, leaving Jones and Hunter alone.

"Thanks," said Hunter. "Nice bunch of people. Are they always this friendly?"

"Ah, they're the same as anyone else, really," the other returned. "Come on, let's find some food. I feel like I haven't eaten in a month."

twenty-three

A pushcart vendor stood at the entrance to the zoo selling kabobs and hot pretzels. "Here," said Hunter, "let me buy you something. What do you want?"

"The gyros look good—with extra sauce. Thanks."

Hunter ordered that and a kabob on pita bread for himself. He also purchased a couple of drinks and, feeling generous, a sack of fries. With food in hand, he looked for someplace to sit and found a bench in front of a fence separating a few sheep and goats from the rest of the world. The trees on either side of the bench along the path had tiny lights hung in their mostly bare branches, giving the foggy pathway a magical quality. Hunter bit into his kabob and leaned back, enjoying the warm food and the nip in the air.

He turned his attention to the young man beside him. He was really just an ordinary guy—didn't take much care with his appearance, wore average bargain-basement-quality clothes, vaguely fashionable in a common sort of way and, like his hairstyle, ultralow maintenance. He seemed comfortable in the silence of Hunter's gaze. They sipped their sodas and munched their sandwiches.

"We were talking yesterday about your cousin John," Hunter said at last, "and whether you thought he might have any enemies, anyone who might wish him harm."

Jones laid his sandwich on the bench beside him. "Who is Washer John that you go to all this trouble over his murderers?"

"It's my job," Hunter replied. "I'm under orders to find out who killed him."

"And where do these orders come from?"

"I should think that much would be obvious."

"Well, then—put another way—why is it so important to find his killers?"

Hunter answered automatically. "They need to be brought to justice."

"Why? That won't bring John back."

"No, it won't. But justice must be done—and be *seen* to be done. Stability must be maintained."

"Fair enough," said the young man. "But why do you do it?"

"Like I said, to maintain—"

"No, *you*. Why do *you* do it?"

Hunter thought for a moment before deciding on, "I like it. It's what I do."

"Why don't you become a street vendor?" Jones retrieved his sandwich and took a bite. "Better job. Easier hours. Grateful public. Don't get shot."

Hunter was becoming slightly annoyed. "Look," he sighed, "I'm a special agent. It's what I'm trained for and paid to do; it's what I'm good at. I work for the good guys and I do what I'm told."

"Do you?"

Hunter realized, too late, that he was getting drawn into a

lengthy philosophical discussion that had no direct bearing on his case. He also resented being interviewed by Jones; having the tables turned on him like this made him uncomfortable.

"Look," he said at last, "let's just stay on the subject. We were talking about Washer John. I think you know who killed him, or at least you have some suspicions."

"You might be able to find who killed him, but keep this in mind—if you go looking for death, you will find death. The powers of evil are great, but it is only in this world that they have power. In the world that comes after this one, evil will be beaten—in fact, it already is."

Hunter dropped his voice and leaned in. "Okay, you can drop the act. You're not talking to one of your intellectual groupies now, all right? It's just me, a very tired ICON agent, and I honestly don't give a rip about this philosophical nonsense."

"Then you're missing what's most important."

"This case is important. What I do is important." Hunter took a bite of his sandwich and chewed a moment to give himself time to cool down.

"Don't you ever think about death, Agent Hunter?" Jones asked.

Hunter paused for a moment and then resumed eating, trying to keep his composure. As it happened, he had been thinking about death quite a lot since the attack; he'd had weeks to ruminate on it when he was in the hospital. By way of reply he swallowed and took another bite of his kabob.

Jones said, "Do you think you're going to care about any of this when you die? What will it matter if you got promoted or won a medal? Your job is important, yes, but it's not more important than *you* are. You can't take your job with you when you go. You leave like you came—with nothing. One second beyond this life and it will all seem like a dream."

"Yeah, sure, whatever," replied Hunter. "Actually, it doesn't interest me one bit."

"Really? You never think about death?"

"No," lied Hunter, anxious to end the conversation. He was getting nowhere in this interview and needed to get it back on track.

"My friend, you do not speak the truth." Jones' eyes became intense as lasers, and Hunter could almost feel them burning through his skin and bones, right through into his soul.

"I just don't see the point, that's all," Hunter concluded.

"There is a way," said Jones earnestly, "—a way to have it all. This way is narrow and it is hard, and you have to follow it to the very end."

"And just what is this 'way'?"

"It's me," said the young man. His grin was sudden and disarming. "You have to follow me."

"Follow you?" Hunter shook his head in disbelief. Now he'd heard everything. "That's it? That's the big secret—the answer to the riddle of the universe?"

"Think about it. We've already established that the things of this world have no lasting value—zero. But if you follow me, I'll lead you to places you've never dreamed it was possible to go. Life will make sense, everything will be beautiful—even pain and suffering."

"So what is it, exactly, that you do?"

"You were at the synagogue—what did you see? And when I was talking to the lawyer, Nick—what did you hear?"

"To tell you the truth, I don't know what I saw in the synagogue this morning," Hunter declared. "And in the park just now all I heard was a load of manure dressed up in a folksy story."

The young man shook his head sadly. "Agent Hunter, there is evil in this world. You know this; you see it. In fact, you wade through it every day. There is a powerful lot of work to do, I won't kid you; and the workers are few. We've only begun to scratch the surface."

He smiled. "But we've made a brave beginning. I've sent people out into the city, into the boroughs, out into the country, and beyond to fight back the darkness and draw the battle lines against the enemy. The greatest battles are yet to come, and the greatest rewards. Come on, join me. You'll never look back, I guarantee it."

"Sounds tempting. What sorts of benefits go with that? Health insurance? Dental? Paid up pension?"

Joshua put back his head and laughed. "Man, you won't need any of that stuff—but that's good. You're trying it on. Good."

Hunter took a bite of kabob. "If it's all the same to you, I think I'll pass on becoming a part of your little religious road show."

Joshua's eyes shifted slightly; his voice became quietly insistent. "You refused my help yesterday, too. All right. Okay. But if you're ever given another chance, don't throw it away. Because even a second chance is more than most people will have after I'm gone." He smiled, and his dark eyes refocused on Hunter's face. "You can find me at any time and follow me. The choice is yours, and I'll never turn you down. You have my promise on that." He stood, threw his sandwich wrapper in the trash can by the bench, and stuck the empty drink can in his jeans. "Thanks for dinner, Alex. I've enjoyed talking to you."

Hunter watched him as he walked away down the sidewalk. Then, suddenly remembering himself, Hunter stood up and chased after him. "Jones!" he called out.

Joshua Jones turned, his expression a question.

"You still haven't told me who killed John."

"Do you honestly think I know?"

"Yes. I do." It was the truth. "I need to know—was it the Kadesh?"

"You have eyes and ears—even a brain. Use them." He smiled again. "I wish you well." With that, he turned and walked away.

Hunter, disgruntled and exasperated, watched him go, then returned to his bench and finished his kabob.

twenty-four

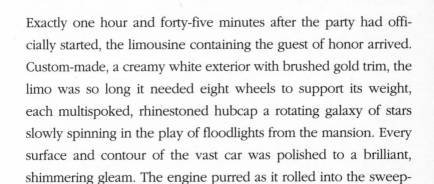

Exactly one hour and forty-five minutes after the party had officially started, the limousine containing the guest of honor arrived. Custom-made, a creamy white exterior with brushed gold trim, the limo was so long it needed eight wheels to support its weight, each multispoked, rhinestoned hubcap a rotating galaxy of stars slowly spinning in the play of floodlights from the mansion. Every surface and contour of the vast car was polished to a brilliant, shimmering gleam. The engine purred as it rolled into the sweeping, circular driveway.

The guests—B-list film stars, captains of industry, minor politicians—stopped to stare as the absurdly stretched limo now halted on the drive. Gossip momentarily forgotten, they all watched in silent anticipation as two footmen in black suits and purple ceremonial capes sprang smartly from the front doors of the vehicle. Chatter died down completely—even within the house—as guests flowed out onto the lawn for a better view of the late arrival.

The footmen took up positions facing one another and opened the rearmost door. After a few long seconds, a white-gloved hand appeared in the open doorway. One of the servants reached out to take it and everyone could now see what a massive thing it was; at least twice as big as the one supporting it. This great paw of a hand was attached to an equally massive satin-sheathed arm. The footman led the mystery passenger out of the car much as a circus master might lead an elephant out of a cage by its trunk.

The late-arriving guest emerged to stand blinking in the brightly lit driveway, his appearance everything that his ostentatious arrival promised him to be. He was a huge, rotund man in outlandish glistening robes bedecked with gaudy and peculiar ornaments, including an enormous gold necklace made of lozenge-sized plates splayed across his considerable chest.

His most arresting feature, however, was not the grand white satin mantle that reached from beneath his wattled chin to the tops of his white brushed-suede shoes and was encircled by a great purple sash; nor was it the small black silk skullcap, edged with rubies, covering his smooth-shaven head. No, it was the great round face of the man himself that provoked most comment, for it was heavily made up with blue mascara, a subtle pink lipstick, and rouged cheeks. The overall effect was not so much feminine as theatrical—as if he had stepped fresh from a Broadway performance of *Die Fledermaus* and had not bothered to remove his makeup. Some of the onlookers, in fact, assumed this was precisely the case.

He posed a moment, his breath steaming in the chill, early November air. Then he turned slightly to the limo as yet another aide emerged carrying a purple, ermine-lined cape, which he draped over the man's round shoulders.

The host of the party, confident and suave in a white tie and black dinner jacket, approached the gilded colossus, who removed his glove and extended his hand. The host took his guest's hand in both of his own, bent low to kiss the massive ring the man wore, then moved a respectful step back. "High Priest Kai, it is good of you to come." He indicated the mansion beyond. "Welcome to my home."

The high priest nodded and allowed himself to be escorted inside. A subdued and respectful applause started up and continued until both men reached the house. The guests then returned to their drinks and conversations, and the festivities slowly recommenced.

Howard Antony Archelon beamed with pride as he conducted the high priest on a tour of his opulent house. The grand entryway glowed under a sparkling crystal chandelier containing two hundred slender white candles that produced a gently shimmering, golden warmth. Glamorous guests thronged a large half-spiral staircase to view a noteworthy collection of expensive postmodern art. Antony led his illustrious guest up the staircase, pausing every now and then to look at one of the paintings—as well as to give the monumentally obese priest a chance to catch his breath. Eventually, they reached the upper floor and the carpeted corridor leading to Archelon's private study, which had been specially arranged that morning to showcase a few of the finer pieces of *objet d'art* in his collection.

The result, after several hours of careful setup, pleased Archelon immensely. He was especially anxious that the high priest should take an interest, but now, as he watched the exalted man stride purposefully down the length of the corridor toward him without so much as a glance to the left or right, Archelon wasn't sure his satin-swathed guest even noticed. *Yes, of course,* he thought, *a man such as the high priest, a man used to the finest of everything, wouldn't notice these trifles. They are beneath his regard. To a man such as the high priest, to notice means something is wrong.*

Consoling himself with this thought, Archelon pushed open the door to his study and ushered his special guest into his office, his inner sanctum. He made a point to remind the servant standing at the door that the room was off-limits to anyone else, and then followed High Priest Kai inside, closing the door behind him.

The lights in the room were tastefully dimmed; a fire flickered convivially in a large fireplace that took up most of one wall. Two large glass cabinets stood at either end of the fireplace, and these—as well as the bookshelves on the other walls and two or three free-standing pedestals—contained objects too valuable to be displayed in the hallway outside.

One of these trophies was Archelon's wife, who waited quietly before the fireplace, a small gift-wrapped box in her hands. Archelon made his way to stand beside his wife, an elegant but not overly glamorous woman several years older, and a few inches taller, than himself. She, like nearly every other woman in the house that night, fairly dripped with expensive jewelry, but unlike the priest, the effect was far less theatrical on her.

"Kai, I would like you to meet my wife, Diana," said Archelon, putting his arm around the woman's bare shoulders.

"I'm honored, sir," Diana purred. She approached the high

priest, who again extended his hand. She took it, lowered her head, and brushed the diamond ring with her lips.

"How remarkable," the high priest said, eyeing the slender length of her body. "I could have sworn that the last time we met you were blond and six inches shorter."

The woman stiffened, bristling at the remark. She turned to her husband with an icy stare. "Anty, are you—" she began.

"Ha, ha!" cried Archelon suddenly. "No, High Priest, that wasn't—you must mean . . . " He trailed off with a nervous laugh and, with a nod, urged his wife forward.

"This is for you, High Priest," she said. With a last glare at her husband, she extended the box.

The high priest accepted the gift with an absent nod and rubbed the paper aside with his thumbs. A black leather box appeared, with the word *Rolex* stamped in gold. He opened the lid and withdrew a handsome gold watch. "My thanks to you, good lady," he said, dangling the watch between thumb and forefinger. He smiled. "Your taste is, shall we say," he licked his lips as he looked her up and down once more, "exquisite—as are you."

Diana smiled. "Would you two like something to drink?" she asked, stepping away. "I will send for Jared, shall I?" But Kai was no longer paying attention. He was gazing pointedly at a man who had stepped out of the shadows and was now standing before the fireplace.

Archelon gave a self-conscious cough. "How lucky I am, to have two guests of honor with me tonight. High Priest, may I have the pleasure of introducing you to Mr. Isaiah Henderson, known to those who love him as 'The Prophet.'" He indicated the dark-haired, silent man who, like himself, was dressed in a black dinner jacket with satin lapels. He wore no tie, but the collar of his stiff-starched shirt was closed by a stickpin with a large sapphire on either end. The two visitors looked at each other like testy cats in an alleyway, and it was several tense seconds before the high priest said, "Ah, yes, Mr. Henderson."

The Prophet's face twitched into a pleasant smile, and he performed a little continental half-bow, keeping his hands at his sides, palms angled toward the heat of the fire behind him. But he remained silent.

Archelon chuckled nervously. "Here, now, why don't we all sit down?" he said, shepherding his guests to a suite of leather sofas and chairs arranged around a low mahogany table. Diana took advantage of the awkwardness to make her excuse and leave. "I'll just see about those drinks," she said, crossing to the door and closing it quickly behind her.

The high priest lowered himself directly into the center of the largest sofa. The Prophet took a seat in a high-backed armchair nearby. As they were settling in, a servant appeared with a tray of glasses and a bottle of wine. He put the tray on the table, poured three glasses, and retired without a word.

Archelon distributed the wine and sat down in a second armchair. "To life, gentlemen!" he said, raising his glass.

"L'chaim!" said the high priest.

They occupied themselves with the wine for a moment, each one eyeing the other but holding his silence. "You know, I think I saw you at my father's reception last month, High Priest," Archelon announced suddenly. "Unfortunately, I was unable to int—"

"Excuse me, Howard," the high priest interrupted, "but what is this about?"

"Ah, well, I asked you to come here tonight in order to meet our friend, Mr. Henderson. Also, I thought we might have a chat about the future."

Kai presented The Prophet with a sour expression, which he then turned on Archelon. "Future?" he asked. "Whose future?"

"*Our* future, High Priest," he said. "These are exciting times. Wars in the Middle East, ICON confidence at an all-time low . . . interesting times, you must admit. Anyone smart enough, and brave enough, to get involved at the beginning—to help *shape* events, if you will—well, that man is going to be in a very comfortable position when the dust settles."

The high priest regarded him coolly, with a wondering expression. "What on earth are you babbling about?"

"The distribution of power!" Archelon exclaimed, with a wild gesture that threatened to splash wine across the Persian carpet.

The high priest turned his squint on The Prophet, who smiled with easy charm. "Power," he repeated softly, making the word sound both attractive and a little illicit.

"That's right," continued Archelon. "You see, The Prophet and I have been talking about the nature of true power—what it is, where you get it, who's got it—a most interesting discussion. And I think we came to a rather interesting conclusion. Most people think that money is power, but that's not true, not true at all."

Kai swirled the deep purple liquid in his glass. "Do tell."

"Of course, money can lead to power—don't get me wrong. The careful application of capital can aid immensely in the acquisition of power. But, in itself? No, money is not *true* power."

"True power," intoned Isaiah Henderson sagely, "I contend, is the populace itself. It is the people; or, to be more exact, the control of the people. No king or general ever won a battle by throwing coins at the enemy. He did it by controlling his troops, by making them lay down their lives for his cause."

"I should have thought it preferable to make the enemy commander's troops lay down *their* lives," observed the high priest. "That seems far more sensible to me." He touched the back of his hand to his mouth as if to stifle a yawn. "But then, I'm a man of peace. What do I know about such things?"

"Oh, you're right, of course," said Archelon. "The point is the same—you must control the people."

"And money controls people," The Prophet continued smoothly, "and that is why it is powerful. Money and power—the two must not be confused with one another. It is people who fight to win wars, just as it is people who make food to live, who build buildings, and who grease the gears of commerce for the world. Therefore, if you control people, by any means at all, you control their production and, hence, the very mechanisms of society."

The Prophet paused to take a drink of wine and judge the high priest's reaction to what had been said so far. But His Immensity sat with his wine glass resting on his paunch, jowls arranged in a frown of bored disinterest.

"An example, if you will allow me," suggested The Prophet, trying a new tack. "Suppose one could control all the farmers in the nation's breadbasket—not so impossible as one might think. By withholding food alone, either bread or meat, one could bring this entire country to its knees in a matter of days. One could tell the starving masses what to do and they would do it. Hungry people are most compliant. War, higher taxes, the removal of human rights—make them hungry enough and they will put up with anything."

"A matter of days—not weeks, or months. Days!" Archelon stressed with satisfaction. "With *farmers* no less!"

There was a long and pregnant pause. Both men looked to the high priest for his comment. "This social studies lesson has a point, I presume?" Kai sighed at last.

"The point, my friend, is this . . . " Archelon said; he crossed one elegant leg over the other and leaned back expansively. "We are powerful men. We are all leaders of men in our own areas of influence. As high priest, you control them through religious rites and teaching. *I,* on the other hand, control them by means of, shall we say, their recreational activities." Archelon allowed himself a self-satisfied smile. "You have them where they worship, and I have them where they live. Between us, I would say, we have them coming and going."

The high priest sneered. His expression might have indicated an ironic mirth at the schoolboy reasoning. He took a last swallow of wine, put his empty glass aside, and turned his attention to The Prophet. "What does *he* control—the tailor's union?"

"Ah, yes," said Archelon, ignoring the jibe. "Now we come to the third important area of concern. Mr. Henderson here represents what might be called a new hand at the table. He . . . well, how shall I put this? Ah—do you remember Washer John?"

The high priest cocked an eyebrow. "Washer John," he spat, his words dripping venom, "was nothing but a trifling annoyance."

"Perhaps," granted Archelon. "Perhaps not."

"Is the end of this tedious exercise any nearer at all?" wondered the fat priest. "If not I shall require more wine." He retrieved his glass and held it out to be filled.

Archelon stood, took up the bottle, and said, "Washer John—now there was a man who knew a thing or two about true power." He poured more wine into the high priest's glass, then topped off the others. "Unfortunately, he couldn't be reasoned with and we had to take him out. But still, people followed him, and that is the point."

Henderson said, "I can see you do not think much of Washer John. You are allowed your opinion, of course. But you must admit he represented a growing faction of the disaffected populace. The world is in turmoil. People are tired of the old regime, and they long for something new and better. The time is ripe for revolution. I think Washer John understood this."

"You still seem to be a long way from the point, Mr. Henderson," said Kai into his glass. He sniffed his wine appreciatively.

"Bear with us, please," said Archelon. "We're merely preparing the groundwork. Now, they say that a visionary is a man who can think out of his time. Well, I would like us all, for a few moments at least, to be visionaries and think into the future. Picture, if you will, a world without ICON. A fairer world where the heavy hand of a power-hungry government has been removed and people are free to think and do whatever they want."

"Sounds ghastly," the high priest said under his breath, raising the glass to his lips.

Archelon's laugh was strained. "Don't be hasty," he coaxed. "Think about it."

"And who would step into the power vacuum the collapse of ICON would create? You, Howard?" Kai gave a snort of derision. "Rebellion. Against ICON. Visionary? You must be insane."

"Think of it as a simple redistribution of power," suggested

The Prophet.

"All right," agreed the priest, "what is this redistribution of power going to cost me? Hmm?"

"We would do all the work," said Archelon. "You would merely continue doing what you do, and we would handle all the rest. There is no risk to you, or the temple, or any of your institutions. In fact, I believe that the Jewish people would benefit greatly from becoming a state-endorsed religion."

A brief spark of interest lit the high priest's small eyes, a fleeting, lustful longing. But he blinked and drained his glass. "You two have some curious ideas on the subject of power," he began, "but I think you lose sight of *control,* of discipline; consequently you misunderstand its importance. The greatest and most powerful engine in the world is of no use if one cannot control it, cannot harness its power." He turned to Archelon. "Your father, Melech Archelon, knows the delicate balance between power and control very well—and that is why he has given you neither."

Archelon stiffened. "I have as much power as my brothers."

The high priest chortled into his chins. "Power divided is power diminished. What did you receive, Howard? Manhattan?"

The younger man frowned, affronted. "Queens," he corrected. "And some of the outlying regions—as you well know."

"Queens," the high priest repeated, derisively. He turned to The Prophet. "And you, a disgruntled man with a knack for rabble-rousing," he scoffed. "Do you think anyone will actually listen to you once their homes begin to burn?"

Antony Archelon became defiant. "I think you underestimate us, High Priest. The Kadesh has many contacts and operatives within ICON already, some very high up in the chain of command. And The Prophet here has spent the last seven years uniting various militant organizations and, shall we say, consolidating the opposition. He has countless heads of militant groups loyal to him. People would follow him. In fact, he *could* be the messiah we've been looking for."

"Nonsense," muttered the high priest, shaking his head slowly.

Archelon, oblivious to the high priest's disdain, charged on. "He's already proven himself at Big Sky. He masterminded the whole op—"

The Prophet coughed and fixed Archelon with a withering stare. Archelon took the hint and stopped. He drained his wine glass and smacked it down on the table. He didn't speak again, nor did The Prophet.

"Well, my thanks to you both," Kai said eventually. He regarded his empty glass with regret and set it aside. "It has been a most enlightening discussion. I can see you are both itching for mischief. As for me, however, I am more than comfortable where I am. But I will give you some unasked-for advice, and if I were you, I'd take it. ICON is a beast best left alone. One day it will grow too big and collapse under its own weight—*then* we shall devour it piece by juicy piece. But until that day it is in the parasite's best interest not to bite too deeply, lest the irritation rouse the sleeping beast."

The high priest heaved himself up from the sofa. He stood swaying for a moment and adjusted his sash and robes. "Unfortunately, gentlemen, your ideas are precisely the sort of irritation ICON finds impossible to ignore. They would swiftly eradicate you by any means possible."

He started toward the door. "I wish you both good night," he intoned, leaving the room without so much as a backward glance.

Henderson and Archelon sat in silence for a moment, staring at one another dejectedly.

"You misjudged him," The Prophet said after a time. "He is neither as greedy nor as stupid as you suggested."

This provoked a dismissive gesture from Archelon. "It doesn't matter. I wanted him on board, naturally. But the temple is history. We don't need him."

"But he knows now. If we go ahead with our plans, he could make trouble."

"That won't happen. He's fat and happy—what does he care?" Archelon emptied the last dregs of the bottle into his glass and drained it with a gulp. "I'll show him how much power we have," he said. He stood and heaved his glass into the fireplace. "I will show them all."

twenty-five

"Agent Hunter?"

He turned around to see a skinny kid in a checked shirt, cheap jacket, and a faded and frayed Yankees baseball cap.

"That's me."

"Could you come with me, please?"

Hunter looked up and down the street, then back at the kid. He had been about to enter ICON headquarters when the youth approached him on the steps. He hesitated. "Mind telling me why?"

"A friend of mine wants to talk to you."

"Does this friend have a name?"

The kid glanced around, then turned the inside lapel of his jacket out. Fastened to it was a small enameled badge emblazoned with the governor's seal. Satisfied, Hunter nodded and followed his guide back down the steps.

He was led a few streets away to a dark red sedan, double-parked with its engine running. Hunter got in, the kid did the same, and the car pulled away.

Not a word was spoken as they drove. Hunter had already guessed where they were going, so he didn't waste his breath asking obvious questions. He just sat back and enjoyed the ride.

Traffic was ferocious; they reached a state office building in Lower Manhattan thirty minutes later. The guard at the gate let them through with a wave as he lifted his eyes from his *New York Times* crossword puzzle. The driver dropped them at a doorway that opened into a labyrinth of hallways, corridors, and antechambers. They rode up service elevators and walked down secluded stairways until they came to a minuscule reception room with a large gray-painted steel door. The kid knocked twice and motioned for Hunter to wait while he stepped inside.

Hunter looked around the reception room. It was a dingy, airless cupboard containing only one very scuffed chair with a padded seat from which the stuffing was trying to escape. On the wall, and looking decidedly out of place, was a portrait of a somber man with an extravagant cravat and high collar. He stared down at Hunter from his gilt frame, his pale, moon-shaped face set adrift on a sea of black cloth. Hunter figured it was a portrait of New York's first chief executive, and judging from his expression, the old bird seemed to disapprove of the way his successors had carried on.

The door opened and Hunter was invited into the next room—only marginally larger than the one he had just left. There was space for a single chrome-and-Formica desk and a battered credenza that supported a fax machine, copier, and wire basket for papers. On the desk were three telephones, a small notebook computer, and a jar of pens. The room's only concession to the high office of its present incumbent was a large leather armchair, and in it the governor himself, P. Horatio Pilate IV, Mother ICON's personal representative for the State of New York. He was growling into the phone and had a cigar as big as a banana clamped between bulging jaws.

The governor was in his shirtsleeves, which were rolled up to reveal the heavy, hairy arms of a teamster. He raised a hand to acknowledge Hunter, rubbed that hand through the day-old stubble of his scalp, and said into the phone, "Morris! Morris, you're killing me. No can do! Got that? No can do. Okay? So get back to me when you come up with a more realistic budget and we'll talk. Love to Anne. Bye."

He threw the receiver into its cradle, stood, and extended his hand in greeting. "Agent Hunter, pleased to meet you. I'm the governor of New York."

"Sir," replied Hunter, "it's an honor, er . . . your honor."

Taking the cigar out of his mouth, Pilate fished a lighter out of his pocket, flicked it to flame, then puffed on the cigar a few times to get it going again. "How do you find New York, Hunter?" he asked, his round head wreathed in aromatic smoke. "Care for a drink?"

"No, thank you, sir. I'm on duty."

"Right answer." The governor grinned through his neatly trimmed mustache and goatee. "I like to know right up front what sort of man I'm dealing with." He reached into a desk drawer and brought out an aluminum tube containing a cigar like his own. "Here, try one of these. They're Cuban—Montecristo Robustos— best you can get."

Hunter reached out a hand, then hesitated.

"Go on," Pilate told him. "It's not a test this time—just a

fine cigar. Take it. Smoke it later if you like."

"Thank you, sir," replied Hunter. He accepted the cigar and read the writing on the container before tucking it away in his jacket.

"If there's nothing else, governor," said the kid, now adopting the more formal tone of a high official's personal aide.

"Yeah, thanks, Jimmy. Stay close; this won't take long."

Jimmy closed the door behind him, and the governor resumed his seat in the leather chair. "I've got the mansion in Albany, an office at the State House, and a penthouse apartment uptown. But this is my little bolt-hole in the city. Not a lot of people know about this room. I'd appreciate it if you didn't blab."

Hunter smiled. "My lips are sealed, sir."

"What it lacks in charm it makes up for in functionality. I get more work done here than anywhere else in the whole blasted state." He spread his hands, as if opening his empire for inspection. "I'd offer you a chair, but there isn't one."

"I don't mind standing, sir," replied Hunter, liking the governor more by the second.

"Okay, Agent," said Pilate, tapping ash from his cigar into a shallow glass bowl with *I♥NY* printed on the side, "here's the deal. What is discussed here tonight stays in this room. Got that?"

"Understood, sir. No problem."

"I say this as much for your benefit as for my own, as you will shortly discover. First, a couple questions. The John Levinson murder—how's your investigation going?"

Hunter was disappointed. Certainly the governor could read his reports if he was interested, couldn't he? "As well as can be expected. It's still in the early days, but I've made contact with certain members of his family. I have yet to establish a credible motive for the murder, but I'm hopeful."

"Anything catch your attention so far?"

"Nothing much. I'm working on the assumption that it was a religiously motivated killing. The best information I have comes from an informant who followed John for a short time."

"Yes. This is the man you met in the Catskills, I believe."

So, the governor *did* have some knowledge of his case. "Yes, sir," agreed Hunter.

"And you even met Washer John."

"I did, sir."

The governor sucked on his cigar, making the tip glow fiercely. "This informant of yours—did he have any idea who might be responsible?"

Hunter paused to choose his words. He knew how odd a condensed explanation could sound to anyone unfamiliar with the specific details. He saw no way around it, so he took a breath and plowed ahead. "Well, sir, my informant indicated a sort of shadow organization which—"

"The Kadesh."

Hunter stopped. He hadn't filed anything about the Kadesh in any of his reports so far. "Yes, sir," he allowed, "that was the name he used."

The governor nodded. "What do you know about the Kadesh?"

"I've had a briefing from a researcher, but it was mostly a history lesson. They seem to be some sort of alternate ethnic government—a fairy godfather group that looks after the Jewish community."

"You'd be smart to keep your history in mind when thinking about the Kadesh," the governor told him. "They hark back to a medieval monarchy more than anything else. Actually, *monarchy* is a misnomer in this instance as there are four separate rulers at the moment, a . . . *tetrarchy,* as a matter of fact. Four of the previous Melech's sons are all jockeying for control of the organization, and they've reached a temporary agreement that divvies up the territory."

Hunter accepted this. "So they do exist."

"You bet they do."

"Do they have any power?"

"The Jewish people have always had great respect for their kings, and the Kadesh is the closest thing they've got at the moment. Yes, I'd say they have some power."

The governor paused, leaving Hunter in a thoughtful mood. "Does this information surprise you, Agent Hunter?"

"A little, sir, yes. Until recently, I had never heard of the Kadesh."

"That's understandable." The governor reached out to the ashtray once more. "Outside the more radical factions of the Jewish community, not many have heard of the Kadesh—they guard their secrets carefully. The Kadesh are also very good at covering their tracks. You may have had contact with them already but were none the wiser."

Pilate took another puff of his cigar, tilted his head up, and blew the smoke high into the air. Hunter let the silence stretch as far as it would.

"The Kadesh has never really been a problem for ICON. We let them do their thing so long as it doesn't interfere with our own interests. They've even been useful to us on occasion. However, I have recently begun to suspect they haven't been playing fair.

"We're looking into the possibility that over the years they've managed to plant their noxious seeds deep into ICON. And now those seeds are beginning to sprout, and I don't like the way our little garden is starting to look."

Hunter smiled at the image as the governor continued. "The Kadesh inside ICON must be ripped up by the roots and tossed out, and the rest has got to be cut down to size." Pilate took another puff on his cigar, eyes twinkling with pride at his analogy. "In short, Agent Hunter, it is time to do a little pruning."

There was a short silence. Hunter took it as a cue to respond. "I'm not much of a gardener, sir. What exactly do you want me to do?"

Pilate smiled. "I need to find out how deep the roots go into ICON. Continue your murder investigation, fine, but concentrate on any Kadesh leads you come up with—and let me know."

"Let me see if I've got this straight, sir," Hunter said. "And forgive me for putting it bluntly, but you want me to use my investigation into the murder of Washer John as a cover for an investigation into the Kadesh—is that right?"

"Got it," smiled the governor.

"Why me, sir, if you don't mind my asking?"

"Because of the Montana meltdown." Pilate paused and his expression grew solemn. "It is this, Agent Hunter, that makes you valuable to me."

Again the Big Sky snafu, thought Hunter bitterly. How long would that dead albatross hang around his neck? "Excuse me, sir," Hunter said, his voice tightening on the words, "but what about the slaughter of all those people in the regional center compound recommends me to you, exactly?"

Pilate heard the pique in Hunter's tone and dismissed it with a swipe of his hand. "Get over it, Agent. It happened. Move on."

"Yes, sir. I am dealing with it. Every day."

"You are valuable to me precisely because you were the one who came out of that debacle holding the bag for all the other screw ups who contributed to it. You took the fall."

"It was my responsibility, sir."

"You bet your pink butt it was," agreed the governor. "But since when did that have anything to do with the price of beans in Borneo? You don't know how many times I've sat here and watched grown men and women squirm out from under their responsibilities, shift blame, deny accountability when disaster reared its ugly head."

Before Hunter could reply, Governor Pilate continued, "I see it all the time, and it makes me sick. But that's not the reason I want you for this job. It's not because you're such a stand-up guy."

"No, sir?" .

"No." The governor chomped down hard on his cigar, chewed for a moment, then took it out again. "No, the reason I want you for this job is because I know you're clean."

"Sir?"

"You can't be one of the Kadesh insiders, because if you were they never would have allowed you to suffer for the disaster. They would have taken care of you; they would have fixed it so you were still sitting pretty when the dust settled. See what I'm saying?"

"Yes, sir, I believe I do."

"Good. Now listen, take my advice and keep Big Sky in the back of your mind—catch that? The *back* of your mind. Also, keep an eye out for anyone planting obstacles in your path, or who takes an unhealthy interest in your affairs. Okay?"

Hunter nodded.

"Agent, you are venturing into hostile territory. You can expect resistance when you get too close. I want you to notify me the moment you discover anything—no matter how unimportant you think it might be—about anyone you think might be in the grip of the Kadesh. And," the governor added with a tone of command, "you will report directly to me. No one else. At all. Got that?"

Hunter raised an eyebrow. He had never heard of an agent reporting directly to a governor. It was a situation designed to put an agent out on a limb, and Hunter knew how precarious his position had just become. He chose his next words carefully. "Are you trying to compromise me, sir?"

"You are already compromised, Agent. I'm trying to help you."

Help me. Right. "Who else can I trust inside ICON?" he asked.

"You can trust me and Police Chief Devlin. Beyond that, consider yourself on shaky ground."

"Very well, sir."

Pilate beamed suddenly, all smiles once more. "Okay!" He stood abruptly and stuck out his hand. "It's a tough nut, but we're going to crack it. And when we do, believe you me, heads will roll."

This curiously mixed metaphor occupied Hunter all the way back to ICON headquarters. He thought about what the governor had said as he prepared a progress report on the Washer

John investigation, and then again before turning out the light for the night. Between uprooting noxious weeds, pruning planted obstacles, and cracking nuts, he was going to be very busy in the governor's garden.

twenty-six

Hunter lay on his bed and stared at the ceiling. He was exhausted, but his brain was humming with restless energy. His thoughts ranged back over . . . what was it? A year ago? Two? It was a distant part of his life now—and one he would rather forget.

But he couldn't forget. It was burned into his soul. He could recite the numbers in his sleep: 1,063 people dead. Of those, 382 were ICON officers and employees; 681 were cult members. Thanks to his own efforts, over two hundred cult members had escaped the death trap and lived to tell about it. He only had to close his eyes to revisit the Big Sky Regional Administration Center; he had memorized every inch of the outer walls. He had camped outside them every night for three months and studied the interior blueprints every day.

It was a standard infiltration assignment, but it had gone horribly, horribly wrong. Hunter had been supervising and coordinating a team of undercover agents who had successfully infiltrated one of the country's most dangerous militia cults. The cult leaders had arranged a rally in Montana, but somehow—and

Hunter was still not sure what had triggered the sudden and irreversible change—the ostensibly innocuous rally had escalated into the armed storming of an ICON stronghold. Almost simultaneously, a Molotov cocktail of civil disorder, political unrest, and bloody violence exploded in the Middle East. Although officially discounted, Hunter subscribed to the theory that the two events were related.

In the chaos following the takeover of the regional center, Hunter had managed to get two of his undercover agents out. The third was not so lucky; she got caught inside the barricaded walls and was forced to endure the siege to the bitter end. Ultimately, she was Hunter's responsibility.

He ran the events of the nightmare over and over in his mind until, exhausted, he fell asleep—waking early the next morning with a rotten taste in his mouth. He treated himself to a ceremonial disposal of his much-neglected sling, a long, hot shower, and a high-protein breakfast at the ICON HQ commissary. Purchasing a very tall cup of coffee to take with him, he steeled himself for his journey into the archives basement, where upon arrival he gave the man at the desk his ID and eased into an empty computer carrel.

Hunter pulled up a dozen of his own reports from a little over a year ago and glanced through them. Then he printed up all his undercover agents' reports—thirty-five of them, including that of the agent who had been trapped inside the asylum with the lunatics. This last document ran to over forty pages.

Hunter also sorted through the debriefing transcripts of the commanding officer of the Rapid Response Unit, and of the captain of the District Mobile Task Force. He scanned them and printed the most useful portions, then pulled up official statements from various politicians intent on minting political capital out of the situation, as well as miscellaneous press clippings—over-heated and sensationalistic though they were. Well, who could blame them? It was, of course, a political gold mine for some, a grotesque nightmare for others, and quite possibly the news story of the decade. That made for a lot of material to wade through.

At noon, he picked up his stack of printouts and headed back upstairs, where he took a dry commissary sandwich and peach tea to one of the reading rooms and sorted the various documents into piles that he spread out on one of the library tables. He occu-pied himself the rest of the afternoon making copious notes about the disaster and trying to read between the lines to see if there was anything he'd missed earlier—especially any veiled ref-erences to the Kadesh. He found nothing significant in the actual statements—they were all fairly straightforward, although a few versions of the situation conflicted.

Hunter couldn't tell if the discrepancy was just the sort of nat-ural differences nearly always found in individual accounts, or if one or more people couldn't keep their stories straight. For exam-ple, in his field report the commander of the RR unit indicated that on the night of the breakout he had ordered each escapee to be interrogated immediately. Their statements were printed up and signed before any escapee was moved. In the official debrief-ing, however, he said the interrogations took place after process-ing at the holding facility.

A minor inconsistency, and nothing to get too worked up over. And, in the horrendous turn of events that followed, such a mistake was all too understandable. Still, Hunter noticed and it made him wonder—all the more so since the governor had planted the seed of suspicion in his fertile brain. The idea that a super-secret organization could have been calling the shots put a wildly different spin on things.

Even so, despite his best efforts at fine-sifting the information, Hunter was forced to conclude, once again, that it all began and ended with the deluded man who had called himself The Messiah. If anyone else had been involved, there was no evidence of covert participation to be gleaned from the files.

Hunter finished all his paperwork by seven o'clock, and although he was much better versed in the minutiae of the event—even considering that he had actually been there—he was no closer to linking any of it to the Kadesh. The trail, if there ever was one, had grown cold and he couldn't pick up the scent.

The last thing he did before he turned off his computer was to look up a certain name and address on the ICON personnel database.

Sarah Nash was now a desk pilot in an ICON law enforcement center in Hartford, Connecticut. The place wasn't far, so by eleven o'clock a train had deposited Hunter right in the middle of town, and thirty minutes later he had located the building and was speaking to the duty officer. He found Agent Nash exactly where he expected her to be—in a cubicle piled high with files and bundles of papers. ICON loved paper; it was life and blood to the bureaucratic behemoth.

Nash was hunched over a keyboard and jumped slightly

when Hunter called her name. Her face turned to him and that almost made *him* jump. It looked like she had aged a decade since he'd last seen her. She used to possess a delicate, almost glowing beauty, but now her eyes were darkly circled and slightly puffy; her hair hung lifeless, and her once-luminous skin had lost its luster. She didn't seem surprised to see him. Swiftly mastering his shock at her changed appearance, he greeted her and cheerily asked if she'd like to join him for an early lunch. She merely nodded, picked up her things, and followed him out.

They went to a diner about a block away from the building and slid into a booth. Neither said a word to the other until they had ordered their food and received their drinks. It was up to Hunter to break the silence, and now that he was here, he found it extremely uncomfortable to do so. He took a slug of his soft drink and plunged in.

"So, how are you doing, Nash?"

"Not too bad, I suppose."

"They treat you okay on the law enforcement side, do they?"

"It's all right. I get a lot of hours, which is good."

"Good." Hunter took another gulp of his soft drink, and no closer to finding a delicate way to broach what was sure to be a painful subject, simply asked, "Do you know why I'm here?"

"I can guess," Nash said, the skin around her eyes tightening with a flicker of pain.

"Something's come up and I need to reexamine the Big Sky incident," he explained.

She lifted both hands and massaged the back of her neck. Hunter waited for her to stop and then continued. "I need to know some details—such as what it was like for you inside the compound."

"What it was like?" she asked sharply, coming alive at last. "It was hell—that's what it was like!"

Hunter let the outburst wash over him. "It could be important. I wouldn't ask otherwise."

Nash stared at him with dull, pain-filled eyes. But he sensed resignation in her voice when she replied, "There's nothing that I can tell you that hasn't been said already—a dozen times over. You can read the reports."

"I have read the reports, Sarah," he replied gently. "Your reports were very concise. But I want you to tell me what you *felt,* what your impressions were. What people said to each other— the rumors, the speculation. I want to hear what you didn't put in the reports."

She looked at him, mystified. "Why?" Her voice was small and childlike. "Why drag it all up again?"

"Start with the night of the rally and takeover."

Nash sighed. She took a drink of her cola. "That was done beautifully. We never saw it coming. It was during the night and we were led through the woods to the meeting point—at least, what we *thought* was the meeting point. But it couldn't have been what was marked on the maps we were given, that's for sure."

"The rally," suggested Hunter. "Let's hear about that first."

"Well, that was the typical thing, nothing special—speeches, a bunch of people getting hopped up and throwing things around—at least at the beginning."

"Describe it."

"Well, The Messiah is wired; he's flying. He's up there ranting away, yelling through his bullhorn, jazzing up the troops, you know—gets the blood pumping. Fight the Great Oppressors, fear is our only enemy, we'll all be martyrs, that sort of thing. It's the usual stuff, nothing we haven't seen or heard before—until he starts handing out guns. I never found out where they got them, and I refused to take one at first, but the guy I was with forced a small handgun on me. Then we discovered we were a lot closer to the Big Sky compound than any of us knew. It all happened pretty fast after that."

The agent's eyes started to lose focus as the memory of that night came back. "The first shots had already been fired by the time I figured out where we were. I tried to miss when I fired. I aimed wide, just slightly off, pretended I'd never held a gun before. . . . " She smiled briefly, but the smile was instantly swallowed in gloom. "But I think there were times when I . . . " She trailed off, despondently.

"What about before—before the rally? Was The Messiah acting odd?"

"*Odd?* Now there's a word," Nash scoffed, throwing it back in his face. "A sick wacko went berserk and a few hundred people got slaughtered! Of course it was odd—it was *nothing but* odd from start to finish!"

"The Messiah," Hunter said patiently, "was he talking to anyone in particular that day—maybe someone you'd never seen before?"

"No." She shook her head. "If he did, I didn't know about it. I've been over it a million times in my head, but I can't remember any tip-offs. Honest, if I'd had so much as a hint of what was going to happen, I would have tried to warn someone. I would have gotten a message to you somehow. Even now, I can't think of anything that might have led me to think they would do what they did. Nobody saw it coming—none of us agents, I mean. It came straight out of the blue. We didn't go up there to do maneuvers or anything like that. The only thing even remotely suspicious was that a lot of people brought their kids along. But I just thought, hey, it's a big weekend rally, people wanted to bring their families. And that's all it was supposed to be, just a rally— a massive chinwag with some of the local activist groups. What happened was . . . totally bizarre."

"Did you ever hear anyone talk about a group called the Kadesh?"

Nash pushed the hair away from her face. "No, doesn't ring a bell. What is it?"

"It's a religious group. Someone suggested they might have been involved."

"If they were, they kept it pretty quiet. I've never heard of them."

Hunter accepted her assessment and moved on. "Tell me what it was like once you were inside the compound."

"Pure disaster, start to finish. The Messiah was in charge, but never in control, not really. I don't think he ever understood what he'd managed to pull off. It's true . . . " she insisted, although Hunter said nothing. "It might sound funny, but I don't think he really had the slightest idea what he wanted. I don't think he had any plans at all."

"Plans for the takeover?"

"No," she corrected. "What to do *after* the takeover. He was like a dog that's always chasing trucks—only this time, he caught one. What's he do with it? Well, The Messiah didn't have a clue.

And the only thing that stopped it all from falling apart long before it did was that everyone was more afraid of ICON than they were of The Messiah, or each other. And you have to remember most all of those folks actually believed what they were being told."

The waiter returned and placed their food in front of them. They both started eating in silence. After a few bites, Nash pushed her plate away, fumbled with her purse, drew out a crumpled pack, and shook out a cigarette.

"Bad habit," observed Hunter. "It'll kill you."

"Yeah?" she shot back. "So will a lot of things."

"Sorry. Go on."

"Look, I don't know what you want from me. Anyway, I don't think I can tell you what it felt like to be in there, Alex. The smells, the sounds, the things I saw . . . dead bodies piled on top of each other . . . some of them people I knew . . . nowhere to bury them. They started to bloat and burst their clothes. . . . It was awful—worse than awful. It was horrific."

"Go back to the first night," suggested Hunter. "When you first got inside the regional center, what happened?"

"The storming was total, appalling chaos. Everyone was ignorant and untrained. They shot at anything wearing an ICON uniform. Just when we thought it was over, that all the workers had been captured or killed, a new group would be found hiding in an office or something, and it would start all over again.

"I tried to sneak away like the other agents, but it wasn't possible. My contact—the man I had become close to—pulled me along and became very suspicious whenever I tried to break free of him. And it didn't stop there. I had to . . . " She broke off and lit her cigarette. She took her time taking a deep drag on it, pulling the smoke deep, and then exhaled very slowly.

"Not everyone was killed that first night—the ICON personnel, I mean. In fact, a lot of them survived. But the next day, The Messiah panicked—I think it finally began to dawn on him what he'd done. He ordered all the prisoners, the survivors of the attack, to be dragged out into the courtyard. He shot them, one by one. Men, women . . . some crying, some begging, all tied up with duct tape—row upon row of them.

"After each execution everybody cheered and sang. I nearly threw up; I told them I felt sick and left, but I could still hear the shots no matter where I went. I knew each one of them ended a life." Agent Nash took another drag on her cigarette and then stubbed it out. "When it was over, they hauled the bodies to a pit in the garden and set them on fire. The smell was . . . " she shrugged. "The worst thing was that you got used to it after awhile."

"I know," Hunter said softly. "We could smell it outside the walls."

Nash nodded, reached for another cigarette, but held it in her fingers without lighting it. "Then ICON cut the water and electricity off, and after that the music started. I got caught in a couple of tear gas attacks. One was bad. I thought I was going to die. The press of people running for the door was so strong. We couldn't breathe. People actually got crushed.

"Then the food ran out. Starvation was terrible. First you're hungry for a little while, and then you're not. You get to thinking that this isn't so bad, and then you get *really* hungry. Your stomach heaves and cramps; you're almost too weak to move. The medical supplies got used up pretty quickly, so if you got hurt or wounded you were just out of luck. I mean, some of the culties would come around and pray for you, but it never did any good so far as I could see.

"And there was the boredom and the terrible uncertainty. With nothing to do, you asked yourself an endless number of questions. For most everyone else it was 'Will they storm us today or tomorrow? Will there be anything to eat? Should I drink the water? If I do, will it make me sick? If I don't, will I die of thirst?' For me it was also 'Will the culties discover who I am and kill me today? Or, if ICON storms the compound will *they* kill me instead, by mistake?' Paranoid fantasies drift through your head, becoming more and more real all the time; you get delusional."

Nash lit the cigarette and watched the smoke curl from the glowing end. "I might have tried harder to escape, but they were killing anyone who tried. They said it was lack of faith, or the Evil Spirit trying to contaminate the purity of the righteous—or some such nonsense. The Messiah would do it himself sometimes. He seemed to enjoy it." She looked at her fingers and then bit the edge off an already short fingernail. "What you have to understand is that most of us lived in constant fear of the handful of really hardcore fundamentalists—the True Believers."

"I know the type," said Hunter.

"These guys followed The Messiah blindly and with such an intense passion that they couldn't be reasoned with. They wouldn't tolerate anything they perceived to be weakness. If you disagreed with any of them, that would be seen as subversion, and you were on the enemy's side. They would haul you in to be punished." She turned her face to stare out of the window.

Hunter let the silence go on for a few moments. He started picking at the remains of his food.

"I was approached once and asked if I wanted to escape," Nash said, still staring out the window. "I didn't put that in the report." She turned to look at Hunter. "Is that the sort of thing you wanted?"

"Yeah, that's the sort of thing. So, why didn't you go along with it?"

Nash frowned and shook her head. "Couldn't risk it. Like I said, you could get killed for that. It was even possible that, at that point, they were looking for victims to make an example of in front of the others. I'd been through so much by then, I just didn't have it in me to risk it."

"Who approached you?" asked Hunter. "How'd it happen?"

"This guy just came up one night and said he was organizing a breakout. He said he had a way to do it."

"This guy—tell me about him."

Nash turned to look at him, her expression blank. "He was just a guy." She shrugged. "In pretty tight with some of the leaders, but nothing special."

"Think," he said. "It might be important. Was there anything unusual about him at all?"

"Well, he was a little different, I guess. Not strange exactly, but . . . it was like he didn't fit in. I'd seen him around. He never said much at the meetings, but he had the ear of The Messiah, that was for sure. He seemed to have a certain amount of influence, but didn't really belong—if that makes any sense."

She lowered her head and gazed at her half-eaten food, cold on the plate. "I found out later that he made it out, so I suppose it would have been smart to go with him. I just couldn't risk it."

"What was his name?"

"I can't remember. David something. Adams, or maybe Abrams. Yeah, it was Abrams. David Abrams."

"I don't remember reading anything about him."

"Well, I remember writing it. Go back and check again. It'll be there—David Abrams. I'm sure of it."

"I'll check it," Hunter told her. "After the escape, what happened?"

"You know what happened as well as I do," she snapped. "The worst day of my life—that's what happened. They killed all those people, and sometimes I wish that I'd had guts enough to drink the poison too, you know?" Tears came suddenly to her eyes and she turned her face to the window again. "Sometimes I wish I had. And then the pain would stop, the terrible memories would just stop."

Hunter thought for a moment. He finished his drink, then announced, "That's enough for now. I might think of something else later. Thanks. You've been a big help."

"You're a liar."

"No, really." Hunter said. "There's just one thing I'd like to check before we go. Do you mind?"

"It's your nickel."

"It won't take but a second." Hunter reached down and pulled up his briefcase, opened it on the bench beside him, and brought out a bulging folder, stuffed with his printouts of the ill-fated incident. He flicked through them until he got to a page of two-by-two-inch photos. He ran his finger down the list, searching for David Abrams.

"I can't find him," Hunter announced, handing the sheet to Nash.

She glanced over it quickly, then paused and studied it more closely. "He's not on here," she said at last.

"These are all the people who escaped and were captured on the night of the breakout," Hunter told her. "The names and details are on the left-hand side."

Sarah looked through the pictures again, taking her time, gazing hard at each one. Eventually she said, "No, this is wrong." She tapped a photo, a middle-aged man with three weeks' scruffy growth of facial hair. "This guy wasn't there. I don't remember seeing him at all."

"You're sure? There are a lot of faces there, and it's been a long time."

"He was never in the compound."

"It's just that I have to be 100 percent certain."

"Look, Alex, what do you want from me? I might not be any great-shakes agent anymore, but I spent eight months with those people and I know what I know." She stabbed a finger at the photo of the stranger. "This guy was never in the compound, all right?"

Hunter felt his blood quicken. "What about his name? Do you recognize that?"

"Armand Deloit?" Nash shook her head. "Never heard of him."

Hunter took back the sheet and circled the picture of the unknown man. "What about David Abrams—what did he look like?"

"He was young—in his midtwenties, I'd say. Dark hair, clean-shaven. About six feet, around 180 pounds. Pretty average, really. Nothing stood out about him. No piercings, scars, tattoos, or anything. But very young to be hanging out with the top-level leaders. He had a lot of closed-door sessions with The Messiah himself."

"And this isn't him?" Hunter held up the photo of Deloit once more.

She shook her head. "Definitely not."

Hunter returned his papers to his briefcase. It could be merely a clerical error—then again, it could be something more significant. "Okay," he said. Hunter clicked the latch on his briefcase and looked up at his former agent. "We can go."

He walked Agent Nash back to her building, said goodbye, and turned to leave.

"Alex?" she called after him.

"Yes?"

"Don't come back."

Hunter considered this. "I can't promise anything."

"Please."

"All right," he agreed. "If I can help it. Goodbye, Sarah."

She opened the door and slipped inside.

Hunter spent most of the train ride home staring at the photo on the sheet—the photo of the man who wasn't there.

twenty-seven

"Well, you've finally caught up with me, Supervisor Riley. Come on in."

"No, let's take a walk."

Hunter blinked at the woman standing in the doorway. She must know how tired he felt. It was close to midnight and his side had begun aching again. Now he was faced with this new torment: a reprimand from his supervisor. He was about to protest and suggest they meet the next day over coffee when the woman turned and started walking down the hall.

"Let me get my jacket at least," he muttered under his breath.

"You won't need it," she said. "This won't take long."

He banged the door shut and let Riley lead him down to the main lobby of ICON HQ. "Would you like anything to eat or drink?" Riley asked.

"Thanks, but no," Hunter declined.

"Then let's just sit here."

They found a nook behind a large potted fern. Hunter sank down into an upholstered armchair, and Riley pushed another around to face him. She carried a small portfolio that she placed neatly on her knees, and raised an eyebrow at him. He sat up straight despite the burning ache in his side.

"How's the arm?" she asked with genuine concern.

"Never better," Hunter replied. "I'll be playing the violin again in no time."

Riley dismissed his impertinence with a frown and folded her hands atop the portfolio. "Sounds like you've been having fun running around the city, Agent Hunter."

"Fun?" Hunter queried. "I wouldn't call it fun, exactly. I've been following a few leads. I'm sorry if I didn't keep in better touch with you. I wasn't sure how much minutiae you wanted to hear about," he lied.

"Forgiven." She nodded, as if ticking off a list. "So, what have you got?"

"I've been filing reports."

"Yes, I know. Where were you today?"

"I was in Hartford, Connecticut."

"Why?"

"Checking on one of my ex-agents," he said. Supervisor Riley pressed her lips into a firm, even line of skeptical reproach. "It's for background," Hunter expanded. "I'm getting a whiff of something in this case."

"Okay," she allowed, "I'll grant you that. What does it smell like?"

If it had not been for the governor's warning, he might have told her everything just then. Instead, he said, "Truthfully? I don't know yet. It just smells funny."

Riley stared at him with a sideways frown. "How so?" she asked finally.

"Ah, well, that'll be in my next report."

Riley flipped up the leather portfolio and balanced it on her knees. "I know you used to be a supervisor yourself, Agent Hunter. And I know you're finding it hard to trust me, but I'm here to help. You can believe that."

"Okay," he agreed.

"So is there anything else you want to tell me?"

"Not at the moment," Hunter said with a smile. "But if I think of something, you'll be the first to know."

"Suit yourself, Agent," Riley said with an exasperated sigh, "but you know what will happen if you don't play by the rules. Unless you give me something to take back to the boys upstairs, I can't go to bat for you."

She obviously didn't know of Hunter's meeting with the governor. *Good.* "Are we done here? I've got an early appointment tomorrow."

"Yes," his supervisor conceded. She leaned back in her chair and gazed at him as if trying to decide whether to skin him where he sat or take him around back. "I guess we're done."

Hunter stood and stuck out his hand. "I'll be in touch."

"You know where to find me."

The next morning Hunter made his way through an icy drizzle to the North American Broadcasting System building. The air was cold, and his feet got damp, but the walk cleared his head and he was feeling better than he had in weeks. He made his way up to a reception room on the seventh floor, where a number of people were milling about, some waiting, some killing time. He snuck up behind a slender young man who was sipping a steaming drink outside large glass doors. He tapped him hard on the shoulder.

The young man jumped, sloshing some of his drink onto his hand. "Argh!" he spun around. "Hunter! You maniac!"

"Not happy to see me Gerald?"

"You could be wearing this right now," said the special teams coordinator, licking steaming coffee off his hand. "Sweet muscular Buddha, don't you ever do that! You know how hopped up on caffeine I usually am."

"Sorry, I couldn't resist. You ready to go?"

"Ready as I'll ever be," Gerald replied.

"Let's get to it."

They pushed through two huge plate-glass doors and into a room full of half-height cubicles with people in them. They started down the main aisle. "So tell me," said Gerald, "what happened to you up in the Catskills? I heard you got shot."

"I don't want to talk about it."

"It's either me or a therapist. Take your pick."

"Yeah, right," muttered Hunter. "I'll take my chances with the shrink."

It was surprisingly easy to gain access to the NABS news archives; all they had to do was flash their IDs, threaten a few lackeys, and sign a sheaf of papers. Once in the archive room— or News Tomb, as it was known to the researchers and secretaries who worked there—they were assigned a technician to help them find the required videocassettes stacked on the miles and miles of floor-to-ceiling metal shelving in the airplane-hangar-sized room. NABS was the best organized and most cooperative news service and the first choice for research like this. Because they traded footage with their competition, they had a wealth of material from other news organizations as well. With hundreds of reporters all over the world, the news footage at their disposal was simply staggering.

Working with the technician, it didn't take long to pull the tapes for what had become known as the Big Sky Suicide Siege. It was a major item, after all, and often requested. There were over 476 eight-hour compilation tapes—interviews, reports, and snippets of things shot on location—and scores of broadcast tapes. The techie loaded box after box of tapes onto his electric cart, hauled them all down to a small viewing room below the archive stacks, and left the two men to get on with it.

The broadcast tapes were of no interest to Hunter. "Let's start with the raw footage from the day of the breakout," he said, when they had sorted all the cassette boxes by date. The first few tapes out of the box were of various NABS reporters offering spot updates on the situation during the siege. There were many false starts and not-for-broadcast camera adjusting, technical misfires, and swearing. There were many miscellaneous establishing shots—a few minutes of the area around the compound, bored RR troopers waiting by their armored vehicles, tear gas attacks, and some of the culties waving signs from the upper windows of buildings within the compound. Gerald fast-scrolled to the end of each tape just to be sure, but found nothing helpful.

Five tapes later they came to some footage of featured interviews with some of the Rapid Response team, most of whom Hunter remembered quite well. Gerald fast-forwarded to the end of the tape and eventually came to some shaky footage of the breakout.

"This is more like it," said Hunter. "Slow it down."

The shot was dark and the cameraman was too far away, unable to pull focus from where he was, so he started to weave his way through the TV and RRU vans with the camera running. He had also been slow off the mark, because by the time he got to the incident site, most of the escapees had been herded off out of view. The last hour of tape was the reporter giving incident summaries, repeating the same script over and over again with slight variations. Gerald ran the tape back to the brief glimpses of the prisoners, slow-rolled through that section, and marked down the time codes before sticking in the next tape.

The front end was full of the standard sort of newscast interviews, but about twenty minutes into it, the image turned dark blue and black. Then, a few seconds later, the screen flashed white and faded down into a green-hued picture. "Nightvision," Gerald said. "Cool. Hey, you know what we can do with this stuff these days? I've got a computer filter that will—"

"Slow it down," said Hunter. "I want to see this."

The camera was about as far away from the breakout as the last one, but the image was much easier to make out. Hunter watched a dozen or so dark green human shapes make their way quickly down a lighter green dirt slope into the hostile hands of the ICON RR team. As the shouts started up, the image exploded into white as floodlights were switched on. The cameraman switched back to normal light and tried to refocus the image.

The focus swung down to the ground as the cameraman lowered the camera in order to weave his way around parked vehicles, just as the other cameraman had done. After a minute the picture swung up to show the last few escapee-prisoners being hauled up off the ground. The view was hampered by the reporter, who kept trying to step in front of the camera to interview one of the prisoners. But the cameraman swung around just in time to see the first prisoners being ushered into a large tent. The screen turned white as a nearby floodlight crept into frame, whiting out the image. The frame jiggled a lot, and then the picture cut out.

"Hmm," said Gerald. "That last part was lens flare. I could take that down to the lab and try to get rid of some of it if you wanted. Might not get a lot, but it'd be something."

"If there's nothing else on these tapes, sure. For now, can you go back and give me a freeze-frame of each of the prisoners?"

"Certainly."

He did so, and Hunter studied each one and compared it with the small head shots on the photo sheet he'd brought with him—pictures taken just after the prisoners had entered the tent. He'd had the photos enlarged, and now he put small Xs by them after he had identified each one.

There were only a few frames of the people going into the tent before the picture washed out due to the flare-up. Hunter was unable to identify the figures, but he did see something strange. He saw an ICON officer stretch out one hand toward a prisoner, while with his other hand out he indicated another direction—as if ordering that prisoner to go somewhere else.

"Slower," said Hunter. "Can you make it go any slower?"

The film slowed down, flashing up individual frames.

"Close up," Hunter said, leaning nearer the screen. "Can you bring it closer?"

"Sorry, not on this machine. If you want, we can—"

"Stop. Go back a frame."

Hunter was staring at the figure of a man with short dark hair as he turned toward the directing officer and then, as the flare of white light started to engulf the picture during the next two frames, Hunter thought he could see the man's feet start to move offscreen. When the lens pulled away from the floodlight, the man was gone and the officer turned and walked off the same way.

"What do you think's happening there?"

"Special Celebrity Guest Terrorist Gets Star Treatment? Hot cup of cocoa and a cookie right this way."

Hunter sat back in his seat. He watched the images again and marked down the time codes of the various actions. This time, as the camera swung to look at the tent, he caught a glimpse of another cameraman and reporter standing in front of the flood-light. He couldn't catch an insignia on either the camera or the reporter but suddenly found himself hoping that the footage from that camera was on one of the remaining tapes.

The next one showed footage taken from another perspective. This time the cameraman had stationed himself in front of the floodlight. Instead of wasting time trying to focus on a dark hillside, he went straight to the RRU main encampment and started filming.

This camera got a shot of all the prisoners on the ground, hands on top of their heads. It filmed each one being searched, cuffed, pulled up, and marched off in the direction of the tent. Hunter slid to the edge of his seat and watched as a man with dark hair, about six feet tall, 180 pounds, was pushed forward. The guy was wearing a gray, hooded sweatshirt and kept his face in an angle away from the camera so his features remained hidden in shadow.

Hunter felt the tension ball in his stomach. It looked like his man, but he had to be sure. After a second or so, the figure moved offscreen. The camera swung around and got a good picture of the ICON officer directing the guy away, but only the man's back could be seen. The head of another prisoner being pushed into the tent moved in front of the camera.

"Get out of the way, stupid," Hunter growled under his breath.

On the screen the gray sweatshirt guy turned and Hunter slammed his hand down on the table. "Freeze it!"

Gerald hit the pause button.

"Go back a frame!"

The screen blinked and Hunter gasped at the image staring back at him.

"Hey," said Gerald. "I know that face. . . . "

So did Hunter.

It was Simon.

twenty-eight

Hunter walked back to his apartment at ICON HQ in a daze. After copying all of the best footage of the pertinent events onto a single videotape, he had sworn Gerald to secrecy and left the broadcasting center feeling shell-shocked by this new revelation that Simon DeVere—his archenemy, as it were—had also been involved in the Big Sky massacre. Seeing Simon on the videotape had rattled him, he had to admit. But now, as the fresh air and exercise did its work, he was able to think more clearly.

The discovery of Simon's intimate connection to Big Sky gave a new pungency to the whole stinking mess. Add to that his connection to The Prophet and Washer John, and the governor's suggestion of a possible tie-in to the Kadesh spread the muck even wider.

Gut instinct told him that Washer John was the key piece to the whole, twisted puzzle. If he could only discover what Washer John had to do with any of this, he might be on the road to solving his case and winning back his rank.

By the time he reached ICON HQ, Hunter had firmly decided that Simon would become his sole obsession. He would hunt him down and put him away forever for all the pain he had caused, for putting him in the hospital, and for selling out who knows how many innocent men, women, and children at the Big Sky compound. He'd do it for the two dead agents, and he'd do it for Washer John. He'd do it because coldhearted, turncoat killers like Simon should not walk free.

But he'd have to work fast. Others would be muscling in on his territory now that it was known that the former ICON agent, Simon DeVere—alias David Abrams—was alive and well, and working for the enemy.

As Hunter stood before the door to the Research Room, he could feel the swells of anger rising up inside him, tightening his gut. The continual dull ache in his side and upper arm flared up and he folded that pain into his rage, feeding the flames.

He found an empty carrel, slid in behind the keyboard, and began pounding out the first of a lengthy series of database searches that would swing his investigation onto its new course.

Hunter worked away in an anger-fueled frenzy, imagining that each jab of a computer key was another nail in Simon's handmade coffin.

Service records, duty reports, assignment sheets, personal information—everything tumbled onto Hunter's growing pyramid of data. One of the first items on the list was Simon's pre-ICON Civilian File, or CF: an administration document kept on everyone that came into contact with ICON for any reason whatsoever, anywhere in the world. Reading between the lines of Simon's CF,

Hunter quickly assembled a working snapshot of his subject's background. Born in Chicago, the only son of a working-class family—father a meatpacker, mother a cleaning woman—Simon had spent a fair amount of time in hospitals due to kidney infections as a child. Unlike so many other young hoodlums from his Southside neighborhood, Simon formed no gang attachments. Hunter guessed that weedy little Simon decided to excel at school instead. Good grades all the way up through high school snared him a place at the ICON Academy immediately after graduation; he excelled there, too.

There was a gap in Simon's file after his entry into the academy and before his official disappearance. This gap, Hunter assumed, would be filled by the ICON duty files. The next-to-last entry was a notation that the agent Simon DeVere had disappeared while on active duty, status and whereabouts unknown. His last supervisor had added a note to Simon's duty file stating that when the agent had failed to make routine contact, the supervisor had followed department protocol for such situations, and after initial attempts to renew contact had failed, a search-and-rescue attempt had been made. Simon had not been found, however, and he was listed as missing on assignment.

The last entry in the file was the update Hunter had initiated through the statements he had given in the debriefings following the Catskills shoot-out. Again, Hunter thought he saw the hand of Supervisor Riley tidying up. The addendum stated that hearsay evidence indicated that Simon was a member of the terrorist organization known as the Zion International Party.

Hunter puzzled over the use of the words *hearsay evidence*. So far as Hunter was concerned, Simon was a dyed-in-blood, card-carrying member of the ZIP gang, The Prophet's right-hand man, and more besides. No doubt Riley refrained from submitting anything more forceful without additional corroborating evidence. So be it. When Hunter captured the slimy devil, there would be corroborating evidence to burn.

Next, Hunter tried to pull up the field reports on the investigation into Simon's disappearance. He quickly found that the files had been corrupted and could not be opened or downloaded. Hunter paused to consider the implications. Corrupted files were not unheard of, but Hunter wondered whether it was only an accident. If the destruction had been done on purpose, it begged the question: What was in the files that made them worth destroying?

He decided to go after the hard-copy files of the online documents and see where that led him. Three hours, four subway stops, five wrong turns, and half-a-mile of industrial filing cabinets later, Hunter came at last to the drawer displaying the first half of the reference code he had tracked down. He opened the drawer with a mighty pull that tugged at the stitches in his side and made him wince in pain. He flipped through a number of blue folders to find the one that matched his code—and this required another painful stretch all the way to the back of the drawer. But there it was.

The folder he retrieved was suspiciously thin. Opening it, he found only a single four-inch square of yellow paper that Hunter recognized immediately as a file receipt voucher—the form used to replace papers temporarily pulled for investigation. The contents of the folder hadn't been stolen, merely borrowed—and recently. Someone else was accessing information on Simon.

The writing on the voucher, which should have indicated the

agent's name and code, was illegible. Deliberately so? That in itself was an offense deserving an official reprimand. However, the date on the voucher was readable, and that was fairly recent. In fact, only three weeks ago.

Returning to HQ Research, Hunter slid back behind the computer terminal he had occupied earlier that morning. He accessed the records mainframe as before, but this time tapped in a code that was not on the menu display. A window popped up indicating that he had entered the Records User Log. It was incredibly simple to find who had accessed Simon's files in the past month or so. The display showed two agent codes for those files in that time period. One was his own, marked today; the other, however, was unfamiliar to him, and it had been logged only four days ago. Hunter jotted down the information.

It was time to call the governor.

Hunter quickly discovered how important he had become to the governor. He phoned Pilate's personal secretary to make an appointment and was told to come up at once.

An hour later, Hunter was once again being led by Jimmy, the governor's aide, into the tiny antechamber that joined the governor's office. Through the crack in the door, Hunter could just make out the shape of an immense, bizarrely dressed black man sitting on a metal folding chair before the governor's desk.

Draped in a flowing red cape secured at the neck by a giant golden clasp, his rotund figure was swathed in a white robe with a wide purple sash and billowing sleeves. He possessed an air of outsized importance, sitting like a live demigod on a too-small throne; he shifted his bulk and peered with vague irritation at being interrupted.

"Bring him in, Jimmy," said the governor. Hunter was brought to stand beside the seated figure.

"Agent Hunter," said Governor Pilate, "may I introduce his Excellency, High Priest Kai." Hunter turned to the man and, unaware of how to greet him properly, gave a stiffly formal ICON bow. The High Priest accepted this with an imperious nod.

"So, Agent, whattaya got for me?" Pilate asked, relighting his cigar.

"You asked me to report anything strange about my investigations." Hunter glanced at the high priest, uncertain how much to say in front of him.

Pilate noted his hesitation. "You can speak freely, Agent. The high priest shares our concerns. We've been having a talk about the Kadesh," Pilate turned to the high priest, "and we've reached an understanding, right?" To Kai, he explained, "Hunter is working on the Washer John case."

The high priest let out a small, slightly surprised, "Indeed." He held his head to one side and gave Hunter a perfunctory appraisal.

Hunter proceeded with his report. "One of the men I came into contact with during my last assignment was also involved at a high level in the Big Sky incident. He escaped two days before the mass suicide. This is the same man who was able to identify me and break my cover."

Governor Pilate took the cigar out of his mouth. "This wouldn't also be the guy who shot you, would it?"

"Yes, sir, it was. It is also possible that this man could be affiliated with the Kadesh."

"I see. We got a name for this guy?"

"Simon DeVere."

The governor looked at Kai. "Name ring a bell?"

The high priest just pursed his fleshy lips and wagged his head from side to side.

The governor turned back to Hunter. "Okay, so, that's it?"

"At the moment, yes, sir. I am in the process of tracking him down. But I have found that there might be another agent looking for him also. Information on the suspect has been accessed, and a file has been removed from records. I'm going to get onto the agent responsible, but I thought you would want to have this update."

"I see. Well, thank you, Agent Hunter." He moved around the side of the desk and took Hunter by the arm. "Keep up the good work." He called to his aide as he opened the door. "Jimmy, Agent Hunter is leaving. Show him out, would you?"

Hunter stepped into the waiting room and pulled the door shut behind him. Just before the door closed, however, he heard the governor say to his guest, "You see? It's time to play ball, Kai. Join the team, or you're batting for the losers. Got that?"

Hunter smiled and closed the door.

twenty-nine

The chief lit one cigar with the glowing bolt of another and squinted at Hunter. "Good to see you, Agent. Take a seat." He brushed some folders from a chair and pushed it forward, then sat back down and laced his hands behind his head, beaming at Hunter. "You look pretty good for a guy who's been used for target practice. I heard it was touch and go for a while there."

"It wasn't so bad," Hunter lied. "The nurses were knockouts."

"Yeah, that's what I hear," Devlin smiled. "Listen, about The Prophet and those ZIP guys—we sealed the bookstore for forensics and dusted the whole building when they finished. We gave it our best shot, but we got bupkis. You should have seen us race out there, though. We were into those buildings in under five minutes, door to door. Still got the tapes if you want to see 'em." He half stood as if to fetch them that instant.

"Thanks," Hunter said. "Maybe some other time."

"Sure, anytime." Devlin leaned back again and sent a puff of smoke billowing toward the ceiling. "I read the incident report on the Catskills fiasco," he continued. "You're one tough nut. Good man to have in a tight spot, sounds like. Shouldn't ever be afraid to ask for backup though. If you had gone in with guns blazing and ten guys behind you—a little Kevlar, a stun grenade or two—it would have turned out a whole lot better."

"No doubt," Hunter agreed quickly, eyeing the file folder on the police chief's desk. "Are we in luck?"

Devlin saw his glance and pushed the folder toward him. "Be my guest."

Hunter flipped open the folder and scanned the contents. Number KMD-765-323-4187-RW. Cullen, David Leroy. Investigations Officer, third class. Three years served. Awards, zero. Citations, zero.

"He's waiting next door," Devlin said.

"Bring him in; let's see what he has to say for himself."

A moment later the investigating officer was standing at attention before the chief's desk. "Relax, son, this ain't the army," said Devlin, grabbing his cigarette from the ashtray. Cullen slumped slightly and turned his attention to his chief, but didn't appear any more relaxed. "This here's Special Agent Hunter; he wants to ask you a few questions."

"What can I do for you, Agent?"

Hunter greeted the investigator and said, "It seems like an assignment you're working on has crossed with mine. I'm looking into the activities of a man called Simon DeVere. What have you got on him?"

Cullen shrugged. "Nothing that you probably don't know already. Former agent, went missing, turned up on the side of the bad guys. I'm trying to get a lead on him, but the trail has gone cold. He's disappeared again. And, from what I can see, he's pretty good at that."

"He's had some practice," Hunter allowed.

"I wish I could tell you more, but . . . " he let his voice trail off, indicating his lack of success.

"Somebody pulled the investigation reports," Hunter said. "Was that you?"

"Uh," he glanced at Devlin, who was watching him with a keen and hawklike stare, "yes, sir, I guess it was."

"What was in them?"

"The assignment number, code name, preliminary contact information, and some summary reports. There wasn't much, sir. The investigation didn't get very far."

"Then why'd you pull the file?"

"I had to check it out. I mean, even if it didn't go anywhere, I had to check it out."

"Who handed you this case?"

"Sir?" Cullen asked, puzzled.

"Who gave you this assignment?" Devlin asked. "It's an easy enough question."

"Right," the young officer blustered, "I misunderstood. It came down from my super—"

"And that would be?"

"Captain Walsh. Forty-ninth precinct." He looked at Hunter and said, "I wish I could help you out. But, like I said, the investigation didn't go anywhere."

"So, what happened to the reports?"

"I took them back."

"You returned them?" said Hunter. "They're not there now, and the last person to see them was you."

"Maybe they didn't get refiled properly," suggested Cullen. "How should I know?"

"You were the last one to see them."

"And I'm telling you I returned them to the archives. I don't know anything about them after that." He looked to Devlin for help, and then back to Hunter. "Anything else?"

"Not at the moment," replied Hunter. He dug a card from his pocket and wrote on the back of it. "Here's my number," he said, handing the card to Cullen. Call me if you get a lead on DeVere— anything at all, day or night. All right?"

"Sure, no problem."

"And I'll do the same for you," Hunter told him.

Chief Devlin thanked the officer for coming in, walked him to the door, and dismissed him. He returned to his chair, lit another cigar, and said, "Well, what do you make of that?"

"Unless they do things differently over at the forty-ninth precinct, I'd say that's the biggest crock I've heard in quite a while."

"Just what I was thinking." Devlin blew smoke upward. "I seriously doubt Walsh came up with this on his own. Somebody yanked his chain." He took a long, hard drag on his cigarette and then stubbed it out. "So, what's next? Want me to reach out to Walsh and find out what he's up to over there?"

"Leave that with me for the time being," said Hunter. "I'll nose around quietly first and see how far I get. I don't know how this will all tie in with the Washer John case, but it's where the governor pointed me, and I'm following that lead for the moment."

Devlin nodded. "Pilate's good at putting pieces together, even if there aren't any pieces lying around." He picked up a remote and clicked on one of his beloved monitors. "Keep your head down out there, Agent."

Hunter rose, thanked the chief for his trouble, and stepped to the door.

"And Hunter . . . " the chief called after him, "you ever get in a tight spot again, just give me a shout and I'll swoop down and save you like the bloody Valkyries."

"You got it."

Hunter endured another late supper in the near-empty HQ commissary and decided maybe it was time to check in at the Belvedere again. It wasn't a vast improvement, but the park was handy, and there was a better selection of cafés and restaurants nearby. He wouldn't have to eat every meal off a plastic tray.

Upon returning to his ICON room, he reviewed the day's activities and meetings, and went to bed with a nagging feeling that he was missing something, that some tiny detail had been stirred up from deep in his memory—a word, a fact, something Cullen had said, something he'd read in a file, *something*—but whatever it was eluded him.

At three in the morning, the elusive detail bubbled up from his subconscious. He awoke full in the knowledge of where to go and what to do next.

As soon as it began to get light outside, he rose, hung up his uniform, and put on his civvies. He was back undercover again, and it felt good to slip his arms into his leather jacket and tuck his gun into his shoulder holster. He grabbed a quick commissary breakfast, then caught the subway uptown, where he wasted not a minute catching up with Eddie at the Carnegie Suites.

This was the bright idea that had awakened him in the middle of the night, and it was thinking about the hotels that had set it off.

Eddie wasn't on the door when Hunter got there, but he flashed his ID at the desk manager, who led him to the employees' changing room behind the front office. "Somebody to see you, Eddie," he called, and let Hunter take it from there.

"Hey, boss!" Eddie exclaimed when he saw Hunter. A wide grin spread across his face. "Good to see you. Back in town, or what?"

"I need some information, Eddie," said Hunter. "It's pretty important."

"Sure, anything."

"When I was last here, I talked to you about a woman who came to see me."

"Uh, yeah, sure. I remember," said Eddie, tapping the side of his head. "Like a elephant, you know?"

"I had a hunch," Hunter said. "When I talked to you the day I checked out, I got the impression that you couldn't tell me who she was or where she came from because the manager was listening. Is that true?"

Eddie grew sly. "Now, this wouldn't be a trick, would it? This is all aboveboard and everything, right?"

"Yeah, Eddie, don't worry about it. This is between you and me."

"It's just that this sort of thing is officially frowned on by the management. I mean, they *know*, but if it ever became an issue they'd have to make an example of someone and it'd probably be goodbye Eddie—y'know what I'm sayin'?"

"It never leaves this room." Hunter removed a fifty-dollar bill out of his wallet and laid it on the table. "Like I said, it's very important."

"Sorry to have to tell you this, Mr. Taylor," said Eddie, eyeing the bill, "but I don't know who she was. Fact is, I thought you found her on your own. I usually wait for the go-ahead from the guests before I make any arrangements—I mean, I offered that once, but you never said anything, so I figured you took care of it yourself."

"You'd never seen her before? You're absolutely sure about that?"

"Never laid eyes on her."

"Seen her since?"

"Nah."

"Okay, now I want you to think even harder. On that same day—it was in the morning, around ten o'clock—a guy came to give me a package—he brought me a book. Remember him?"

Eddie's brow contracted, furrowing heavily. The elephantine recall system was struggling.

"He was tall, blond, midtwenties . . . "

Eddie squinted his eyes and looked up into the air, as if observing the man himself. "Yeah . . . yeah," his face brightened, "I remember now. Spiky hair, and a couple pierced ears and a pierced eyebrow, right?"

"Bingo!" said Hunter.

"Ha! Steel trap!" crowed Eddie, tapping the side of his head again.

"When I came back, I saw you two talking together. What were you talking about?"

"Uh—you, I guess. Yeah, we was talking about you."

"Did you mention that I might be looking for female company at all?"

Eddie thought. "No, no, I don't think so. But even if it did come up, everything would have been in strict confidence. A job like mine, you gotta make those connections, right? It's all about who you know, you know?"

"Did it come up, or not?" Hunter asked, his voice growing firm.

"Yeah, I think maybe it came up."

"Okay, Eddie, that's great. The important thing now is that I have to find the woman again. Do you know how I might go about doing that? Her name was Rosa."

"Well, now, let me see," he glanced at the fifty on the table. Hunter added a twenty to the fifty and handed both to Eddie, who said, "As it happens, I think I might be able to help steer you in the right direction."

thirty

As soon as it grew dark, Hunter hit the streets. He surfaced from the subway in Times Square and started working his way east into club land, the nightlife district, home of licit and illicit fun and games. In his pocket was the card Eddie the doorman had given him. "Dulcinea—it's a club, not a girl," he'd said.

It took Hunter twenty minutes to find the Dulcinea, a small, dingy-looking residence hotel. He walked up the steps to a well-beaten door and tried the doorknob, but it was locked. He rang a buzzer set into the wall.

"Yeah?" came a raspy, possibly female, voice.

"I, um—Eddie sent me."

"Who?"

"Eddie the doorman."

"Second floor," came a reply from the speaker as the door lock buzzed.

Hunter entered a small elevator, and when the doors opened onto the second floor he found himself in a waiting room that didn't fit at all with the building's drab exterior. There were low leather sofas along the walls and a chrome-and-glass desk at the far end. A beefy bouncer with a spiderweb tattoo on the side of his neck was sitting on one of the sofas; he had a small paperback crunched between his meaty hands. Lining the rose-colored walls on either side of the room were large photos of young women. Hunter scanned these quickly. They were professional model composites with a head shot of each girl, as well as a full-length shot of the same girl in an alluring posture superimposed to one side. He found a photo that looked like his girl second from the last on the left-hand wall near the desk. His heart started to race. He stepped closer. Definitely her.

The bouncer looked up and said, "You want something?"

"I'm here to see one of your ladies."

"Bell on the desk," said the man. He resumed his reading.

Hunter moved to the desk and pressed the button marked "Ring for Service." A moment later a grumpy matron appeared. She took one look at Hunter and said, "It'll be a hundred—in advance."

Without a word, Hunter counted bills onto the desk in front of the bouncer. Spiderman swept the bills off the desk and into a drawer. "Which one?" asked the matron.

"Rosa," said Hunter.

"Rosa?"

He pointed to the photo on the wall. "That one."

The woman nodded and then went through a doorway behind her. A couple of minutes later she returned with Rosa behind her. She was perfectly made up and wearing a short, pleated red skirt, translucent white blouse, and a trim, form-fitting black crushed-velvet jacket.

Rosa stopped in the doorway the instant she saw Hunter, a small cry of surprise frozen on her well-painted lips. The momentary hesitation made the older woman turn around in concern. Spiderman put his book aside and stood up.

"You okay, hon?" he asked.

"Yeah," said Rosa, recovering herself with a smile.

"You know this gentleman?" the matron asked, eyeing Hunter up and down.

"Yeah, it's all right. I thought he was somebody else for a second." She gave the older woman a peck on the cheek and adjusted her jacket.

Hunter led her to the elevator.

"So, what'll it be—your place or mine?" said Rosa, looking up at the ceiling of the elevator car as the doors slid closed.

"Neither," replied Hunter. "Actually, I'm starving. Want to get something to eat?"

"Sure. Whatever. It's your call," she pressed the button and the elevator started down. Ten minutes later they were sitting at a table in a small, smoky, dimly lit Spanish restaurant nearby. Rosa was picking at a limp seafood salad and trying not to make eye contact with Hunter as he chewed a piece of steak.

"So, do you know who I am?" he asked after a moment.

"Yes. Well, no, not really. But I know you weren't who you said you were. You're an undercover ICON agent."

"Not so much undercover anymore," he said. Retrieving his wallet, he flipped it open to reveal his ICON ID. "Special Agent Alex Hunter."

"Nice name," she said.

"And you are?"

She looked down. "I'd rather not say."

"Fine, whatever. Listen, what were you doing when you came to see me?"

"Just trying to get a little information."

"Fair enough," granted Hunter. He nodded, thinking how to phrase the next question. "Would it bother you to know that the information you provided resulted in me getting shot? They shot me up pretty bad, in fact."

Rosa shook her head in emphatic denial. "I don't know anything about that. I had nothing to do with it, okay?" She read the doubt in Hunter's eyes, and added, "Believe it or not, I'm telling the truth."

He took a sip of coffee. "I'll assume you want to help me," he said evenly, "and you assume I'm not blaming you for anything."

"Okay," Rosa said, sounding none too certain. "So, what do you want to know?"

"Why were you sent to me?"

"Just to find out about you," she replied. "Like I already said."

"Who sent you?"

She looked away, her eyes darting to the windows.

"The man who sent you—it was Simon DeVere, right?"

Rosa looked down at her salad and nodded.

"Are you afraid of Simon?"

She brushed back an errant lock of hair. "I've known worse."

"He won't know that we talked. In fact, I'm pretty sure he's skipped town."

Rosa looked up at him. "You got shot, huh?" The note of sympathy in her voice was genuine.

"I did." Hunter nodded, looking into the dark pool of blood

from his rare steak. "Simon tried real hard to kill me. He shot me in the arm and in the gut. Cracked my skull. I was in a coma for weeks, and this close—" Hunter held a thumb and index finger an inch apart—"to being worm food. I'm one lucky guy." He forced another smile. "At least that's what they tell me." There was a long pause.

"I need to find him. I need you to tell me where he is."

"So *you* can kill *him* this time?"

Hunter looked at her, then shook his head. "I wish it was that simple. But it isn't. The thing is, Simon's mixed up in some pretty rough stuff. I have to get to him before anyone else gets hurt."

Rosa turned her face away again. "I wish I could help you."

"I'll pay you for any information you give me."

"Look," she said sharply, "you're not listening. I don't know where he is."

"When was the last time you saw him?"

"About two months ago, I guess."

"*Where* did you last see him?"

"His apartment."

"Give me the address."

"You won't find him. He changes addresses. Usually he tells me, but not this time."

"The address?"

"Eight ninety-six Fulton Street. It's an apartment house over in Brooklyn," she said, then reached across the table and touched his hand. "I'm sorry about what happened to you, Alex." She said in a low voice, "I could try to make it up to you if you like."

"It's history. Forget about it."

Hunter stood and tossed some money down on the table. "Come on, I'll walk you back."

They returned to the Dulcinea in silence. Hunter left her at the door, said goodbye, and headed back toward Times Square. She watched him walk away, then called out, "Hey!"

Hunter stopped and turned around.

"My name is Maggie."

He started back to her, but she was already disappearing through the door.

thirty-one

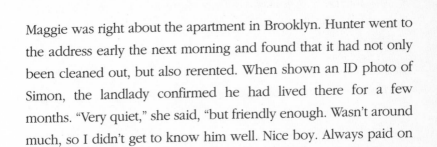

Maggie was right about the apartment in Brooklyn. Hunter went to the address early the next morning and found that it had not only been cleaned out, but also rerented. When shown an ID photo of Simon, the landlady confirmed he had lived there for a few months. "Very quiet," she said, "but friendly enough. Wasn't around much, so I didn't get to know him well. Nice boy. Always paid on time, kept the noise down—not like a lot of people these days."

"When did he move out?"

"This would have been six weeks ago. A Tuesday I think—or Wednesday, maybe. I don't know. All I got was a phone call saying he wasn't coming back. He hadn't been around much for about a week before that though. I told him he'd lose his deposit because he wasn't giving me thirty days' notice, but he said that was okay, *plus* I could keep whatever he'd left in the apartment—which wasn't a lot."

"Do you still have it?"

"Most of it I sold, but I kept the VCR and portable TV. The clothes I gave to the homeless shelter. He had some nice things."

"Didn't you think it was a little odd?" Hunter asked. "Just up and leaving like that?"

"Not really. I take short-timers—they pay a little extra for the flexibility, you know? Now that I think of it, he might have said something about Pennsylvania—probably a job or something. That's usually what happens anyway."

"And you haven't seen or heard from him since?"

"Goodness, no."

"And he left no forwarding address?"

"Nope." She shook her head. "You could check at the post office—maybe they forward it from there. But I haven't had any letters for him."

Hunter thanked the woman for her time and headed back across town.

There were two voice mail messages waiting when he got back to his room at ICON HQ.

The first was only a few minutes old. "Hunter, this is the governor," the gruff voice announced. "You're about to get a call from Mike Arnolds in Intelligence. Do whatever he says. Something is happening and we need your help. I'll leave it to Mike to fill in the details."

Hunter stabbed at the button to bring up the next message.

"Agent Hunter? Commander Mike Arnolds here. We've got a developing situation, and I need to pick your brain. Call me as soon as you receive this—extension 4543."

What could it be? All 4000-level extensions were high-security departments. He punched in the number. The phone was answered on the first ring.

"Ah, great, Agent Hunter," came the reply from the other end.

"Listen, we need you in the ICC—pronto. Take the central block elevator down to sublevel six. Just use your ID; I've cleared you for entry."

"I'm on my way."

The elevator opened onto a completely bare security chamber. There was a stainless steel swipe pad next to a steel door, and Hunter ran his ID through the slot. The red light next to the swipe pad switched to green, the door clicked, and Hunter pulled it open and entered the humming nerve center of ICON New York.

The Intelligence Command Center was a ring of eight connecting rooms around a central core—a large octagonal doughnut with a steel-and-glass center. It began six levels under ICON HQ and occupied three subbasements. In the room Hunter entered, banks of computer desks fanned out in front of a giant plasma-screen monitor. Looking through the glass partitions into the next rooms in the ring, he could see a similar arrangement of desks and screens. The entire city and half the Eastern seaboard could, theoretically, be run from the ICC.

Hunter stood for a moment, taking in the quietly urgent activity: people sitting at computers, rattling keyboards, and talking intensely on telephone headsets. The air reeked of burned coffee and stale cologne.

Although he had never been in this particular command center, there were situation rooms like it all over the country, one in each of the larger ICON administration regions. Hunter realized now how much he missed the feeling of power, of being in the loop, of having up-to-the-second information at his fingertips and the ability to command many different agents all over the country. He missed the crackle of energy, the adrenaline rush, and the fact that here, at least, he was never shot at.

A big, shambling man with coal-black skin and graying hair came breezing up and clasped his hand in a hearty grip. "Hunter? I'm Arnolds," he said. "Thanks for coming so quickly."

"No problem. What's up?"

Commander Arnolds rubbed a hand over his face. He had the permanently tired eyes and raspy voice Hunter had seen in many ICC commanders. He looked slightly frayed around the edges, but still game for a fight. "I honestly wish I knew. Here—we're using the conference room."

Arnolds led Hunter up a freestanding metal staircase to a room inside the central core. As he ascended the stairs he looked out over the room below, trying to glean from the general tenor of the activity an indication of what was going on. It was hard to read, but something in people's movements, their faces, told him that they were more confused than busy. The room lacked the highly tensed atmosphere and quick, darting movements of a calamity-in-progress, but there was an undeniable undercurrent of anxiety that told Hunter something big was going down. A man carrying a box of computer disks caught his attention as he walked quickly through the room placing a handful of them on each desk.

Stepping into the conference room, Hunter found that from inside the glass core, he could see into each of the rooms around the ring. In the center of the room was a large, oval conference table and next to it a bank of plasma screens similar to those in the workrooms outside. The conference table itself supported all the latest technical paraphernalia: laptop network hubs, multifeed satellite phones, individual scrambler phones, backup power supplies, individual lighting—and also pads of paper, marking pens, white boards: everything and anything anyone might require to aid communication.

There were four other people in the room, and three of them were introduced to Hunter as Incident Specialists—experts who were flown around the country to handle "extreme situations." Usually that meant terrorism. The fourth person was a techie whose job it was to keep the gadgets and humans on speaking terms.

"What seems to be the problem, sir?" Hunter asked Arnolds as he was shown a seat.

"We're under attack," he answered. "Cyber attack. It started a few hours ago when the main system began one of its daily backup routines. We got error messages out the wazoo, indicating that all our backup systems were nonoperational."

"All of them?" wondered Hunter. He related to computers from the user end, not the systems end, but knew that one backup was never enough.

"All of them," confirmed Arnolds. "The data bunker in Nevada, the one in Ottawa, even the secure facilities in Ireland and New Zealand have been compromised—not to mention the smaller regional facilities nationwide. But that's not all. Add to that the discovery of a host of extremely malicious viruses, worms, and whatnot spreading through the system, and it's looking very much like an act of terrorism."

"It sounds like it," agreed Hunter.

"No one could have got into our system without insider help. I mean, until yesterday you could'a counted the number of people that even *knew* about the New Zealand facility without taking off your shoes. And the bunker in Silverlode Mountain is, or was, considered impenetrable. Even if you knew where to find it, you couldn't get near it—physically *or* virtually."

"We've got a mole problem," concluded Hunter.

"A serious mole problem," agreed Arnolds. "Right now we're just trying to figure out how to keep the system up and running because if it goes down . . . " The intelligence chief made an exploding gesture with his hands to indicate his estimation of the damage.

Hunter found this alarming enough, but also somewhat mystifying. "So, where do I come in, exactly?"

"The techs have quarantined one of the viruses, and they found what we believe might be a signature embedded in the code. There's a line of text that reads, "The words of The Prophet are written in blood." We're pretty sure we were meant to find it and we're pretty sure that it actually *was* The Prophet who arranged this nasty little surprise, because this particular virus directed its attention to destroying the files in the terrorist database."

"I see."

"We've been giving the governor regular updates, and when he heard about this development, he said to call you," Arnolds concluded. "Seems you've met this Prophet character a few times."

"Only twice."

"Well, we need to know whatever you know. Naturally, his files were the first to be deleted by the virus."

"Naturally."

The techie placed a steaming mug of coffee in front of Hunter. The Incident Specialists turned to him expectantly, waiting for information. Ignoring one female specialist who was drawing furious circles with her clogged ballpoint, Hunter started to recount all the details he could remember about The Prophet. When he was finished with that, he started on the story of his blighted undercover mission.

All listened quietly and without comment to everything Hunter had to say. When he finished, he sat back in his chair. "That's all I can tell you," Hunter concluded. Aware now how very little it was, he added, "I wish it was more. I really do."

"Did you ever hear The Prophet issue any specific threats or name any targets?" asked one of the Incident Specialists.

"No, ma'am, I never did. He seemed generally hostile to ICON and everything it stood for, but there was nothing in particular that stood out."

"Peachy." Arnolds took a sip of his coffee, "Well, thanks for your help, Agent Hunter. We'll call you if we need anything else."

Hunter stood up and straightened his uniform. He unbuttoned his collar, as the room had become stuffy and warm. "Sorry I couldn't be of more help to you all."

"That's fine, Agent. You've given us a few things to think about." Arnolds tapped his scribble-filled notebook. "I'll show you out."

They walked out onto the gangplank and down the stairs into the main room, which was sweltering.

"AC's busted again, Chief," whined the techie as they passed. "On top of everything else!"

They returned to the outer room's steel door. "Sorry I couldn't have been more help," said Hunter, swiping his ID through the slot to let himself out. When nothing happened, he tried it again. Still nothing.

"Here, allow me," said Arnolds impatiently. He crossed to a small keypad on a nearby stand and quickly tapped a code on it. The machine buzzed at him harshly. He keyed in the code again and still the red light blazed and the door remained locked. "What next?" he muttered.

The intelligence chief picked up a phone built into the keypad stand and put it to his ear for a moment before slamming it down angrily. "Wait here a sec." He charged off to the next room in the octagonal ring.

Hunter waited for about five minutes, then made his way to the next room, where he found Arnolds fuming over a technician's computer.

Arnolds glanced up irritably. "We've got real problems now," he said. "Scott has just been telling me that none of the keypads or card readers in the entire building are working. But I think we've managed to—" At that instant, the phone at his elbow, as well as every other phone in the room, started to ring. Arnolds stared at the tech. "Did you do that?"

"Sorry, no."

Arnolds picked up the receiver. "Nothing but a busy signal," Arnolds said. He put the phone back down and it immediately rang again. "Oh, come on!" he cried, picking it up again. He put it to his ear and then laid it on the desk. The ringing of the other phones continued sporadically for a while, and then gradually stopped.

Arnolds sighed. "Might as well put your feet up, Hunter. It looks like you're going to be here for a while."

thirty-two

Seven hours later, Hunter was back in his room. The hallway was dim, lit only by emergency lights. The power was off throughout the entire building so that the systems could be debugged and reset one by one. Lights and air circulation to the living quarters were, apparently, a low priority. Without the fans to keep the air moving, the heat rose to the upper floors, making the temperature almost unbearable, even in winter. Hunter couldn't wait to open some windows.

As he stepped into his apartment he found that it was already being aired out by a man who was sitting on the couch. The visitor rose quickly as Hunter entered.

"I hope you don't mind me coming in, Agent Hunter," said the young man as he stood. Hunter could see it was the governor's aide.

"Not at all, Jimmy," Hunter said wearily. "Be my guest."

"I tried to call you, but—"

"Sure. What's up?"

"The governor wants to see you."

"Let's go."

Hunter closed the door to his refreshingly cool apartment and followed Jimmy back into the stifling, dark corridor. So now the governor wanted to see him. *Why wasn't I this popular in school?* Hunter mused to himself.

Jimmy led Hunter to the state office building, but to a different office this time. They both waited on one side of a long, glass-topped table heaped high with notebooks, files, and papers while the governor paced up and down the opposite side of the table, talking into a cell phone. As he started the walk back toward them, he caught sight of the two men; he waved Jimmy away and Hunter forward.

"Look, I'll call you back in ten minutes," he said, terminating his call. "Hunter, glad to see you. I heard you got stuck in the basement over there. Bad luck—I needed you here hours ago." He put the phone on the table and stuck his hands in his pockets.

"Sorry, sir, there was nothing—"

"Forget about it," the governor said. "We've lost time here is all I'm saying." He pulled out a silver lighter and reached under a stack of papers for a large ashtray, retrieving a half-smoked cigar from it. "The Jewish high priest called me a few hours ago and wants to see you."

"Me?" *Yet another admirer,* thought Hunter.

"He got word of the HQ shenanigans, and since you seem to be the only person in the whole city who knows anything about The Prophet, he wants to talk to you. Go figure."

Hunter nodded, trying to estimate just how big a bog he was getting sucked into. The governor relit the cigar and puffed emphatically to get it going again; he then pointed the glowing tip at Hunter. "I assume you've worked out what's going on here."

"I think so, sir."

"Washer John, The Prophet, and the Kadesh." The governor held up three fingers. "We can put those three together and crack this case wide open."

"Can we, sir?"

"I'm betting that the high priest is holding the ace card in this game, or he wouldn't bother stepping up to the plate."

Hunter nodded.

"The high priest is a smart one, Hunter. He's basically throwing us a meaty bone here—not just Washer John, but a chance at The Prophet before he makes an even bigger nuisance of himself. It's in his interest, sure. There's nothing he'd like better than to see the Kadesh and The Prophet disappear, but still he's doing us a favor. Treat him with respect; he's an important man." The governor took a draw on his cigar and added, "We'll pay for it in spades later—he'll want concessions, he always does—but that's my concern."

"Yes, sir."

"Jimmy is going to take you to Kai's place now. Find out what he has to say and report back to me. Got that?"

"Got it, sir."

"Get going," grunted Pilate, picking up his phone. He returned his cigar to the ashtray and started pushing buttons with his thumb. "Good luck, Agent." To the person on the other end of the phone, he said, "Okay, Morris, where was I?"

Hunter left the room without a word.

The high priest's palace was situated on Manhattan's Upper West Side in a district comprised of lavish residential hotels and exclusive apartment houses. The high priest lived in a genuine palace, the architecture of which was a curious blend of Mediterranean and Gothic—high, narrow windows and massive stone walls with buttresslike projections supporting a terra-cotta-tiled roof. The front entrance was at the top of a steep flight of stone steps, guarded by two purple-and-white robed doormen who stood in two small alcoves on either side of the impressive cast-bronze doors. One of the doormen stepped out as Jimmy and Hunter approached and, without a word, opened a smaller door that was cut into the larger one—part of an inset panel sculpted with vines and grapes. They were ushered into an enclosed, climate-controlled marble-paved courtyard complete with palm trees, bubbling fountain, and carved stone pillars. A riot of flowering tropical plants filled the humid air with heavy fragrance.

Jimmy waited by the fountain as Hunter was led up a wide spiral staircase to a high-ceilinged reception room, and then to a smaller and more intimate study. The obese priest sat in a large, softly upholstered chair, looking far less grand and exotic than Hunter had last seen him. Dressed in a plain cloth robe, and lacking the flash of jewels and golden baubles, the high priest appeared haggard. "Ah, Agent Hunter," Kai purred lazily. "Here you are at last." He gestured for the doorman to draw a chair closer. "Please, have a seat."

Hunter thanked the servant and sank back into a well-worn leather chair. "What can I do for you, si—I mean, Your Excellency?" he asked.

The high priest leaned back, staring at Hunter. After a few seconds he said, "I have come across some information that I believe will be of some use in your murder investigation."

"Yes?"

"Mmm, yes." He raised the back of his hand to his mouth to stifle a yawn. "I believe I know the identity of Washer John's killer."

"Oh?" asked Hunter. "And how would that be?"

Kai's small eyes quickened at the hint of impertinence in Hunter's voice. "I heard him confess it."

"I see."

"It might interest you to know that Isaiah Henderson was also in the room at the time."

"Are you saying you think The Prophet was involved in some way?"

"That is my distinct impression, Agent Hunter. The proof, I fear, you must discover for yourself. . . . "

There was another lengthy pause. Hunter let Kai continue at his own pace. "How well-versed are you in the lore of the Kadesh, Agent Hunter?"

"I'm learning more every day."

Kai nodded. "The man you want to interview is named Howard Antony Archelon." The high priest looked out the window as a small flurry of snow started up. "He rules part of the Kadesh 'kingdom' here in the city, but he resides upstate on a large and rather ostentatious estate near Monticello."

"If you don't mind me asking, High Priest, how exactly di—"

"I heard him speak of it at a party."

"Okay . . . " said Hunter, hoping more would be forthcoming. But the high priest seemed to be drifting into some weird, staring reverie. After a moment, he asked, "Can you tell me anything more?"

Kai started as if returning from a dream. "Howard Archelon is a spoiled brat. John Levinson had the audacity to denounce him in public—something about marrying his brother's wife."

The high priest drifted off again, so Hunter guessed the rest. "So, this public accusation made Archelon angry and Washer John paid the price—is that it?"

"Precisely." The high priest closed his eyes. "If you want any more, you'll have to ask Archelon."

"All right," said Hunter. "I think I've got enough to go on. But there is one more thing, High Priest."

The large man opened his eyes.

"Forgive my ignorance, but is the Kadesh connected to the temple in any way? I mean, the religious beliefs and all . . ."

The high priest rolled his head from side to side. "No, not even remotely. They wish they were, and they have tried for years to make inroads, but no. They have nothing to do with the temple. Nor does the temple have anything to do with them. If you ask me, they are a bunch of pathetic little men living in an imagined past, using their strong-arm enforcers, two-bit thugs, and heavy-handed brutes to create an illusion of power where there is none." Kai yawned again and sank even further into his chair.

Taking his cue to leave, Hunter stood. "Thank you, High Priest; your help has been invaluable."

"Tell the governor I wish him well."

"I'll do that, Your Excellency." The high priest lifted a hand in farewell, and Hunter left him to his dreamy stupor.

Hunter replayed his conversation with the high priest word for word when he got back to the governor's chambers at the state office building.

The bald governor rubbed his bearded chin and thought for a minute. Then, with a growl that might have been a command, he bowled from the room. "C'mon."

Hunter trailed him to the small office downstairs, his bolt-hole, where Pilate slid into the large leather chair and dug out an address book from the innards of the battered desk. He pawed through it to a page with no names, only a narrow column of numbers. He ran his finger down the list. Tapping the speaker button on the phone, he dialed one of the numbers.

Hunter listened to it ring a few times before it was answered by a low, monotone voice. "Yes, who is it?"

"This is Governor Pilate. I want to speak to the Melech."

"One moment, please."

There was a clicking sound and another voice answered.

"This is Melech," came a richly accented voice that put Hunter in mind of a bad Count Dracula impression.

"Melech, it's Pilate. How are you?"

There was a nervous mumbling from the other side of the line. "I am well, Governor . . . as well as you might expect . . . yes, and you?"

"I won't lie to you, Melech. I could be better. Tell you the truth, I've got a headache I wish would go away."

"I am sorry to hear it. Is there something I can do?"

"I was hoping you'd say that." Pilate smiled at Hunter. "It

seems someone has been indiscreet with some very sensitive information. It has caused a lot of damage and made a lot of people very upset."

There was a pause. "I see." The words were flat, without expression. Nevertheless, Hunter clearly understood that through the Kadesh, Melech already knew about the attack on ICON HQ.

Pilate leaned back in his chair, drawing out the awkward silence, forcing the other man to speak first.

"And this is the cause of your headache?" came the other voice after a few moments.

"Couldn't have said it better myself," replied Pilate. "I hope this won't come as too much of a shock, Melech, but it seems that your son Antony may be mixed up in something he shouldn't be."

"Really? Hmm, is that so?" The man on the other end of the line didn't seem shocked or offended, but spoke like someone trying to solve a tricky conundrum.

"It's a fact," Pilate declared. "We're going to have to ask him some questions, and I don't want there to be any trouble over this. Got it?"

"I understand."

Pilate paused. "My concern is that if he should attempt to resist arrest . . . well, someone could get hurt and I know neither of us wants that."

"Governor, I have told you I understand. There will be no trouble."

"I have your guarantee? Thing is, the agent I'm sending is very valuable to me."

"Don't worry, no harm will come to your agent. You have my word."

"And you'll make the necessary arrangements?" confirmed Pilate.

"It will be done. But there is just one thing I need from you, Governor." The Melech paused. Pilate held his cigar suspended halfway to his mouth, waiting for the shoe to drop.

"Yes?"

"I would like to think that this gesture I am making will be appreciated for what it's worth. Antony is my son, after all. It may be that one day I will need a favor. I would like your assurance that I could call on you, Governor Pilate, as you have so freely called on me."

"You know me, Melech," said Pilate. "I do not make promises I can't keep. Let's just say I set great value by your gesture and that it goes a long way toward smoothing the rocky ground between us."

"Thank you, Governor Pilate. I'll accept that."

They both hung up and Pilate turned to Hunter. "It's as good as done. Go pick him up."

"Excuse me, sir," said Hunter, "but you didn't mention anything about the Washer John murder investigation."

"You don't use a sledgehammer to crack a peanut, Agent. Anyway, we've got bigger fish to fry. Before this is over, I'm going to have 'em all twisting slowly in the wind. Got it?"

"Yes, sir," replied Hunter, smiling at the governor's free and easy way with everyday aphorisms.

"Good luck, Agent. It's your show from here on out."

thirty-three

The man in the lodge beside the entrance to the estate waved the Humvee through the open wrought-iron gates. The vehicle rolled up the drive and into the floodlit forecourt, where eight ICON Rapid Response troops in full body armor and wielding M4 assault rifles had already taken up defensive positions around the lead Hummer. Their weapons were trained on four men standing in front of the house in heavy coats.

Rushed by helicopter to Stanton Airfield a few miles from Monticello, Hunter had been met by the Albany RR unit captain and quickly outfitted with his own body armor before piling into the Humvee and driving through the winter darkness to Howard Antony Archelon's country estate. The entire journey to this point had taken less than two hours.

Once the troops were positioned, the captain gave the nod to Hunter. "Ready when you are, Agent."

Hunter picked up his bullhorn and climbed from the vehicle; he walked toward the house, stopping in the arc of light from the Humvee headlights. Raising the bullhorn to his lips, he pressed the trigger and said, "This is ICON Special Agent Alexander Hunter. I have a warrant for the arrest of Howard Antony Archelon. He is wanted in connection with the cyber attack on ICON Headquarters in New York."

His declaration was met with utter silence. The men on the front steps remained motionless. Hunter waited a moment, then added, "If the suspect does not present himself immediately, we will be forced to come in after him. You have three minutes."

Hunter raised his hand and noted the time on his watch, beginning his countdown.

An uneasy silence settled over the courtyard. The seconds slipped away.

"You have two minutes!" Hunter said, speaking slowly into the mouthpiece.

Another minute ticked by, and Hunter announced, "You have one minute!"

Two of the men on the front steps turned and went inside. A few seconds later, indistinct shouting came from inside the house and the mansion's front door opened. The two men emerged once more, hauling a third man between them. "Let me go! I demand—!" shouted the reluctant prisoner. His eyes went wide when he saw the ICON troops lined up and waiting for him. "No! No! You can't do this!"

The two Kadesh enforcers stopped a few paces from where Hunter waited. Hunter nodded to the captain and stepped forward to meet his prisoner, with two RR troopers behind him.

"Howard Antony Archelon?"

Archelon stopped squirming. "That's right," he spat belligerently.

"I have a warrant for your arrest. I'm asking you to come with me for questioning." Hunter regarded the man before him: a smooth, well-dressed businessman with dark hair and a round, boyish face. He felt not the slightest ounce of anger toward the man who had killed Washer John. Mostly, he just felt a low-grade loathing. "You are advised that you have the right to remain silent. Anything you say in my presence may be used against you in a court of law . . . " he began.

"Skip it," Archelon said. "I know my rights better than you do, and I'm not saying anything without my lawyer."

"Cuff him," Hunter ordered.

Archelon squirmed uselessly until the handcuffs were on him. He was then led across the courtyard, through the line of ICON troopers, and into the Humvee. Having delivered their prisoner, the two Kadesh enforcers returned to the front entrance of the house, where they stood looking on.

The ICON RR team closed around the armored vehicles and one by one climbed in, the captain and four troopers in one vehicle, and Hunter, Archelon, and three troopers in the other. The doors slammed shut and the vehicles backed from the drive.

Things couldn't have gone better.

Archelon stared out of the bulletproof glass into the blackness of a night lit only by the occasional farmhouse or yard light. Flanked by two armed ICON troopers, he looked small, crumpled, and wretched.

Hunter, in the jump seat, gazed with disdain at the preposterous poser in his expensive suit, then leaned back and closed his eyes for the drive back to the airfield and the waiting heli-copter. He listened to the heavy tires on the road and heard the driver's check-in with the waiting chopper pilot. His mind drifted back to when he was an agent in the Midwest and Rocky Mountain district, and he wondered when everything had become so complicated. His job, his life—everything—seemed more straightforward back then, he thought; at least, more things made sense. Or, then again, maybe it just seemed that way.

Lulled by the darkness and the whir of the tires on the pave-ment, Hunter felt the tension of the day start to abate. His head had just touched the headrest when he felt the Hummer begin to slow.

"What the—!" exclaimed the driver. The vehicle lurched for-ward as the driver downshifted fast and skidded to a halt.

Hunter, jolted upright, turned around and looked through the hatch that allowed communication between the passenger com-partment and the driver's cab. "What's going on?"

"Looks like a truck jackknifed in the road, sir. About a hun-dred yards ahead."

Hunter squinted through the steel mesh grate and the wind-shield beyond. He could see part of a large semi-truck trailer sprawled across both lanes. It must have been a recent wreck; there were no other cars around. He looked out the side win-dows. From what little he could see, there were stubble fields to the right and, to the left a narrow band of unharvested corn—a few dozen rows left standing to help fatten pheasant and deer for hunting; beyond the field, it looked like woods.

"What do you want us to do, sir?" asked the driver.

Just then the radio burst to life with a blast of static. The driver picked up the handset and said, "Vehicle one. Go ahead, two."

A voice buzzed over the speaker. "We're turning back. Follow us, one. Proceed to I-90 junction with eighty-seven."

"Roger, two. Behind you all the way."

The driver backed up and executed a tight three-point turn on the highway. The driver had no sooner shoved the vehicle into gear once more when he loosed a hot stream of obscenities. Hunter looked out the front window and gave a yelp of surprise. Bearing down on them at high speed was another large truck. He shouted a warning to the troopers and braced himself while the driver gunned the engine and swerved the Humvee off the road.

An instant later, the Humvee shuddered violently as the semi sideswiped them.

"Get us out of here!" shouted Hunter. He heard the gears grind and felt the vehicle jolt forward. Through the passenger window he saw the truck reversing. The Humvee slewed sideways and tilted, sliding downward into the ditch beside the road.

The driver tried to ease the Hummer up out of the ditch, but the armored vehicle had become hung up on something. Grass and mud flew in every direction as the driver struggled to get back onto the road. The spinning front wheels slipped further into the muddy ditch.

There came another violent, bone-rattling shake as the semi rammed into the rear of the Humvee, spinning it sideways and tilting it precariously. Hunter found himself looking up at a terrified Archelon and a grimacing trooper as the vehicle pitched wildly and rolled over onto its flat roof.

Suspended by their seatbelts, the passengers hung upside down. Hunter clawed at the harness release and dropped to the roof, which was now beneath him. He twisted around and began to yank Archelon free of his seatbelt; the trooper in the backseat of the Hummer opened the rear door.

Above the angry blast of invective from the radio speaker, Hunter heard the sound of the truck gunning its engine on the road. "Out! Out!" Hunter cried. "Everybody out!"

"This way!" shouted the trooper in the back as he scrambled out. Hunter grabbed Archelon by the arm and pulled him toward the exit.

Two RR troopers were already outside, weapons drawn, kneeling beside the road. "Get going!" Hunter said, shoving Archelon out the open doors.

"All right! All right!" squealed Archelon, sliding down and out.

As Hunter swung his legs around to slide out, he heard the troopers outside open fire in short, controlled bursts. The shots were returned from the direction of the semi. Over the radio he heard the captain radioing for assistance, but who knew how long that could take? They were trapped beside a narrow country road between two semis and couldn't wait for the cavalry to show up. He had to get Archelon to safety. Drawing his sidearm, he clambered from the overturned Hummer, grabbed his hand-cuffed prisoner, and ordered the troopers to defend their retreat.

Pushing Archelon into the ditch, he took a last look at the situation on the road. The second Humvee was stalled in the middle of the road, its front end smashed. The troopers were on the ground around it, shooting at unseen attackers hiding in the darkness to the left of the jackknifed trailer. To Hunter's right was the cornfield and wooded hill that would probably provide them with the best cover.

"Fall back!" he shouted to his troopers. "This way!"

He dropped down the side of the ditch to grab Archelon and called again for his team to follow. His voice was lost amid a sudden high-pitched whine. He had only a heartbeat to wonder what it was when the road erupted upward in a searing ball of white flame.

The troopers on the road were blown off their feet, and Hunter was thrown against the side of the ditch. Fiery pain shot through his body, radiating out from his injured arm; his head filled with a dense, numbing ring. Shaking his head to dispel the fog, he raised himself up to the level of the roadbed and looked around to see who was still alive. In the headlights of the semis, he saw that one of his troopers was little more than a crumpled heap of disjointed limbs, and another was lying on his back, smoke rising from his chest. The third was nowhere to be seen. Hunter turned to check on his prisoner, but Archelon had disappeared.

There was a rattle of dead leaves from beyond the far side of the ditch, and Hunter looked up just in time to see Archelon dive headlong into the cornfield. Hunter slid down the bank and splashed across the water-filled ditch, then clambered up the other side, racing for the shelter of the standing corn.

Weighed down by his body armor, Hunter found it difficult to run. The uneven ground swayed up and down beneath his feet. He stumbled and fell to one knee as another explosion lifted the second Humvee from the road and flipped it end over end.

Hunter put his head down and dove into the standing cornstalks as the first bullets ripped through the broad, dry leaves.

thirty-four

He tumbled in among the standing stalks, sprawled forward onto his hands and knees, but managed to keep his feet moving. Using his hands, he pulled himself deeper into the field. There were shouts from the road behind him and the crackling discharge of automatic weapons.

Hunter hit the dirt as one burst shattered stalks near his head. He rolled onto his back and began ripping at the straps to his armored leggings. They were heavy and holding him back. He took off the arm protectors too and flung them aside. His fingers hesitated on the straps of his chest protector; he decided to keep it. As soon as the gunfire let up, he rolled to his feet and resumed his pursuit of Archelon.

The corn was dry and the stalks brittle. Bullets plowed the ground and rattled the stalks on either side of him. Lurching, lunging, leaping from row to row, he ran.

When the shooting stopped, Hunter stopped too. He crouched and listened for sounds of pursuit as well as those of the escaping Archelon. Apart from the rattle of dead leaves in the wind, and the voices of his pursuers shouting directions to one another, the night was eerily silent. Behind him he could glimpse the bright haze of vehicle lights on the road. He considered circling back for a look at what was happening at the Humvees, but the possibility of being seen was more than he cared to risk.

Instead, he moved on and took stock of what he had.

He still possessed his cell phone and the radio transmitter attached to his chest armor. His gun, however, had been lost when the explosion threw him into the ditch. He had his wallet with a little cash and credit cards; and in a side flap of the chest protector were a Swiss Army knife and two packets containing bandages and painkilling tablets. He wished now he'd worn a coat; the night was cold and getting colder. Still, all things considered, he was not in such bad shape. True, he couldn't use the radio or phone without giving his position away, but he was mobile and alert, and ready to give the goons on the road a run for their money.

There came a sound of a splash behind him, quickly followed by two more. The goons were on his trail. His main objective veered sharply onto a new course: save his own skin. He'd run and live to fight another day. Archelon would have to wait.

Hunter picked up his pace, trying to make as little noise as possible. But every step over every furrow ridge was onto crackling dry corn, and every slide sideways through the brittle foliage produced a clattering sound, which, he imagined, could be heard a mile away. Those behind him had no such worries; he could hear them crashing through the plants at will. Every now and then his pursuers would stop and send a volley of gunfire blindly through the standing corn, shredding some stalks and decapitating others where they stood. But the aim was wide and moving away from him, so he kept going, slowly working his way toward the wooded hill bordering the far side of the field.

One row, then another, and another—step by careful step he edged his way past the standing stalks until he had finally stepped over the last row and out into knee-high grass. Ahead, in the darkness, he could just make out the beginning of the wood thirty yards away. He heard a crashing sound off to his right and darted back into the cornfield just as one of his pursuers charged out into the corridor of open ground that ran the length of the field.

Crouching low, Hunter poked his head out to see that the goon had a flashlight on his rifle and was shining it this way and that as he waited in the clearing for Hunter to emerge.

He yanked back his head and edged his way further down the row. When he judged he had put sufficient distance between himself and the gunman, he knelt and risked another look down the outside of the row.

The gunman was still there with his AK47, poised for action—and this time he spotted his target.

Two quick salvos sliced the air just above Hunter's head. The shooter hollered to his comrades and started running to where Hunter had disappeared once more.

Hunter ran along the row a few yards and then crouched down, hoping against hope that the gunman had marked his previous spot accurately. He had. Hunter heard the sound of his running footsteps pounding on the soft turf. Between the stalks he saw a dark blur of movement—his pursuer rushing for the place he'd last seen his target.

As the goon passed, Hunter launched himself from the cornfield.

His flying tackle clipped the gunman from behind. The assault rifle flew from his hands and both men went down. Hunter scrambled free, drew back his foot, and kicked his assailant hard—once in the stomach and once on the side of the head. The man grunted and lay still. Hunter fell on him and started going through his clothing for weapons. The man was dressed completely in black special-ops-style urban warfare gear—top quality, regulation issue; all that was missing was the ICON patch.

Finding no handguns or other weapons, Hunter made a swift and furious search for the rifle in the long grass. It couldn't have gone far.

Given time and a little light, he might have found it. But as he combed the grass with his hands, a sizzling rip sang through the air beside him. It was followed instantly by the crack of the rifle. Hunter glanced to his right to see another gunman taking aim for a second shot. He dived into the grass, crawled to the edge of the clearing, and then ran like a rabbit for the trees. The gunman shouted directions to his fellow assassins and charged after him.

The woodland promised better cover than the cornfield, but first he had to get as much distance between himself and the goons as possible. Swiftly and steadily, Hunter worked his way into the heart of the winter-bare wood. Though the inky darkness made progress more difficult, he was grateful for it. Here and there he found evergreen bushes that allowed him to stop a moment to catch his breath before moving on. Gradually the shouting and shooting grew more distant; he could hear the echoing cries and sporadic gunshots in the wood on either side, but he continued on and these soon faded. After a while, he could no longer hear any sound of pursuit at all.

"City dogs," Hunter murmured. He drew the night air deep into his lungs and started walking.

He had no clear idea where he was or where he was going, but he aimed to keep moving away from the scene of the assault. Questions now buzzed in his brain like insistent wasps: *Who ambushed us? Where is Archelon? Where's the nearest farmhouse? Who do I call for backup?*

This last question was particularly pointed.

At the moment, Hunter couldn't say if the attack was a rescue attempt for Archelon or an assassination. Whatever the motive for the ambush, however, there had to have been a tip-off. They had been betrayed.

Through the bare branches overhead, Hunter glimpsed a cloudy night sky with a few faint stars showing in the gaps between clouds; over the wooded hilltops far to his right, a pale half-moon was rising. The little light it cast was much appreciated, and Hunter stopped to look around. The surrounding trees were mature hardwoods with a few cedars and spruce evergreens. The ground beneath him was soft, damp, and covered with leaves and dry grass. He didn't know how far he had gone, but he felt that it was not far enough. He scanned the wood behind him but saw nothing in the shadowy blackness.

He shivered and moved on. His clothes were wet from his roll in the ditch, and even his short pause to reconnoiter had given him a chill. He'd have to keep moving in order to stay warm. So he walked and jogged and walked again, picking his way through the wood, stumbling over fallen branches and tree trunks, tripping over roots, all the while trying not to make too much noise.

The ground rose steadily, and eventually Hunter reached the top of a long, sloping rise and stopped again to listen. He heard the faint whir of tires on pavement some distance away to his left. He turned and made for the sound.

Weary and heavy-footed, he eventually reached the two-lane blacktop. His limbs felt wooden, unresponsive. Exhaustion was setting in. Shooting pain coursed through his arm and side; his hands and face were scratched from encounters with unseen bushes and branches. Drained from his adrenaline high and cold to the bone, he squatted down to see what had passed on the road. Shortly, though, his body began to convulse with chills, and he realized he'd have to keep moving.

Hunter crossed the ditch and started walking along the shoulder. Stuffing his hands in his pockets for warmth, he found his cell phone. Would it be safe to call for assistance? Could he trust anyone at ICON? Devlin? Pilate? Steiner? Riley? The moment he called any one of them, his position would be revealed, and he'd become, once again, a target. Having just eluded the hit squad, he was in no hurry to have them renew the chase.

He decided his safest course was to get to civilization and then back to New York, where he could begin sorting out this mess.

He walked for twenty minutes to a crossroads where the blacktop met a farm lane. In the distance, a mile or more down the dirt track, he saw a small, glowing light—perhaps that of a farmhouse. As he stood trying to decide whether to turn aside to the farmhouse or keep heading toward the highway, he felt the first wet flakes of snow strike the side of his face. He looked up. The moon was gone; low clouds had moved in on a cold east wind that sent snowflakes swirling. Tired and dispirited, Hunter decided he'd try the farmhouse. He started down the dirt track.

The heavy, wet snow fell harder. His uniform was soon soaked through and he was shuddering. He was seriously considering giving up and seeking shelter in the wood, when he heard the distant hum of an engine on the blacktop behind him. He turned and started jogging back the way he'd come. He reached the blacktop and saw, off to his right, a faint light growing on the horizon.

What to do? The vehicle could be a harmless local, or it could be a truckload of ambushers searching for him, aiming to finish what they'd started. With snow and cold and exhaustion on one hand, and a truck filled with black-clad attackers on the other, Hunter decided to press his luck to the limit.

He moved to the center stripe and took up a stance in the middle of the road. The sound of the engine grew louder, and the light glowed brighter.

Then, over the crest of the hill two headlights appeared. Hunter began waving his arms and walking slowly down the center of the road toward the oncoming vehicle.

The vehicle slowed as it approached. A few seconds later, a two-toned GM pickup rolled to a halt a few dozen paces in front of him. Hunter sighed with relief and hurried to the driver's door. He tapped on the window and the glass slid down a few inches to reveal an apprehensive woman in a denim jacket.

"I need a ride to the nearest town," he announced.

The woman gaped at him.

"I'm an ICON officer," he told her, indicating the logo patch on the front of his armored vest. "It's an emergency."

The woman bit her lip. "Okay, sure," she replied at last. "I guess." She leaned over and unlocked the passenger door. "Get in."

Stepping quickly around the front of the truck, Hunter opened the passenger door and slid in. "Thank you," he sighed, as a tidal wave of relief rolled over him. "You just saved my life."

thirty-five

The pickup sped along the highway, flurries of snow swirling before the headlights. Hunter slouched in his seat and watched for any sign that the road was being watched. Who could tell? They rolled along, passing harvested fields and the occasional farmhouse and barn, but all seemed calm.

The driver seemed scared. A slightly built woman in her thirties with a frizzy poodle perm and kindly dark eyes, she was obviously not used to picking up battered ICON agents on the highway in the middle of the night. The woman stared straight ahead at the road and gripped the steering wheel so tightly her knuckles were white in the dashboard light. Her foot was heavy on the gas pedal, and Hunter feared they might as soon end up in a ditch as at their destination: Haupton, a small town a few miles ahead. He figured they'd both be mightily relieved when it was over.

They soon reached the highway and then the outskirts of the darkened town, which Hunter vaguely remembered passing through on his way to pick up Archelon. That seemed like a lifetime ago.

The woman dropped Hunter off at a dark motel on the outskirts of town and sped off. He stood for a few moments in the parking lot, trying to decide how to handle the next step. He needed to sleep. Using one of his credit cards would be like sending a radio beacon to Mother ICON. Probably not the best idea.

Instead, he decided to use his status as an ICON agent to commandeer a room at the motel. Advancing across the parking lot, he took in the general demeanor of the place. It looked nice enough in a homely way, not sleazy or run-down. The door was locked and the office dark, but he pressed a button labeled "Night Porter," and soon a teenager in a Linkin Park T-shirt and tartan flannel pajama bottoms came to answer the door.

"We're closed," he complained.

"Not anymore," replied Hunter; he opened his wallet and pressed his ICON ID to the glass.

"Oh, man. . . . " the kid whined and opened the door to let him in.

"Just give me whatever room you got," Hunter told him. "I'm not fussy. And get me some food—a sandwich, scrambled eggs, anything—I don't care. And make it snappy. I'm starving."

"Look," said the kid, rubbing his hair. "Do we gotta do this?"

"We do," Hunter assured him. "We most definitely do."

"Oh, man. . . . " The kid moved behind the desk and brought out a key attached to a chunk of wood. "You can have room twelve. It's up the stairs over there and down the hall."

"Does it face the highway?"

"No."

"I want one that does."

"I thought you said you weren't fussy."

"I lied."

The kid withdrew the key, rummaged through the drawer, and tossed out another. "Take number eight then."

"Thanks," replied Hunter, snatching up the key. "Just bring the food when it's ready. And something to drink—bottled water is fine. Orange juice would be better."

The kid nodded and shuffled off. Hunter went up to his room and stripped off his armored vest, shirt, and trousers. When the kid arrived with the tray of food, he found Hunter wrapped in a blanket and leaning against the heater beneath the window. "Just put the tray on the table," Hunter told him. Then, pointing to his clothes on the floor, he said, "I'd like to have those dried right away."

"Housekeeper's gone home," the kid informed him.

"Yeah, but you know how to work a dryer, don't you—smart guy like you?"

"Do I get to know what this is all about?"

Hunter shook his head. "Sorry."

"Oh, man. . . . "

The kid scooped up the clothes and shut the door. When he returned thirty minutes later, Hunter had finished his soup and sandwiches and was lying on the bed, wrapped in his blanket like a mummy. "Clothes are ready."

Hunter rose and took the clothes, pushed the kid from the room, and wished him a good night.

Hunter awoke the next morning stiff, sore, and ravenous. He looked out the window. In the early morning light the highway was clear and dry; the snow had stopped, leaving only a light dusting along the roadway and sidewalks. He showered quickly and dressed in his uniform—it was still smeared with dirt, but dry at least. He decided against wearing the chest protector—it was just too bulky and heavy. He also decided against using the phone. He'd forego making any calls before he got to New York. The way things stood, if anyone was looking for him, they couldn't have much of an idea where he was right now and he wanted to keep it that way. He went downstairs.

There was a different clerk than the night before—a heavy-set middle-aged woman in a bright pink sweater and long denim skirt. Hunter talked to her briefly and asked if anyone had been around looking for ICON agents. The woman told him no one had been in yet this morning; she spoke with an honest expression Hunter found reassuring. He thanked her for the use of the room and asked for directions to the nearest diner or café.

He needed to get back to New York as quickly as possible, yes, but he needed breakfast more. The diner was across the highway, a few blocks from the motel. He hurried out into a brisk winter day, crossed the highway, and jogged to the diner. The place was mostly empty; he took a booth in the back and ordered coffee and the pancake platter with an extra egg and ham on the side. The food came quickly, and while he ate, he watched the diner fill up with its average morning crowd. When he finished, he went to the counter and, raising a hand in the air, called out loudly. "Excuse me! Please! Excuse me, everybody!"

Conversation stopped; all faces turned toward him as he asked in a loud voice if anyone was driving to New York. A trucker in a tan cowboy hat put up his hand. Hunter joined the trucker in his booth while he finished eating, then paid for the driver's breakfast, ordered another coffee for himself to go, and ten minutes later was out of town and on his way back to the city.

As soon as they hit the turnpike, Hunter drifted off to sleep for a few hours. When he awoke they were well into the suburban sprawl of New Jersey, and he could see the towers of Manhattan looming on the horizon. Traffic became heavier; smaller capillaries joined the main arteries leading to the congested heart of the city, slowing progress to a crawl.

"It's always like this," the trucker volunteered. "Except when it's worse."

The truck advanced in fits and starts, eventually reaching the Hudson River. Upon emerging from the Holland Tunnel, they were greeted by a giant electronic billboard: *Welcome to New York . . . City of Dreams.*

"Yeah," mused Hunter bitterly, "and all of them bad."

The trucker dropped Hunter at Canal Street, which was as good a place as any. Hunter hailed a cab and rode toward midtown. Traffic was all but gridlocked. The cab inched through the city, horn blaring in concert with every other cab, car, and truck on the street. Hunter didn't mind the lengthy delay; he used the time to think through his next moves. His plan, such as it was, involved a few phone calls to judge the heat of the water he was in. Beyond that, he'd have to wing it and see how things developed.

Upon reaching Times Square, he tapped on the plastic divider and told the cabby, "Let me out here." He paid the fare and started walking up Broadway. Glowing neon, overpowering the watery winter sunlight, splashed gaudy color onto the damp pavement. Stone-faced pedestrians hurried by, clutching briefcases, backpacks, and shopping bags; cars, buses, and taxis juddered along, horns blaring in staccato beat; commuter jets whooshed low overhead. Hunter felt the New York buzz in his blood and reached into his pocket for his cell phone.

He brought up the governor's private office line, pressed speed dial, and muttered, "Here goes nothing."

thirty-six

The phone rang, there was a click as the call was automatically rerouted, and then it rang again. It was answered at once. "Hello, the governor's office."

"This is Special Agent Alex Hunter. I need to speak to Governor Pilate immediately."

"I'm sorry, Agent Hunter, the governor isn't available right now."

"Forward this call," Hunter said. "It's an emergency."

"I'm sorry, Agent, but that won't be possible."

"Look, it's urgent. He'll want to talk to me. Just tell him it's about the Antony Archelon incident. Please, could—"

"It doesn't matter what the call is in regard to, Agent; the governor simply isn't in."

"But he'll be expecting my call. My name should be on a list or som—" Hunter swore as the line was disconnected.

Okay. There were other ways to the governor. He quickly improvised a Plan B. He dialed his supervisor, Janet Riley, as he continued to float along with the flocks of shoppers and office workers crowding the sidewalks.

"Riley, this is Hunter."

"Hunter? Where have you been? Where's Archelon?"

"I can't explain now. You have to get me through to the governor."

"I don't think I can do that. I don't have—"

"You can, Riley, and you'd better! My life is on the line here."

"What's going on, Hunter? Talk to me."

"Sure thing—*after* I talk to Pilate."

Riley paused. Hunter could sense her weighing the possible ramifications of her various options. "Okay," she agreed at last. "Give me your number. I'll call you back."

Good. That was more like it. Hunter gave her the number and disconnected the call. He continued moving with the herd as it migrated along Broadway toward Fifty-seventh Street. About four minutes later his phone rang.

"Hunter? Is that you?" The voice brought him up short. It wasn't Pilate.

"Commissioner Steiner?" He asked, warily.

"Thank goodness you're safe, Hunter. You had us all extremely worried."

"Steiner, sorry. I thought the governor was going to call. Can you put me in touch with him right away? It's urgent."

"Relax, Agent," said the commissioner quickly. "I'm coordinating the situation. The governor and I are working hand in glove on this one. Listen, we're both very anxious to talk to you and find out what's been going on. I'm sending a car for you immediately. Tell me where you are."

Hunter thought for a moment. Could he trust Steiner?

When he didn't reply immediately, Steiner continued. "I

understand your hesitance, Agent. Is there anything I can say that will help?" Steiner's voice was calm and collected, reassuring.

"Yes, sir, put me in touch with the governor."

"He's in a sensitive position right now, Hunter. Please understand that. No can do. Sorry."

Hunter thought. "All right, then I want you to come in person."

Now there was a hesitation on the other end of the line.

"It's difficult," replied the commissioner, thinking. "But, okay. Sure. Where are you now?" Hunter gave him the address of the theater across the street. "Right. Stay put. I'll be right there."

Hunter hung up and crossed the street, taking up a position next to the box office of the Ed Sullivan Theater. As he waited for the car to arrive, he gave some thought to the questions that needed answers before he gave out any information.

He waited—and then waited some more. He watched the traffic; cars rolled by endlessly, but none of them stopped. He was on the brink of abandoning his post to go buy a coat and some gloves when a black Town Car pulled up. There were three men in it—two in front, one in back. Hunter made no move to meet the car. Finally, the rear door opened and Commissioner Steiner stepped out onto the pavement and beckoned him over.

So far, so good, thought Hunter; he approached the car cautiously.

"It's good to see you, Agent Hunter," Steiner said, clapping him on the back. "I'm glad you made it back safely."

Hunter nodded and got in the car. Steiner climbed in beside him.

The car pulled back into traffic. Hunter sat patiently as the vehicle moved down the street; he waited for the commissioner to speak first.

After a moment Steiner sighed heavily. "It's been an absolute disaster, as you can imagine. A total nightmare." He turned to Hunter and said, "You can't believe how glad I was to hear you'd survived. Can you shed any light on what happened out there?"

"It was an ambush," Hunter replied, trying to keep his voice level, his tone objective. "Two squads of heavily armed attackers, and they were waiting for us. We walked right into a trap."

Steiner sighed again. "I'm afraid you're probably right. It would seem we have a double agent in our midst." He looked out the window, and then slowly back at Hunter. "I don't suppose you'd know anything about that?"

Hunter caught an undertone in the police commissioner's words and a whiff of uneasiness wafted over him. The air seemed suddenly dark and heavy.

"We were picking up a high-ranking member of the Kadesh. We were on our way back and stopped for a jackknifed semi that was blocking the road," Hunter said, his voice rising slightly. "We were attacked by men in urban assault gear, automatic weapons, and some sort of explosives—possibly rockets. My team was blown away, and I barely escaped with my life." Hunter returned the commissioner's gaze and added bitterly, "I guess that's about all I know."

"Take it easy, Agent. I was merely asking." Steiner nodded and turned once more to the window.

"There is one thing I can't work out," Hunter continued, watching the commissioner closely for his reaction.

"Only one?" wondered Steiner. "What is that?"

"Whose men were they?"

"Devlin's," replied the commissioner evenly and with conviction.

The two men in the front seat exchanged glances. Hunter saw the look that passed between them, noted it—and then wondered why the two weren't wearing uniforms. "I would have thought," continued Steiner, "that much should be obvious."

"Not to me," said Hunter.

"It had to be someone at the top, someone with the governor's complete trust, in order for The Prophet to organize an operation like that."

"The Prophet," said Hunter. "I wasn't talking about The Prophet."

"It's all connected, Agent Hunter. It's all of a piece. We have been tracking this for some time. Archelon has been supplying The Prophet with the money and equipment he needs to perpetrate his crimes—the cyber attack on ICON headquarters, all that computer mess, and now this. Devlin made it possible. He opened the doors and agreed to turn a blind eye for reasons best known to himself alone."

Hunter sat in silence, calculating.

"But I wouldn't worry about Devlin," Steiner said. "The noose is tightening around his neck even as we speak. The governor and I have gathered most of the evidence we need. Devlin's living on borrowed time."

The pieces suddenly fell into place for Hunter. He looked out the window. They were in the middle lane of a three-lane street and coming up to a stoplight at the corner.

The commissioner turned narrowed eyes toward Hunter again. "Now that you're here and can confirm what happened out there, we can move. There's just one or two more loose ends to tie up first." The car was slowing to a stop. "You've made it, Hunter. All your problems are solved."

"It's a great relief to hear you say that," replied Hunter. He looked out through the windshield, his eyes fixed on the stop-light. The red circle seemed to burn into his eyes. He forced him-self to keep his hands in his lap. Waiting . . . waiting . . .

The light turned green, and as the driver pressed the acceler-ator and the car moved forward, Hunter's hand flicked to the door handle. The door swung open, and Hunter threw himself from the moving vehicle. He hit the pavement, rolled to his feet, and lurched away, falling against the car in the next lane. He spun, kept his feet, and scrambled around the car as it screeched to a halt. Hunter dived across the next two lanes, where the oncoming cars were just rolling into the intersection. Dodging the slow-moving traffic, he made it to the far side of the street, darted through the rank of parked cars, and gained the sidewalk. Seconds later he was once again running for his life.

thirty-seven

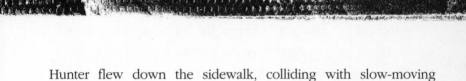

Hunter flew down the sidewalk, colliding with slow-moving pedestrians, ducking and diving, sliding through knots of people jamming his way. Assuming Steiner had already issued an alert and broadcast his description to every car and foot patrol in the area and throughout the city, he needed to steer clear of all ICON contact. *Think! Think! Think!* He forced himself to slow his pace to the casual yet purposeful gait of an ICON special agent.

Crossing West Fifty-second Street he saw, too late, an ICON cruiser sitting four cars back from the intersection. He hoped the officers hadn't seen him as he sharply turned the corner and walked on.

That tenuous hope died in the screech of tires and siren wail that started up instantly behind him. Without a backward glance, Hunter ran, swerved into the nearest alleyway, and headed down the dark passage between two buildings.

The cruiser skidded to a halt, blocking the alley entrance. Hunter heard doors slam and then the dull crack of gunfire. They were shooting already? What had the commissioner told the dispatcher? Another shot echoed down the alleyway. A bullet dug into the brickwork above his head, sending a shower of dusty fragments over him. He pressed himself close to the near wall and edged along it. The only cover was a rank of Dumpsters fifty yards ahead.

The alley narrowed as he approached the Dumpsters. On the street behind him, the cruiser door slammed again, and a second later the headlights swung into the alley. Hunter ran for the cover of the huge metal bins, searching furiously for a doorway, a fire escape, anything.

Behind the fourth Dumpster he saw a niche in the wall closed by a steel door. Shoving between the bins he flung himself against the door; it rattled but did not give. He moved on.

Edging along the wall, he glanced toward the street. The patrol car had entered the alley and was rolling toward him, its spotlight playing along the alley walls. When it reached the row of Dumpsters, it would be blocked. Hunter figured he still might have a chance to elude the patrol if he could just find a way out.

Keeping the Dumpsters between himself and the car, he ran to the far end of the alley, which was blocked by a building with a high iron fence protecting its rear entrance. Hunter raced to the fence and flung himself upon the gate. It was locked, but he heard whistling coming from behind the door. Presently, a man in kitchen whites emerged from the building with a black trash bag in his hands. Hunter crouched low and held his breath.

A moment later, there was a click and the gate opened a crack. He leapt for it, throwing his shoulder into the steel mesh of the gate. It bounced wide to the surprise of the very startled cook. Hunter shoved past him to the door of the building.

"Hey!" shouted the cook. "You can't go in there!"

Hunter leaped through the doorway, spun around, and

shoved the heavy door closed. Outside he heard the cruiser doors slamming and the officers shouting.

Glancing around, he saw he was in the fire exit of a restaurant. He grabbed a mop from a nearby bucket and jammed the metal handle in the push bar, hoping it would stop his pursuers, or slow them down at least. He jogged down the tiled hallway. At a T-junction, he was confronted with a choice: a large kitchen on the right, a passage with several doors and a stairway on the left. Hunter went left.

He passed the first door, skidded to a halt, and then backtracked. This was a laundry room—perfect. He needed a change of clothes.

He upended the nearest of several large laundry bins, dumping the contents onto the floor. Dozens of white laundry bags spilled out, each with tags pinned to them. He started tearing them open. *There has to be at least one businessman with a suit that needs cleaning,* he thought, tossing aside a second bag with a dress and women's underwear in it.

Reaching for a bag that seemed to have something more substantial in it, he found what he was looking for: a dark blue blazer jacket of similar color to his uniform; there were also two shirts: one white, one gray. Swiftly stripping off his uniform jacket and the shirt beneath, he threw them aside and pulled on the white shirt—ignoring the rank body odor—and stuck his arms through the sleeves of the jacket.

Next he pulled the cuffs of his trousers out of the high-topped boots and shoved them down to his ankles. He was still buttoning the shirt as he cautiously reentered the hallway.

The police were pounding on the alley door and shouting. It

was time to make himself scarce before someone came to see what was going on.

Hunter turned and raced down the hall and up two flights of metal stairs. Upon reaching a set of double doors with "Reception" stenciled across them, he pushed through them and entered a foyer leading to the large, plush, marble-tiled lobby of the New York Hilton. Hunter slowed to a dignified walk. *All you've got to do is act natural,* he told himself. *Act like you belong in polite company.*

Calmly moving through the lobby, looking neither right nor left, he approached the large revolving doors. Two doormen tipped their hats while he passed through and out onto Sixth Avenue. He strode down the red-carpeted path that crossed the sidewalk and climbed straight into a waiting taxi.

"Where to, pal?" asked the cabbie.

"Take me to Central Park."

"Hey, it's a big park!"

"Okay—East Drive. The Boathouse."

"Right you are!"

Hunter sank down in the seat as the taxi pulled away from the curb. He didn't think anyone had spotted him but he kept his head down just the same. As the taxi put more distance between him and the hotel, he began to breathe easier.

His mind turned at once to Steiner and what it was that had given the police commissioner away. Small things mostly—the easy way he preyed on Hunter's trust, welcoming him into his confidence when there was no way he could have known that Hunter himself was not responsible for the ambush and massacre on the highway. Also, the easy way he had accused Devlin raised a qualm or two.

Now that he thought about it, he should have seen it from the very beginning. In fact, he had tried to co-opt Hunter from their first meeting—with his "great minds think alike" speech and the unnecessary appointment of Riley.

Hunter had been compromised from the start. "But we won't let a little collateral damage worry us," the commissioner had told him. "Things happen in the field—I know that. All I ask, Agent Hunter, is that you keep me informed. I want to know what my agents are up to. That way I will always know how best to help you . . . if something unfortunate should happen. Understand?"

And then there was the subway shoot-out incident. The shooters had carried Steiner's personal number in their cell phones. Why would they do that? And why would the commissioner concern himself with the antics of low-level cops like the two Hunter had caught that night?

They were working outside channels with the commissioner's blessing. One of the most powerful men in the city police force was using them for his own dark purposes. And from the very beginning Hunter had been encouraged to work outside official channels, too—something neither Devlin nor Governor Pilate had ever suggested. It was Steiner all the way. Steiner was the high-level ICON mole, he'd bet his life on it.

In fact, it occurred to Hunter that he already had.

When the cab came in sight of the Central Park Boathouse, Hunter gave the driver his ID code and hopped out, hurrying across the pavement and into the park. He stayed to the lesser-used paths and kept on the lookout for foot patrols.

The gray winter day had turned gusty and there were few people around. Confident now that he had given his pursuers the slip, his determination to bring down Steiner strengthened with each step. The odds were stacked against him, as they most always were, but he wasn't beaten yet.

Near an outcrop of stone boulders, he found a secluded bench and sat down. It was biting cold, and his borrowed blazer didn't offer much in the way of warmth. He'd have to find something else soon, but that could wait. First things first.

He pulled out his phone and punched in Devlin's number.

The call went through to a secretary. Hunter told him he needed to talk to Chief Devlin right away.

"Certainly, sir. May I have your name and ID number?"

"No, I can't give you that. But I can tell you he's waiting for my call."

"I'm sorry, but I can't put you through without either a name or an ID number."

"Okay, listen—can you put me through to the duty officer?"

"Just a second."

Hunter waited, scanning both directions along the deserted path. "Come on," he muttered. "Come on, come on, come on . . . "

There came a click on the other end of the line. "Who is this, please?" a female voice asked.

"I'm a special agent. I need to talk to Chief Devlin right away. I can't tell you my name. But, please believe me, it's very urgent."

"Special agent?" inquired the voice. "When was the last time you saw the chief?"

Hunter thought. "Last Wednesday." It seemed much longer than that.

"Hold on for a second." There was a long pause on the other end of the line, and some muffled talk. "What is the name of the man you were going to meet?"

"Howard Antony Archelon. Nicknamed Anty."

"I'm putting you through now, Agent."

Hunter exhaled a sigh of relief. A second later a gruff voice was on the other end. "Devlin here."

"Devlin!" Hunter nearly shouted.

"Hunter, what the thunder is going on? What's happened to Archelon?"

"I don't know. We were ambushed on our way back to the city."

"So I hear. Are you hurt?"

"I'm okay—for now. I tried to call the governor as soon as I got back, but Steiner showed up. I think he was planning to kill me too."

"You *think?*"

"Yes, probably. He's the mole."

The line went silent.

"Devlin?" inquired Hunter. "You still there?"

"I'm thinking," he paused. "Commissioner Steiner?" he asked incredulously. "Are you serious?"

"Serious as a cemetery. I've had officers shooting at me for the last hour."

There was another pause.

"Look, if you don't believe me, check and see if there's been an all-points alert put out on me in the last half hour or so. Then check who called it in."

"Okay, I'll do that. But right now, just tell me where you are and I'll pick you up."

Hunter got up and continued walking along the paths. The thin, gray twilight was fading toward evening. "How do I know I can trust you?" demanded Hunter. "How do I know that you and Steiner aren't running this scam together?"

"And how exactly do I know *I* can trust *you?*" Devlin shot back. "How do I know it wasn't you who let Archelon escape?"

"Why would I do that? Ask yourself that. What possible reason could I have for doing that? And even if I did, why would I be calling you about it?"

"Okay, fine. I don't blame you for being cautious, but you have to trust me. I can protect you, but you gotta come in."

"I can't do that yet. Let me talk to Pilate."

"He's been making himself scarce since this went down."

"I'll call back in ten minutes."

"Hunter, be reasonable—"

"I can't be reasonable right now. I want to trust you, and I probably should, but I just can't. Nothing personal," Hunter added. "I hope you understand. Don't worry, you'll hear from me."

"Look, stay where you are. I'm tracking your number. I'll come and get you. We'll talk. You don't have to come with me if you don't want to. But we've got to talk."

"I'll call you." Hunter cut the connection and turned off the phone. Was it possible to track a cell phone when it was off? With Devlin's gadgets it was best not to take the chance. He tossed the phone into a nearby trash can and hurried into the thickening shadows.

thirty-eight

He moved quickly through the park to put distance between himself and his phone, from which his last known position could possibly be fixed. He jogged now and then to keep warm and watched the dull day end in a hazy blue twilight. An odd thought surfaced in his mind, something that someone said to him not too long ago: *If you go looking for Death, you will find Death.* Who had said that? And why was he thinking about it now?

Hunter came out of the park at Fifth Avenue and began walking north. At Seventy-second Street he saw two ICON officers standing beneath a streetlight, talking to an old homeless man. Hunter ducked off the sidewalk and back into the park, where he found a stand of short, black trees. Keeping close to the trees, he continued north, passing an open area that he skirted until he had circumvented the policemen. He jogged to the street once more and paused to look both ways for any sign of either cruisers or officers on foot.

Crossing Fifth Avenue at a trot, he continued crosstown to Lexington Avenue where he turned north again. It didn't matter so much *where* he went; it was more important merely to keep moving, to stay one step ahead of the game until he could work out how to play the next move.

He headed into more familiar territory in the neighborhoods of the Upper East Side. There were trendy bars and restaurants along the street, which was beginning to show signs of life as the club crowd emerged in party mode. At a faux-Irish pub, the golden light against the steamed-up windows made the place seem so inviting that Hunter went in to warm himself at the bar. He drank an Irish coffee and contemplated walking off with a fellow patron's coat, but the coat rack was in full view of the bar and tables, and he couldn't work out how to make the snatch without being seen. He contented himself with the hot whiskey-laced coffee and soaked up the heat.

Out on the street again, he saw a group of guys on the sidewalk ahead of him. He picked up his pace until he had joined the stragglers at the rear. They were young, between sixteen and twenty-five, and dressed to party. But they were also loud and rambunctious, obviously looking for action, and Hunter swiftly concluded they might draw too much attention to themselves. He had already decided to abandon them when he saw two more ICON officers on foot, heading the same direction.

The group reached the intersection and turned the corner; Hunter went with them—and so did the ICON policemen, tagging along a few dozen yards behind. Hunter decided to duck into the next bar or café he came to; there was nothing close by that he could see, so he remained with the kids. They crossed another intersection and joined another group of kids—this one mostly girls and only slightly quieter—walking in the same direction. Up ahead he could see other groups of people—all of them seemed to be making for the same place: maybe a party, maybe a concert. *Terrific,* thought Hunter, *just what the doctor ordered.* He would lose himself in the crowd.

He continued on for several more blocks. The clusters of people became more numerous—and more raucous. The party atmosphere was strong, spirits high. Hunter felt the buzz in spite of himself. He cruised along, happily lost in the moving throng until, all at once, they came to a bottleneck at their destination: the entrance to an empty parking lot.

Could this be the place everyone was heading for? A stout chain-link fence formed one side of the square, and brick apartment buildings towered over the other three sides. Hunter stood in the press of bodies, planning his next move—whatever it was it would have to include getting hold of some warmer clothing. The prospect of standing around on cold concrete listening to blaring music held no particular appeal; he decided he'd followed the crowd far enough. It was time to move on.

He turned and began shoving his way back against the flow of people trying to get into the parking lot. It was then the ICON cruiser appeared on the street. It drove by slowly and then stopped. Hunter whipped around again and rejoined the flock trying to get into the parking lot. Nobody seemed to have any tickets, and no one was there collecting them; everyone just filed in through the open gate. Music started up—fast and loud, with a driving beat. Hunter reached the gate and saw, far too late to do anything about it, that ICON was already present: two troopers were standing just inside the entrance.

Were they on to him?

He felt the surge of adrenaline hit his bloodstream; his heart-beat ramped up a notch, and he had to force himself to remain calm. It occurred to him that he was probably constructing some sort of paranoid fantasy, seeing policemen at every turn and thinking "they" were all out to get him. Then again, maybe they were. Or, maybe he was just losing his mind.

He decided to take no unnecessary chances. He could check into an asylum later—right now it was simple survival. He turned away from the guards and pretended to take an interest in one of the young women next to him, who made a face as if she didn't entirely welcome the attentions of a smelly, unshaven guy in a wrinkled blazer.

"Come here often?" Hunter asked the girl as they moved by the gaze of the policemen.

"Get out!" said the girl.

"Believe me, I'm trying." Hunter could feel their eyes on him as he passed, but he wasn't stopped. They shuffled on a few more paces, and then they were in. "Well, it's been great talking to you," he said, pushing away into the crowd.

"Pervert!" sneered the girl.

The flood of bodies carried Hunter into the parking lot, and he slid further into the crowd and away from the cops at the gate. At the far end of the empty lot a Portacabin had been set up and a stage erected; there was a curtain backdrop and massive speaker cabinets on either side; trees of bright colored spotlights lit the night. The music was cranked, booming off the nearby buildings, making the concrete reverberate to the rhythm.

Up onstage was a sound desk, but no musical instruments were anywhere in sight: no drum kit, no amps, no keyboards or microphone stands. It came to Hunter then, that it wasn't a concert, it was a rave—a flying disco. A here-tonight-gone-tomorrow mobile club, which would be tolerated by the authorities until it got too loud, too late, or too wild with drugs. Then ICON would swoop down and pull the plug.

Hunter didn't want to be there when it happened.

He began planning his exit. He couldn't go back the way he came but reckoned he could slip out behind the stage. He pressed his way through the crowd, working his way toward the far end of the parking lot.

Halfway to the stage, Hunter glanced back at the entrance, and what he saw made him groan. "Not good," he muttered. "Not good at all."

There were now at least fifteen ICON troopers at the gate, and he could see the multiple flashing lights of cruisers on the street outside. One of the gate cops was pointing into the crowd. As Hunter watched, two more patrolmen took up positions at the entrance, and the rest pushed their way into the crowd, fanning out among the congealed throng of revelers.

He had been marked, and they were coming after him!

thirty-nine

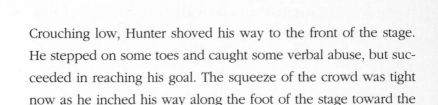

Crouching low, Hunter shoved his way to the front of the stage. He stepped on some toes and caught some verbal abuse, but succeeded in reaching his goal. The squeeze of the crowd was tight now as he inched his way along the foot of the stage toward the side and, he hoped, a rear exit.

Suddenly, the crowd cheered. He glanced up and saw that someone had come onto the stage, microphone in hand.

Hunter ducked and shoved his way farther along.

A voice erupted from the stage. "Welcome, friends!"

The sound of the voice—even blaring over the speakers— brought Hunter up short. He knew that voice. Staring back at the stage, Hunter saw a slender young man step into the blue glow of a spotlight: It was Joshua Jones.

Jostling people right and left, Hunter elbowed his way to the side of the stage. If he could get behind it, he might yet escape unseen. At the side of the stage he came to a ring of low metal fencing that had been erected to keep the crowd from doing exactly what he had in mind. Without hesitation, Hunter vaulted over the barricade, landing with a thud on the concrete. He dived for the edge of the stage and was about to crawl under when he felt two large, powerful arms around his chest.

He squirmed in the grasp of an extremely hefty young man with short dark hair and the arms and chest of an Olympic weight lifter. The fellow didn't say a word to Hunter but picked him up and lugged him back to the barricade.

"Hey! Hold on!" cried Hunter, trying to avoid being thrown back over the fence to ICON. "I'm here to speak with Joshua."

"No way," the weight lifter replied. With a grunt, he hefted Hunter over the barricade and dropped him back on the other side. "Now stay there."

Ignoring him, Hunter continued down the fence line, working his way along the side toward the back of the stage. He could see a chain-link gate that he guessed must be the rear entrance. He had almost reached it when two ICON policemen appeared and took up places on either side of the gate.

Hunter shrank back and ducked into the press of bodies, returning to the fence once more. The weight lifter was still on guard beside the stage, and he was talking to another man. Hunter decided to try again.

Hunter yelled, but the two men ignored him, so he leaned over the barricade as far as he could reach and snagged the nearest man by the shirt. "Hey!" he shouted, trying to raise his voice over the music. "You have to let me in."

The weight lifter looked up and the second man's head whipped around. His eyes met Hunter's and for a second the two stared at each other, recognition flashing in their faces simultaneously.

"Simon!" he gasped.

"Special Agent Hunter," the other man said, but Hunter was already pushing back, trying to get away from the barricade. His mind reeled, his feet stumbled.

Simon DeVere . . . impossible!

Shock, anger, desperation roiled inside him, blurring his vision. He had to get away! The tight-packed crowd held him in place. He couldn't move.

"Hunter, stop!"

"No!" he shouted. He tripped and fell backward, landing on the concrete. It was impossible! Simon couldn't be here. Not him. Not now.

His mind raced. He had to get away from the stage!

Dodging, scrambling, crawling backward, Hunter squirmed through the crowd. Simon vaulted the fence, striding into the crowd after him. Hunter struggled to his feet, lurching wildly like a wino. There were too many people in the way and he couldn't dodge them all; he tripped and went down again.

"Where are you going, Alex? What are you running to?"

Simon was standing over him now, his hands spread before him. He said something, but his voice was lost in the sudden din as the crowd erupted into a cheer that instantly became a chant: "He-ro! He-ro! He-ro!" they were shouting.

Hunter, unable to hear above the noise, climbed to his feet. He craned his neck to see the two ICON policemen moving toward him along the fence line. Simon saw where he was looking. He stepped closer and stretched out his hand.

Fearing a gun, Hunter flinched away instinctively. But looking down, he saw that the hand was empty.

Simon took his arm and drew him closer. "You're in trouble," he said, nodding toward the police officers. "I can help."

"Like you helped me last time?" sneered Hunter, finding his voice at last. He pulled free of Simon's grasp. "No thanks."

"I'm sorry."

"You're sorry?" Hunter said, his voice thick with rage. "You ruined my life!"

Simon edged closer. He pointed to the stage and at Joshua, who was now talking into the microphone. "We can help you, whatever it is," he said. "But you have to trust me."

Hunter glanced over his shoulder at the policemen, who were advancing.

"You've got to trust somebody," Simon said. "Time is running out."

"That's good," snarled Hunter, "coming from you."

"I know what you feel, man," Simon assured him. "And I know it isn't easy. But it's me, or it's them." He indicated the cops, who were wading toward them, closing the distance.

Desperate, writhing with indecision, Hunter could not make himself accept Simon's offer. He pulled away, deciding to take his chances with the devil he knew.

"Don't do it, Alex," Simon said, grabbing him by the arm again. "Who are you going to trust? It's time to decide."

Hunter turned back to Simon. "All right," he snarled. "But if you try anything, I'll kill you with my bare hands. I swear it!"

"Fair enough. Now stay calm. I'll get you out of here," said Simon. Turning to the cops, he shouted, "This guy is sick. Do you want to deal with him, or should I?"

Hearing this, Hunter quickly doubled over, opened his

mouth, and stuck his fingers as far down his throat as they would go. He gagged, and as his stomach heaved, he swung around to give the ICON guards a good look at himself vomiting his Irish coffee onto the ground.

"Stupid drunk," he heard one cop mutter. "Get him out of here."

The other cop lingered a moment, then waved them on, and the two continued stalking through the crowd. Simon put his arm around Hunter's shoulders, gathering him in like a long-lost friend; together they walked slowly to the barricade beside the stage where he helped Hunter climb over.

Numb with astonishment, Hunter regarded Simon. "You," he murmured, "of all people . . . how? Why?"

"You can relax now. You're among friends. I'll come get you when the coast is clear, okay?"

Hunter nodded. Simon called across to the weight-lifting giant. "Hey, Petrov, I want you to take care of my man here. Keep him out of sight."

"Sure thing." Petrov gestured Hunter over. "Follow me."

Hunter fell into step behind him and was led to the portable cabin behind the stage. Petrov pounded on the door; Hunter surveyed the area nervously. The ICON officers at the rear gate appeared more interested in the crowd than what was going on around the stage. "Hey, open up!" called Petrov, smacking the door again. A moment later it was opened from the inside and Petrov stuck his head in. "Hey, girls," he called, "would you mind looking after this guy for a few minutes?"

And there she was, standing in the doorway, long hair swept back, her dark eyes searching expectantly. "Maggie," he said, and reached up to her. Surprise turned to pleasure as she realized it was Hunter.

Taking his hand, she led him up the short flight of metal steps and drew him inside. She closed the door, saying, "Welcome to the side of the angels, Alex."

authors

STEPHEN R. LAWHEAD is a best-selling author of mythic history and imaginative fiction, having sold over five million books worldwide. His works include *Byzantium,* the five-part PENDRAGON CYCLE, and the award-winning SONG OF ALBION series. Stephen makes his home in Austria with his wife, Alice. His website is www.stephenlawhead.com.

ROSS LAWHEAD studied screenplay writing for film and television at Bournemouth University in England. He is the cowriter and penciler on the !HERO comic books and graphic novel. Ross lives in Oxford, England.

The action explodes in books two and three of the !HERO novel trilogy.

When an über-terrorist faction, *Rogue Nation*, detonates dirty bombs in cities across the country, something must be done—and fast! Hunter stays undercover with Hero and his followers until he can make his move on the terrorist leader known as The Prophet.

Rogue Nation
by Stephen R. Lawhead and Ross Lawhead
1-57683-508-1

Coming Spring 2004

Read the awe-inspiring conclusion of the !HERO novel trilogy. Hero boldly faces off with those who want to see him dead. Betrayal, murder, and the utterly impossible ensue, forcing Hunter to decide—once and for all—if Hero really is everything he claims to be.

<table>
<tr><td>

World Without End

Coming Fall 2004

</td><td>

World Without End
by Stephen R. Lawhead and Ross Lawhead
1-57683-538-3

Coming Fall 2004

www.herouniverse.com

</td></tr>
</table>

To get your copies, visit your local bookstore, call 1-800-366-7788, or log on to www.navpress.com. Ask for a FREE catalog of NavPress products. Offer #BPA.

NAVPRESS ®

BRINGING TRUTH TO LIFE
www.navpress.com